Deceptive Silence
Hailey Arquette Murder Files
Book Two

REILY GARRETT

Acknowledgments

To Gunther... This series, as is the case with much of my writing, is inspired in part by my four-footed companions. Dogs have always been a part of the Garrett household. I recently met one who has reminded me so much of my long-coat shepherds that he deserves a mention. Gunther is a 200+ pound ball of love and fur who shares some of the same mannerisms as my fur kids. Yes, I used *who* instead of *that* because in our home, dogs are considered people too. Thank you, Gunther, for keeping all my fur kids alive in my memory.

To Rosie Amber for an in-depth assessment of character and plot, thank you for all your help. You can find her blog and services at rosieamber.wordpress.com/beta-reading-service.

To my editor RE Hargrave, tireless and always patient. Thank you for keeping me on the straight and narrow. You can find her services as www.rehargrave(dot)com.

To my readers, each one of you who selects and reads one of my books, thank you for the opportunity to share my work. If you've enjoyed it, please consider leaving a review. They are the best way to help your author share her work.

Chapter One

Hailey

Before the sun peeked over the horizon's rim to separate the lush greens, golds, and browns that would comprise the best picture in Hailey's portfolio, misty gray held the bayou's secrets tight within its obscure and deadly grasp.

The occasional *pew, pew* of a baby gator replicated the sound of a science fiction gun blasting over open water. No doubt the growl heard thereafter came from the mother warning off other ambush predators.

In self-preservation mode, her fingers tightened on her bang stick. Only one shot, the .44 magnum proved an effective weapon while the long handle ensured she maintained a little distance from creatures intent on catching their next meal.

Dusk and dawn proved the most dangerous times for exploring the bayou and the best hunting times for apex predators. This morning, she was one of them. Natural light would help obtaining her best shot—with a camera.

On a recent excursion, she'd witnessed a black panther—reported to inhabit China, Southern India, and Malaysia, but nowhere in the US—prowling in search of prey. Without her camera, she could not prove its presence.

Her current position deep in the thinly treed forest allowed her to keep a decent 360 visual while viewing the narrow passage where her trail cam had caught her current target.

After checking for snakes and other meat eaters who enjoyed human flesh, she and Gunther settled behind the broad base of a cypress tree, a sentinel of the swamps. If not for the early start to their dry season, she would've had to hunker down in a boat.

Any amount of discomfort was worth the picture that would put her photo on the front page of *Wildlife Ezine*. Private investigative work earned her paychecks. This picture would establish her place as a photographer.

Beside her, Gunther perked his ears with the grumble of low voices in the distance. She wasn't the only bipedal creature around; though, running into others this far along the inlet was rare.

She couldn't hear the gist of the exchange.

Two men argued as they walked parallel to her position. They stopped and faced the water with one using his hands to emphasize a point. Their exchange heated and rose in volume until both startled as branches snapped to their left.

Using her hooded telephoto lens, she scanned the acreage bordered by three intersecting canals. Estimated distance put them at the edge of the largest waterway, a dangerous place to stand and not pay attention to surroundings.

Because she was generally curious and considered nosy, she snapped a few bursts to capture the moment on digital media. Both men stood canted toward the water, their profiles silhouetted by the rising sun. Shoulder-length hair pulled back in a ponytail swung to the side when the stockier of the two pivoted to face the woods.

His companion also wore jeans, but a hoodie covered his head. Shorter and wiry, his accent pegged him for a local.

Ponytail spoke with a stiff northern accent. He also wore a long-sleeved tee, common for maintaining a barrier between skin and biting insects. An eagle's head on the back of his ball cap proclaimed him a Philadelphia baseball fan.

From his back waist, Hoodie pulled a gun and took a step back, gaining distance between himself and his opponent, shaking his head.

Beside her, Gunther growled when a sharp crack filled the morning air, not the type issued from an alligator or the horrendous pop from a pistol. It was louder and lingered longer.

Rifle shot.

Ponytail, so animated a moment prior, fell back on his butt, his hands clutching his chest. Maybe she imagined the raspy breath before he slumped down in the marsh grass without further moving.

Hoodie was behind him and couldn't nail Ponytail in the chest. A third person shot him.

Gunther's presence during weapon's training assured he wouldn't react without conscious thought. Still, he didn't like guns and voiced his displeasure with zealous appeal.

Her hand on his collar kept him from bolting forward but also proved a distraction. In the split-second it took to quiet him, he'd given away their position, to both Hoodie and whomever shot his companion.

Hoodie's gaze swung in Hailey's direction.

"Duck!"

The harsh command in her ear startled her into hunching her shoulders. She dropped down and behind the tree trunk in the next second.

Someone had snuck up from behind her. Her gaze swiveled to either side in her half-pivot.

No one was there.

To prevent light from glinting off her lens barrel, she kept it low and tucked under her tee. The bang stick wouldn't aide her now. In order to fire, it required pressure, as in slamming it against an adversary.

Hoodie's gaze searched for a target. If he thought she'd shot his companion, he wasn't considering the angle of origin.

If he realized he'd left a witness after hearing Gunther bark, he'd face a murder charge if identified. His gaze swung between the direction of the shot and Gunther's warning, confirming her status as a witness.

"Hailey, move it." Something touched her shoulder, like a prankster who struck and disappeared. She ducked and swiveled her head, again finding no one.

A heartbeat later, another crack punched through the morning haze, the type of sound that accompanied lead boring through skulls at high velocity. The bullet tore bark from the tree she used as cover. Splinters cut her cheek.

The bastard is either lucky or an excellent shot. On the heels of that realization came, *Who saved my life?*

Who was the word coming to mind, not what. The directive had been unmistakable and precise, spoken inches from her ear.

Her four-footed companion strained against his collar. No doubt, he'd bring down the shooter if not stopped with a bullet. Neither scenario was acceptable out in the swamp when facing two guns.

"No, Gunther. We run. We're outmatched." She wasted no time grabbing her bang stick and urging him away. "Truck, boy. Load up. Go."

Running wasn't her first inclination, but it was the safest.

Gunther understood the objective and kept pace with her sprint through the maze of trees. Fear and another two shots fired motivated her to increase speed. She couldn't shoot the bastard, but she could damn sure outrun him.

In quick succession, return fire suggested Hoodie found a target. He'd obviously figured out the scenario. Staccato pops from his pistol was more distinctive than the rifle's discharge. Both were deadly.

She didn't imagine the perspiration melding her t-shirt to her skin or the wild thump of her stampeding heart. Each precious breath came with an increasing pain in her side. Twice she stumbled over weed clumps and struggled to remain vertical.

A boat's engine roared to life as she ran. With the amount of scrub brush along the waterline, cover was abundant. At least one of them got away.

In the distance, water sloshed. Maybe Hoodie ran along the waterline, or a feeding frenzy started with Ponytail for breakfast. The last scenario was rare but did happen.

She'd parked her truck a hundred yards east, which now put the rising sun in the shooter's eyes, not that she had hopes of hiding her identity. Many throughout the county knew her pony-sized wolf dog.

Another engine roared to life. From her angle, she couldn't see whether Hoodie fled or gave chase.

At the moment, neither mattered. She paused behind the base of a broad trunk at the edge of the forest to listen for the dwindling sound of the motorboat.

Unlike Gunther, who sat by her side, her breaths came in short pants and blocked out the normal sounds of waking wildlife. Exhaustion had bent her into a hands-on-knees position with adrenaline washout forcing to seek support in leaning against the oak.

"Looks like they're gone, boy. I wonder if the murder was planned or spur of the moment?" Either way, carrion predators would dispose of the remains in short order.

Gunther nudged her thigh until she tunneled her fingers through his long fur. In her mind's eye, she ran over the scenario again. It all happened too fast to get a look at either man's face.

When able to take her breaths in slow drags, she gathered her thoughts and determination.

"Okay, fella. They're gone. Let's go back and see what we can figure out before the evidence disappears."

It made sense for Hoodie and Ponytail to have come in different vehicles, both approaching from the water. Were they arguing about who they were supposed to meet?

A quick swipe of her phone revealed no cell service.

Go figure.

The satellite phone she'd wanted for months just became top priority. That and maybe a long talk with either her mom or a psychiatrist. Hearing a voice that sounded so real worried her as much as someone using her for target practice. One was a quick death, the other, a slow decline into madness.

In counterpoint, the verbal warning had saved her life. How was she supposed to reconcile that?

Town gossip long declared the Arquette family rife with Vodou practices and anything occult. Little did they know how close yet how far off they were.

Her grandmother had heard voices, the psychic ability manifesting as a teenager. She'd refused to offer details until Hailey reached adulthood. Unfortunately, cancer removed her from the living years ago. Hailey had celebrated her twenty-fifth birthday, well past the age expected to develop new abilities.

Her mother refused to discuss the matter until the time was *right.*

Once back in her original scouting spot, she checked her camera for specific landmarks while listening to nature. Crickets, frogs, and morning birds returned to their vocal routines after their rude awakening. Business as usual, except for the dead body in their midst.

Using the familiar misshapen tree as a reference point, she hiked to where Ponytail fell. Lack of water splashing dictated natural predators hadn't discovered him, yet.

There was little hope of getting cell reception and making an emergency call before they did. Since the victim hadn't landed in the water, maybe he still drew breath. Stranger things could happen, and usually did.

"Help me."

Low, almost inaudible, the gravelly base echoed behind her. The male's voice wasn't what she heard earlier.

She pivoted in a 360 but saw nothing.

"Where are you?" Jeez, she was talking to, what, a tree five feet away?

"I'm right in front of you."

"No, you're not." Hailey swept her hand out as a blind person might when treading in unfamiliar territory. Nothing.

Her hearing wasn't defective. Her mind—maybe.

"Ouch! Stop that."

"Stop what? I can't see you." Three steps back and almost tripping reminded her to turn and keep an eye on the waterline. Gators were incredibly fast for short distances.

Each step closer to her objective tripled the bile in her stomach until the wave of nausea threatened to eject her rushed breakfast of coffee and beignets.

"You can *hear me. So, you can help."*

Ahead, she saw a face among the tall grasses. A man lay supine, face up with the end of his ponytail draped over one shoulder, a pool of blood collecting beside his body. She knew in that moment he was dead. She also knew he'd spoken to her.

Directly to her.

Her fingers went slack, the bang stick dropping to the ground. Gunther edged forward and sniffed at bloody jeans, then up toward a mouth slackened in death.

Lifeless. Yet the man spoke to her. Yep, she was ready for a padded room and white jacket and hoped the long sleeves that wrapped around her torso were comfortable.

Why didn't Grandma talk about this?

"Mister?" Hailey prodded his lower leg with her booted foot. If she touched his skin, she might learn a lot, but that emerging ability was new and sometimes backfired due to misinterpretation.

The visions she received with contact were always jumbled, stronger when touching flesh, but chaotic just the same.

With no response, she grew bolder, kneeling to shake his shoulder, careful to protect herself by only touching his clothes.

Still, no response. Either from him or a vision.

Black cotton wicked up the crimson expanded to encompass a softball size stain on his chest. Rivulets down his flank led to a pool of bloody grass. Death had arrived and taken his soul, leaving wide-staring eyes accusing her for not returning sooner.

It wasn't morbid curiosity that made her take a picture of his face. No, the likelihood of this body remaining intact until the police arrived was nil. He was too heavy for her to move far enough from nearby carnivores.

Every murder victim deserved justice.

"Some son of a bitch killed me."

Hailey shoved back with her legs and dropped her bang stick. Gravity and the angle with which she pushed off dictated she thudded on her butt. Her right hand landed in a hill of mud and leafy debris before her mind registered what her fingers invaded.

Oh, shit... Eggs? In September?

Not impossible but very dangerous. She looked to the waterline less than twenty feet away and wasn't sure which spooked her more. Landing on top of an alligator's nest or hearing voices.

"Who are you?" If she could verify anything from the victim, she could prove her sanity was intact.

"Nobody now. If I tell you, it will bring you nothing but death. Go to the local police. Show them my picture. Tell them I was here. They'll do what they can and notify my family." There existed a sadness in the tone that transcended the otherworldly realm.

Shit.

In her scramble to stand, her hand brushed against something hard, something metal. Her fingers tightened around it. In a pinch, anything could be a weapon.

Not long ago, a female alligator had treed her for the worst night of her life. Now, she'd come full circle in finding a gator's nest.

I didn't just find it. I disrupted it.

Smaller predators such as raccoons destroyed a third of gator nests for the succulent eggs within. Hailey had no such ambition.

In standing, she saw what her fingers had inadvertently clutched. A gun. It could've belonged to Hoodie or dropped when Ponytail fell.

Her mind flashed image after image of it firing in slow motion, but shock blurred the horrific aftermath. She couldn't tell if he'd hit his target or even see a face.

The familiar warning hiss and growl of an approaching threat energized her into action. In her haste to get clear, she flung the gun, which landed on top of the dead man's chest.

Sorry, fella.

"Gunther, run." At least this encounter didn't include a sprained ankle. There wasn't time to retrieve the weapon and see if it was loaded. She didn't care to face off with a pissed-off momma gator either way.

Holding her camera lens in one hand and her bang stick in the other, she didn't stop running until reaching her truck.

Once she and Gunther were inside, she settled her equipment and rested her head against the steering wheel.

Neither of her best friends would believe the voices were real. They'd chalk her timely duck to subconscious warnings. They did however, know of her gift for psychometry, to learn about an object or person through touch. That would inspire questions.

As members of the local sheriff's department and FBI respectively, Trenton and Leigh would seek justice for the victim when shown proof of death, her photograph.

It was unfortunate she'd left the gun behind but didn't intend to wrestle it from a gator's clutches. If it belonged to Hoodie, it might be the only method of identifying him.

Another thought came to mind. She wasn't the only one with a strange ability. A teen she'd recently met could not only converse with spirits, but see them too.

A joint effort might be the only way to catch the killer. In the end, she wouldn't risk taking a teenager out on the bayou, even if she was uniquely qualified and technically an adult at eighteen years of age.

Casper could still help. If she could call the dead man's spirit to her, they might solve the case without risk.

On the heels of that came, *Ponytail's killer saw my face.*

Chapter Two

Hailey

Gunther's tail sweeping side to side signaled growing excitement as Hailey parked on the grass shoulder in front of her loft. His soft chuffing and short yips turned her gaze to see Casper striding out the office door.

She hadn't yet stopped to call her.

The teen's unrequested presence foreshadowed their insertion into a hornet's nest. Timing, depth, and duration were yet to be determined. Casper held more secrets than any government agency, which brought to mind her connections.

Months prior when Trenton stuck his FBI nose in her business, he received a sharp reprimand from his superior. The young woman was off limits for reasons unspecified, and the two hadn't seen eye to eye since. Neither would back down or give quarter.

Lucky for Hailey, she didn't work for the county or the feds, and as such was able to bypass the teen's resistance to authority figures. Since extricating them both from the local antique store when trapped by a thug months ago, Casper had begun offering tidbits about her life.

The teen's psychic talent went beyond anything Hailey could imagine. The ability to phase through any attack was an invaluable asset.

She'd remained aloof when discussing her family from Pennsylvania or past experiences.

Trust takes time.

The passenger door opened to admit the black-haired enigma wearing jeans and a t-shirt bearing KISS in bold red letters.

"Looking for companionship or promoting your favorite band?" Hailey nodded to the emblem.

"Acronym. 'Keep it simple, stupid' has become my motto." Casper blew air between her lips before giving Gunther his due of attention. "A friend from PA gave it to me, encouragement and a warning built into one. She thinks I tend to act before I think."

"Imagine that. Someone knows you well." Hailey grinned.

"Yeah, something we have in common other than long black hair, according to your friends Trenton and Leigh." A calming hand on the wolf dog's head soothed when he whined and sniffed her right shoulder. "It's okay, boy. S'all good."

There'd be time to puzzle out her wolf dog's constant fascination with the teen's shoulder later. For now, they had work to do. "What brings you to my door?"

Casper shrugged. "I hear you were on the wrong end of a shoot this morning." The teen nodded to the camera case on the back seat. "And not that kind."

"How'd you find out? I just got off the phone with Leigh before I parked."

Casper ignored the question in favor of asking one of her own. "You gonna take me out there, or do I have to find it myself?"

"Leigh will kill me if she sees you at a crime scene. Trenton might have a stroke."

"So, we'll get there first, do what we need to do, then get out. There's something we need to find."

"Which would be?" Hailey knew the answer before she spoke.

"The gun you left behind." A hurry-up gesture of her hand signaled impatience. "C'mon. You know I can phase us through any animal attack. We'll be safe. In and out before your badge-toting buddies come to the rescue." She rolled her eyes as only a teen could do.

"Both Leigh and Trenton have been riding me about why we're together so often." She hadn't found the right way to tell her friends that Casper would be the C in H&C Investigations at the end of the spring semester.

Despite hitting the legal age of eighteen, Casper was enrolled in the Gifted Elite school, pretending to be seventeen. Securing proper documentation to pull that off required significant backing. Another secret not yet shared.

"So, tell them the truth. We're partners."

"I can't. Not without telling them you're eighteen. Not only that, they both want to know how we got out of the antique store when Henri cornered us this past spring."

Casper studied the fields in passing, making a small noise in her throat. "Best that they never know. The group I work with, well, they protect their anonymity with a vengeance. Trenton knowing about me would lead to many questions. Not a good scenario."

"Understood, but I get the feeling there's more to you than the ability to walk through walls."

Casper grinned. "Yeah, there's always more to us than meets the eye. In time, we learn what we need to know."

"So, what's new at the school for the Gifted Elite? How're classes going?"

"I hate school, but it gives me the cover I need. Clannahan is holding that investigation over my head. I came down here to find information on my family. He won't spill it until this school business is over. I did find something interesting, though."

"What? Another pervert like Armond Boyer?"

"No. From the vice principal's office, we found some records. Encrypted communications between him and a school board member."

"And?"

"I'm not a digital prodigy but, luckily, I do know the best in the field."

"What's the VP involved in? Drugs?"

"Not sure yet. In tracing the emails up the chain, his buddy in the school board has frequent communications with someone associated with a local mob boss. Big money involved."

"How'd you find *that* out?" Hailey wondered about the apparent extensive resources of one so young.

"A friend of mine is a hacker, the equal of which you'll never meet. Wyatt can break through any firewall given the time."

Casper offered details and known money exchanges as they traveled farther into the remote sections of southeast Texas. Bayou country. Home of the superstitious, the religious, and the adventurous.

Trimmed lawns gave way to wilder country dotted with switchgrass, bluestem, and Indiangrass. There wasn't a part of the land Hailey didn't love. Though, the farther out they went, the more cautious they'd need to be. On a normal day, four-footed and slithering predators were more dangerous than their bipedal counterparts.

Miles after turning off an unpaved road, Hailey guided her truck along a four-wheeler path used by biologists supervising the wildlife management areas.

She parked and cut the engine near the same sward from which she'd run earlier.

"It's several hundred yards west." The tree line offered a minimally traveled path to the horrific scene. "Listen, Casper, the man is dead. You're only eighteen. I think—"

"Don't sweat it. I've seen dead before. Believe me, been there, done that. This is a piece of cake." Opening the door, she slid out and waited for Gunther to follow.

Succinct and casual, the statement pegged her as an old warrior trapped in a young soul. It also declared the circumstances didn't involve a funeral home or hospital. One day, Hailey would learn those secrets, hoarded like fire ants storing prey beneath their mound.

Details behind their strange relationship unfolded at a snail's pace and only when necessary. Casper didn't trust easily and didn't appear to socialize much, at least not like a normal teen.

Time and patience Mom always says.

Hailey took the lead through the woods with her bang stick in hand. Though she preferred the novelty of Casper phasing their bodies at a second's notice, she didn't want to burden her soon-to-be partner. Nor did she want her sense of self-preservation to grow lax.

"Did it look like a planned murder, 'cuz Donny wasn't expecting it."

Hailey stopped so abruptly Casper had to phase or stumble against her back. A shudder rippled from shoulder to shoulder as her silent partner phased forward then pivoted to face her.

"You have a name already?"

"Yeah. Donald Fitzpatrick. Didn't have time to look him up, but I sent it to Wyatt, my hacker friend. He'll have something soon I'm sure."

Gunther barked then lowered his shoulders to play-bow position, his tail sweeping the tall grass aside and a big doggy grin in place. He loved to play with Casper when she phased through solid objects, although it drove him nuts when he had to use hallways and stairways to find her. The ultimate hide and seek partner.

"How'd you know his name, Casper?"

"He talked to me. Didn't give many details. He's a cagy sonofabitch."

"What'd he say?"

"Asked me to help you get the gun. It might be very important and lead to bigger things."

"Damn. You knew I heard spirits? How?"

"They told me. Welcome to the club, and no, we're not related. Not that *I* know about, anyway. I've no clue who I'm related to down here, or if any relatives still exist."

"You're right... I heard something else just before a bullet struck inches from my face. Someone told me to duck, knew that I was the target."

Casper grinned, looking at the space beside Hailey. "You don't say."

"Who saved my life, Casper?" Hailey twisted her mouth in frustration when the teen shrugged and fell in step.

"Not for me to tell. If she wants you to know, she'll tell you."

"You know her identity. You said *she* and not *he.*"

"Focus, Hailey. Distractions get you killed." Casper stopped before exiting the tree line and pointed toward the creek. Thirty yards away, a half dozen alligators fought over something bigger than a raccoon or wild pig, something decidedly human shaped, or had been at one time.

"Oh, crap. They got into it fast." Hailey knelt to address her furry companion. "Gunther, stay. I don't want you getting excited and land us all in trouble."

Casper held out her left hand. "Here, take it and I'll phase both of us."

Hailey grasped at the offering, knowing the weirdness factor was just beginning. With contact, dozens of images assaulted her mind.

A ferocious battle took place beside a large mansion. Dozens of men and women lined up to protect their home. Weird flashes of light, electricity, fire, and things she couldn't identify contrasted the night blanketing the earth. Men screamed in agony from knives, guns, and swords.

Hailey snatched her hand away, knowing she'd viewed a scene from Casper's life and not a twisted dream. "Wow, you have experienced a lot, haven't you?" One day, she'd quiz her new friend about prior experiences.

"Yeah. Some days were tests of survival, saving the world and that kind of shit." Casper again held out her hand.

This time, Hailey caught a vision of four people buried in what looked like a shallow grave but wearing an oxygen mask.

"You sure you can hold us phased against this many?"

She'd never seen a feeding frenzy but knew the numbers could be much greater. Sometimes—gators attacked each other.

"It's not the number we're against that taxes me. It's how many I'm phasing." Casper trudged forward, a grimace on her face at the gruesome scene coming into view.

"The body... he's mutilated." When Hailey had left earlier, she knew there was a chance this would happen, especially considering the time of day and location.

She wasn't prepared to see most of one arm lying yards from its body and the subject in a tug of war.

Two more gators fought over the chest and torso.

The teen didn't flinch when three more reptiles erupted from the creek and joined the fray. "Damn filthy carrions have no respect." To make her point, she unphased her foot and kicked the closest tail in passing.

The gator whirled then growled as it tried to attack. Inability to make contact elicited continued hissing, soon joined by others.

"There's no way to find the gun now." Hailey couldn't help but flinch when the animals snapped strong jaws at her leg yet didn't connect.

"Yeah, we can. It's just harder to do, and messier. I hate messy options." Casper's gaze swiveled to the side, where a familiar figure stood. "Which one?"

"Ohmygod. Ponytail? I-I mean Donald?" Hailey flicked her gaze between the grotesque scene of alligators feasting on the corpse and following the line of Casper's gaze to the translucent figure—the man she'd seen shot.

"*The big one.*"

The voice, recognized from earlier, startled Hailey two steps back, stopped with Casper's jerk on her hand.

"Oh, God. I can see him, minus the wounds and dismemberment. He's watching these things tear him apart?" She couldn't step away without losing contact with the only form of protection, hence twisted and emptied her stomach where she stood.

At the moment, she wanted nothing more than to kick the closest predator in the head, poke his eyes, or shoot him. Unfortunately, she'd left her bang stick with Gunther in favor of helping Casper find the pistol.

On the heels of that thought came a realization. "Wow How long have you been able to see and talk to spirits?" She'd just entered a new dimension where nothing seemed real, except the smell of blood and gore permeating the air.

The teen shrugged. "Big one? They're all big, Donald. That doesn't help much."

A long sigh signaled a rough time ahead.

"Fine. It's not like I haven't done this with a shark before." The teen dipped her phased hand through the largest gator's body.

The creature gave no indication of feeling anything different—until going utterly still.

"It ate the gun? Why?" Casper asked as if a normal question for the scene.

Hailey noticed that not only did the teen take the work in stride, she did it without turning a sickly shade of green. "Consider it a small feeding frenzy scenario. They'll tear into each other at times, biting anything they get their jaws around. Smaller prey get eaten whole, other stuff... not so much."

"I'm trying to find its stomach."

"So, uh, Donald, saw this one eat the gun?" Hailey's world just got a bit darker.

"Yeah, and I hope it broke a bunch of teeth in the process."

"Donald? Why don't you tell us who shot you? And maybe why you were out here to begin with."

"No. Leave it for the cops. I don't want to get a woman and kid killed."

"Listen, moron." Casper berated the spirit. "We're here. We're on the case. And we're your best option for getting justice."

"There's a whole lot more behind my story, half-pint. I don't want either of you involved, regardless of how special you may be." The tone suggested there'd be no middle ground.

"Fine. We'll do it on our own." Casper blew bangs from her face with a huff. "What in hell does a gator's stomach feel like? I've not studied their anatomy."

"I've no idea, but if we're going to identify Donald through fingerprints for the police, we'll need his hand." Hailey pointed to the two gators still fighting over the arm.

"First, the gun. It's in this guy's belly. You've got his picture... I know some sharks have J-shaped stomachs that expand quite a bit since they swallow prey whole."

"*Gators have two stomachs,*" the noncorporeal being said. "*You'll find gastroliths, or stones, used to grind up their food in the first. The second is extremely acidic, so as to, you know...*"

The teen didn't apparently object to taking instruction from a bodiless spirit. The descriptions alone turned Hailey's stomach. "Casper, you are way beyond your years."

"Yeah, I've been through a lot."

Hailey followed the light tug on her hand and helped search the gator's stomach. Though she hadn't had much practice with phasing, what little she'd experienced would haunt her dreams. She felt a tingly sensation at her fingertips.

She wondered exactly what type of experiences Casper had in respect to searching for bodies and weapons.

"Ah, I've got something. Let's see." The gator in question roared when Casper pulled her hand out.

"Damn. It's a belt buckle. Let's try this again." Scrunching her nose, she delved back through tough hide like it was nothing but air.

A minute later, she grunted and pulled hard on something. "Got it."

This time, she pulled out a gun.

"Okay. Let's get out of here. Your cop friends will arrive soon."

"If Trenton and Leigh catch you out here with me—"

Gunther issued an excited yip from where he sat. With his gaze facing the trail and his tail wagging, his entire body quivered with excitement. A normal response to both Trenton and Leigh.

"Damn. I shoulda posted a guard." Casper handed the gun to Hailey and wiped her fingers on her jeans. "They're here. We need to scoot. Now."

Hailey gripped the hand keeping her in one piece as two predators again clamped their jaws on nothing but each other. "How am I gonna explain your presence? I shouldn't have brought you out here." Retrieving her bang stick after tucking the gun in her waistband didn't make her look any more responsible.

"I'd be more concerned about them finding a gator's stomach acid all over the gun." Casper snorted. "You could tell them I'm your new partner, that we're both into Vodou. They'd believe that. 'Sides, I am eighteen."

"But they don't know that yet. Whoever altered your records did a damn good job." Hailey stared, deadpan. "No need to invite more questions."

"Yeah, Wyatt's the best. Married to my best friend, who saved my life and brought me into her family."

"I hope someday—"

"You'll meet them at some point, I'm sure."

The path grew quiet once they'd left the feeding gators behind.

It was too much to hope they'd reach her truck before Trenton and Leigh saw them.

Fate showed little mercy. The badged duo met them at the head of the trail.

Hailey's thoughts dissipated at the first sight of Trenton's furious glare.

"You brought a kid to a crime scene? Are you nuts? What in hell are you thinking?"

"Hey, listen up, Fed. I don't know who doused your last condom in hot sauce, but I'm eighteen now, and if I'm not mistaken, you've been warned by your superior to not mess with me." Casper edged around Hailey to stand toe to toe with Trenton, showing no hesitancy in meeting his glare.

"I'm not messing with you. I'm trying to protect you! Damn, kid. Have you no sense of self-preservation?" Trenton roared.

Casper's fists clenched and relaxed at her sides. "I can take care of myself."

Trenton gripped the teen's upper arms. "You're right about one thing. The SAIC told me to leave you alone. You're just a kid." Bending to within inches of her face, he continued, "But you're at a crime scene now. That makes you fair game. You will answer my questions, and you will give a formal statement. Nothing can allay that. Got it?"

Casper fumed silently, the only outward sign a twitch in her jaw. As if flipping a switch, she smiled, not in a friendly way. "Yeah, I got it. Tell me something, are you a sound sleeper?"

Hailey stilled, keeping her hand on Gunther's head and giving Leigh a warning shake to not interfere. "Ah, Casper? How 'bout we head out and let them do their job?"

She envisioned Casper's ghostly following tormenting Trenton's nights. She'd have to find a way to cool the rising animosity between them if she wanted peace moving forward.

Leigh, a detective with the Jefferson County Sheriff Department, stood and watched the interplay then cleared her throat. As a long-term friend, she knew when to adopt the *wait-and-see* modality of life.

"I sleep just fine, *Olivia*." Trenton emphasized the teen's adopted name. He released his hold and softened his tone. "Look, Casper. I just want to make sure you live to graduate."

"I don't need your protection, don't want it, and won't stand for it." Her mien changed in an instant. "However, if you have anything else on your mind, since I am legal now and all," she fluttered her eyelashes and adopted a shit-eating grin, "...I am available."

Beside him, Leigh giggled, aware of the saucy, provocative strategy.

On cue, Trenton back stepped so fast he lost his balance, twisting at the last minute and sidestepping a large clump of cordgrass to remain upright.

"Now that we've cleared the air and gained some distance, Hailey, wanna hand over the evidence to your hottie?" Casper smirked when Trenton made a low rumbling noise in his throat.

Hailey quickly produced the gun and offered it to the federal agent who'd been her friend since childhood. The anger swimming in his gaze didn't abate despite the smooth façade overtaking his expression.

"Where?" Was all he said.

"Follow the trail, but keep your guns handy. You'll need them." Casper flashed a sweet smile before directing her attention to Hailey. "I know we have to give a statement, but I'm feeling a bit lightheaded." Placing the back of her hand to her forehead in a dramatic parody of shock, she added, "I think I need a shower and some food."

Leigh snorted.

Trenton stared, then grabbed Hailey's bang stick to examine it. "I hear the gators. How is it you went among them to retrieve the gun yet never fired a shot? They wouldn't be swayed by your beauty."

Comments like that derailed her focus. They were friends, yet the intensity of his gaze coated her in a thick layer of gooey emotion she wouldn't define. He stepped closer, within inches, such that she caught the scent of his aftershave. He intentionally used the heat and electricity between them to offset her. And it worked.

Until she took a step back and smiled.

"We asked them nicely, Trent. How else?" Hailey snatched her stick back and ushered her young friend toward the truck. Once out of earshot, she chuckled. His valiant effort almost worked.

"I just antagonized the hell out of a federal agent. Dumb move. Worse—I raised his curiosity to DEFCON One. You're the one who likes getting a rise out of him."

"You're the one who *should* be getting a rise out of him. Damn if he isn't fine looking with the body to match. Why haven't you indulged?" Casper stumbled over uneven ground, muttering something about norms.

"Trenton and I are friends and have been, like, forever. I did think about it at one time, but didn't want to ruin what we have. We're good." In her heart, she knew they could be great together. Fear kept her from taking that leap. Hailey opened the driver's door to usher Gunther inside, staring back at the trail leading to the horrific scene of death.

Instead of hopping up, the wolf dog issued a low rumbling growl that morphed into a round of ruckus barking.

"What's wrong, boy?"

On the back seat beside her camera, a thin gray blanket covered a lump.

"That wasn't there before." From the passenger side, Casper threw back the cover. "Um, *ew*? Do you have a secret admirer that you're keeping from everyone? If so, please don't introduce me. I'm not into that kind of kink."

The bloody head of an alligator took up the width of the seat, its soulless gaze rooting her feet to the soft earth. Blood wicking over the cloth signaled recently dead status.

"Damn. We'd only been here a half hour before Leigh and Trenton arrived."

Casper grasped the amulet around her neck and briefly closed her eyes, saying, "Donald Fitzpatrick, did you see who left us this present?"

A minute passed.

Gunther continued sounding his verbal alarm.

"No. I was... elsewhere."

Hailey faced where she'd heard the voice, next to Casper. To call specific spirits to her side marked a vast advancement on the scale of psychic ability.

From the wood line, Leigh ran with her gun in hand, pointed at the ground. "What's got Gunther in an uproar? And why would he alert with an intruder's alarm when—oh, Hailey. What've you stepped in now?"

"Damn it, Hailey!" Trenton pushed both Leigh and Hailey back as he surveyed the item left on the seat.

"Don't you dare say it, Trent. I don't want to hear it. This is not Vodou."

"Then, what is it? You must know. You always know more than you let on. Wait, is this related to her?" Trenton cast a suspicious gaze in Casper's direction.

"She's got nothing to do with this. Really." Hailey jumped when a low hum sounded in her ear.

"It wasn't left by my killer. I can tell you that much."

Hailey dropped her chin to chest. "I don't know who left it, Trent. I honestly don't know."

What she did know, was that Donald Fitzpatrick was dead and holding secrets.

Chapter Three

Hailey

Shadowed arms of the maple tree in her backyard fluttered their fingers against the rear block wall of her loft. The first hint of autumn announced itself with a tinge of orange caressing the leaves and reminded Hailey of the warm, spiced pear gin cocktails she and Leigh enjoyed.

Gunther hop-skipped by her side, expending energy stored during a morning at the police station giving her statement. The time had proven entertaining if nothing else.

Even Lieutenant Colson, Leigh's supervisor, snickered at Casper's virtual thumbing her nose at them all. The lieutenant was wise enough to not agitate the situation and took the time to choose his words with care.

Trenton, not so much.

Instead of heading up the stairs to her loft, she led Gunther down the hallway and entered the first-floor reception area to touch base with her part-time receptionist.

Gunther bolted through the door to greet Elizabeth as soon as it opened.

"Hey there, boy. You miss me?" Elizabeth crouched, her long hair sliding forward with the new colors illustrating an ability to match any outfit, this one showcasing her affinity for blue, yellow, and red. The rainbow hues began at her shoulder and changed every few inches until reaching her mid back.

"Hey, Liz, how're college classes going?" Hailey noted the open grammar book on the desk. Positioning suggested it the perfect support for her snacks.

"Grammar rules are confusing. I mean—an apostrophe means possession, right? Except with the word *it*. Sometimes you could be referring to a specific *thing*, but sometimes you could use it either way, and it still sounds right. Who thought up these stupid rules, anyway?" The receptionist huffed out a breath and rubbed foreheads with Gunther. "You don't care, do you? As long as you get attention and people are kind, they could say anything, and it wouldn't matter."

"You'll get the hang of it, Elizabeth. Any messages?"

The scarred wooden desk groaned under the weight of the young woman using it to push herself up, not that she was heavy or needed it for support.

"Yeah, right after that nosy kid left, this woman called all in a huff. Ya know, I don't know why Casper keeps coming around. You'd think she'd have better things to do. It's not like she's ugly or fat. Maybe she's got a personality quirk boys can't handle."

"She's actually a big help. I think that—"

The younger woman's careless shrug declared the answer rhetorical and not worth finishing.

"For that matter, Hailey, *you* could have any man you wanted if you'd just wear contact lenses to disguise the weird color. It's not like a guy could see them in the dark, unless they glow? I bet even—"

Hailey crossed her arms over her chest and twisted her lips to the side.

"Oh. Oh! She calls herself Casper!" Elizabeth palmed her forehead and scrunched up her nose. "I didn't recognize the connection before. Is she gonna be the C person in H&C Investigations?"

"We're talking about it."

"Oh, my God. You mean I'll have a *kid* for a boss? That's inhumane, Hailey."

"Nothing's etched in stone. Also, if she does join us, she's pretty laid back and still attending classes at the Gifted Elite. You'd get along just fine."

"She's sarcastic as hell, arrogant, and in general, a pain in the ass. What makes a high-school senior appropriate to work here?"

Elizabeth had never been subtle about fishing expeditions, most of which went ignored.

Hailey held her hand out expectantly, not about to explain why she refused to hide her unusual eye color any more than she'd discuss Casper's strange abilities.

On occasion during an investigation, it became necessary to wear sunglasses during an interview. Otherwise, people could make their own assumptions about physical attributes and questionable heritage.

"Elizabeth? The message?" Keeping the receptionist on track was a full-time job.

"Um." Several papers slid from desk to floor during the questing search. "Yeah, here it is." Dusting the donut crumbs from the paper, she handed it over. "Pushy as hell. The woman said I should go find you right away, like I know my way through the swamps."

It wasn't worth the breath to deliver an admonishment that Elizabeth would misunderstand. Instead, Hailey took the paper scrap to her office and read it en route. It was marked "urgent," in no less than three places, the last one underlined twice.

Retrieving her phone, she dialed the local number.

Instead of an introduction or greeting, a blistering string of invectives soared through the airwaves.

"Hello? Ms. Teaman?"

In the next breath, a flood of expletives arrived from the other end of the line.

"Oh, yes. Hello. Is this Hailey Arquette? This is Charlotte Teaman."

Hence began a normal conversation where the owner of Upward Bound, a youth center on the town's outskirts, detailed her need to find a specific young man, missing since the prior day.

"Okay. I can pop over in a few minutes."

After disconnecting the call, Hailey knelt to offer Gunther a cuddle session. Life had gone from scary to grotesque before venturing into loony. AKA a somewhat normal day.

She'd witnessed a murder, watched alligators eat a man, then walked *through* said alligators to find a gun, all in the course of her morning.

It was barely noon.

What more could happen? If earlier events didn't freak her out, nothing would.

Grandma always said to never invite the gremlins.

"C'mon, fella. Let's go for a ride. It's ambassador time for you." She kept his service vest in her truck for easy access. Due to the wolf side of Gunther's heritage, she'd never obtained official documentation, but he'd earned his certificate for canine good citizenship.

The short drive didn't settle her thoughts about what she'd seen that morning. In counterpoint, Casper had taken it all in stride, like just another day at the office, which begged the question, *What has her life been like, and who trained her?*

A lifetime of contemplation wouldn't answer the odd questions. However, several things became abundantly clear in short order.

Conversing with and taking advice from ghosts lay in Hailey's future. That realization ranked right up there with *creepy situation of the year* with a side order of, *How do I deal with that?*

Perhaps her mother could shed some light if she gathered the courage to open the topic. Her grandmother had encouraged conversations about spirits and legends, but Cecile Arquette had drawn a hard line, declaring the topic closed until the time was right. The only thing Hailey knew for certain was that her grandmother had strong psychic abilities.

Ghosts?

A second shock during the prior months included Casper proving game for any challenge, if lacking forethought. She not only spoke to spirits, she saw them, which begged the next questions.

Since Hailey now conversed with spirits, would she see them too at some point? Did she share a blood relative with Casper somewhere in their past?

To her knowledge, she had no siblings, except the sister who died shortly before birth. Her mother had withheld that information until the discovery of her father's body, which led through a tangled web of deception and conspiracies.

None of which could've involved Casper, the enigma who'd only recently moved from Pennsylvania to investigate the school for the gifted.

Since discovering the teen's unique abilities, Hailey hadn't risked an in-depth conversation with Trenton or Leigh for worry of giving away some juicy tidbit. Trenton was a skilled interrogator, usually unflappable, and Casper horded secrets like an NSA analyst.

Another peculiarity came to mind.

Each time the teen and Gunther came into close proximity, the dog's agitation morphed to excitement with continued efforts to sniff her shoulder and neck. Immediately thereafter, he'd close his eyes and rest his head before issuing a low doggy groan, the same as when she stroked his forehead.

Despite age difference and their approach to problems, it seemed fate expected Hailey and Casper to join forces. It just felt... right.

Seven years difference wasn't a stretch when considering the visions experienced after taking Casper's hand at the crime scene.

She's had her hand in a shark's stomach.

It didn't bear thinking about *those* circumstances. Could she breathe underwater?

Focus on the now.

The severed gator's head proved effective motivation to identify the killer before meeting the same fate as Donald Fitzpatrick. She'd been targeted with a totem left in her truck and the recipient of an attempted "crushing by gargoyle statue" months prior.

Her entry to Upward Bound paused for a family of foxes crossing the dirt road straddled by fields of wild grass. A wooden sign hung from a foot-wide brace spanning the driveway supported with six-by-six posts, reminiscent of an old western ranch. Custom made, it sported metal horses and elk on either side of marsh grass.

Hailey wound her way up the twisting lane and parked beside a four-wheel drive diesel. No doubt it pulled the horse trailer seen beside the barn fifty yards from the house.

Post-and-rail fencing cordoned off a good fifty acres in front of the barn with roughly the same size to the rear. A half-dozen quarter horses grazed in the back pasture.

A golden retriever barked once and wagged his tail in greeting as she slid out and shut her door, offering her hand for sniffing. "Afternoon, girl. Aren't you pretty? Are you friendly to other dogs?"

One lick preceded another before the golden moved on to the next visitor. She rested her paws on the driver's door to greet Gunther through the open window. Seeing there was no conflict, Hailey invited her furry partner out.

The two romped around the front yard with play bows, sharp turns, and dodging in their game of tag until a whistle stopped the golden in her tracks. Changing course, she raced passed the wooden steps leading to the two-story ranch-style house to her handler.

"Hailey? Hailey Arquette?" The voice belonged to a slightly older woman who bore no fear of dogs, evidenced when she knelt to greet Gunther with her hand out.

"Hi. Yes. You said it was urgent, so I—"

"Yes, thank you for coming right away. I'm Charlotte." Dusty blue jeans and a worn cotton shirt revealed the owner's hands-on approach at her facility.

The hand offered in greeting was calloused and firm. The woman wasn't afraid of a hard day's work. Deeper lines on her forehead declared she scowled more often than smiled.

Charlotte's pause when meeting Hailey's gaze equaled a frequently encountered response. The unusual shade of blue generated a wide range of comments, conjectures, and slight gasps.

Hailey fixed a tight smile on her face before acknowledging the young woman toting three bridles toward the house.

"This is my assistant Juliet. Let's sit on the porch so I can explain what I think is happening." Short with wavy brown hair, the owner was in her late twenties or early thirties and presented a business demeanor. "Juliet, why don't you take a break before finishing up?"

Short with a layered blonde pixie cut, the assistant suggested, "How about I grab you both some tea before I call the vet?"

"Great. We'll sit on the porch." Charlotte led them up the stairs and gestured Hailey to sit. "I have a file with the information you'll need."

Hailey nodded her assent. "Thank you." Sweeping one hand wide, she said, "This is quite a place you have here. I've heard of it, but have never visited."

"It's a work in progress. We fight for every soul who walks onto this property, and let me tell ya, it's usually one hell of a battle."

Charlotte opened her folder, revealing the snapshot of a young man tossing a bale of hay from the back of a truck. Further details of his life formed a picture of one who'd shed an old life for a new path.

"I assume you've contacted the police?" Hailey leaned forward in the wooden rocker to accept the photograph then used her phone to capture a digital picture.

"Yes, but they're reluctant to jump in so soon. Babtiste used to belong to the local gang, so the police assume he has returned to them. I want someone who's fully invested in finding him. I know damn well he didn't return to the Jackyls."

"You've helped quite a few kids leave that life behind. They can't be too happy about losing members. How do you keep them at arm's length?" Hailey wondered about the inner strength needed to persevere against such hatred and asked.

"The ones who've come tend to share secrets. The Jackyls know this and don't want their dirty deeds returning to roost. It's been a battle, and we have to keep security tight."

"When did you last see Babtiste?"

"Yesterday afternoon. He's one of the few who live here. The others come for the day. I encourage each new arrival to reconcile with their families if appropriate. Unfortunately, that's not always possible."

Details on personal and family history of the missing young man accompanied another picture of him smiling at the photographer. Handsome in a rugged sort of way, it was hard to imagine him a member of the gang until noticing the scar along his right cheek.

"He's helping me keep new arrivals safe, but it's hard. That group is evil personified and rule their members with an iron grip."

Every town had its share of thugs, the larger the population, the bigger the gang, according to Leigh. For reasons unknown, Hamchet had a disproportionate number of those willing to pledge their lives to whatever cause dictated to them.

"The Jackyls are basically drug dealers and couriers. They have an integrated system with those along the *pipeline* so to speak."

"And nobody's been able to shut them down?" Hailey knew drugs were part of any culture but hadn't known much about the gang taking a foothold in her county.

"They've been growing in numbers and ambition, more so over the last few months. I'm not sure what's spurred it."

"Growing in ambition? In what way?" Drugs were bad enough. Hailey retained a small scar after a face-off with Henri, a major drug runner taken out of the equation by a teacher at the Gifted Elite.

"They want a piece of the gun smuggling operation." Juliet said as she let the screen door close behind her. She set down a tray with three glass mugs of tea before taking a seat.

The tea was sweet with an unknown spice, savored as they contemplated the larger scenario of drugs and guns. She hadn't heard Leigh or Trenton mention gun smuggling as a major issue, probably to keep her out of any current investigation.

Sparse population along the intricate and complicated waterways of the bayou provided good rendezvous points for illegal transactions. A perfect setup for criminals.

"Two of our kids were killed last year by the Jackyls when they tried to leave the gang. Police found a gun that someone wiped clean, and no witnesses stepped forward. It came from a shipment slated for destruction in Florida." Juliet rocked in her chair, patting Charlotte on the shoulder. "It was hard on us all, but you most of all. That young man could've pulled his life together with a little help."

"Running guns doesn't sound like the work of a local gang," Hailey murmured. "That takes connections to a larger organization."

"You're right. Rumor mill says organized crime sects are combining to challenge local factions wherever encountered. If successful, this could be the beginning of a war, one that'll cost many lives," Charlotte added. "There aren't many around here who would tangle with that crowd. One of the victims had been Babtiste's best friend."

"Yet you don't hesitate to jump in." Hailey admired the farm owner's strength and perseverance.

Those who've faced great adversity in their lives either break under the pressure or obtain a hardened shell with the perseverance to endure whatever life throws their direction. It was obvious strong demons rode Charlotte's shoulders. Only a few years older, she had clear goals and the guts to see them through.

"As a former Jackyl, does Babtiste have other friends who are still active members?" Several possible scenarios came to mind, none appropriate to mention until gathering further information.

"I suppose so. He doesn't talk about those days much. Said he'd found a better way of life and wanted others to share it, to feel the freedom he'd earned." Charlotte watched the dogs romping around the yard. "Freedom, denied to some, simply enjoyed by others." The setting was almost idyllic, if not for discussing murder, drugs, and gunrunners.

"Did Babtiste have any enemies or recent entanglements with anyone *not* in his former gang?"

Charlotte made a low sound in her throat. "Not that I know of, but he did learn some disturbing information."

"About gun distribution?"

"Yes. Whoever is transporting them is trying to extend the route along the Texas coast. I don't know how or where, or even what else he knew. He didn't share any further details." Charlotte's fingers tapped a soundless rhythm against the armrest of her chair.

"Where did he say he was going yesterday? On the phone, you said something about preparations for a festival?"

"Yes." Juliet's excitement over the upcoming affair dimmed with her eyebrows lowering and her lips pursing. "We intended this to be our first of many celebrations, an annual event for those who've joined us. Babtiste left to pick up the proper permits and permissions for fireworks."

Charlotte raised her hand to make a point. "But that was early in the afternoon. When he wasn't back yesterday evening, I thought maybe he got caught up with some friends, but he hasn't returned or answered his phone. This isn't like him. He wouldn't abandon this place, not with all the work he's put into it. He just wouldn't."

Retrieving her cell phone, Hailey took a photo of Babtiste's driver's license and other detailed information in his file. "Okay, now that I've got a starting point, I'll call you with a progress report in a few days."

In standing, she called Gunther to her side, now laying in the grass beside his new friend. "C'mon, boy. Time to roll."

With several threads to pull, she'd need both Leigh and Trenton's help. No doubt, Casper would insert herself into the thick of things, regardless of where her own investigation into the Gifted Elite school led.

Before loading Gunther in her truck, she removed his vest and laid it on the back seat. "Good boy, Gunther. You did just fine."

From the center console, she grabbed one of his treats and held it up. Once he hopped in and over to the passenger seat, she tossed it to him, grabbed in midair with a soft *woof.*

"What'd ya think, fella? Is this Babtiste the golden boy Charlotte says, or has he slipped back into old patterns?"

Gunther leaned against her shoulder and chuffed once.

"Yeah, I don't know either, but how about we go get some ice cream from Á La Mode before we dig into this thing? Your buddy promised to keep a stock of peanut butter frozen treats just for you, and I could use a little sugar rush."

Animal loving locals knew and welcomed Gunther's presence wherever he went. Others were skittish of the startling contrast of blue eyes and black fur. Some went so far as to suggest a black-magic connection.

A familiar jingle from her phone aired through her truck's speakers in turning out of the facility's lane. Tapping the screen of her phone, she waited.

After their third encounter, Casper had borrowed Hailey's phone and created a new contact. The ghostly theme hadn't registered at the time.

Now, she laughed.

"Hailey."

Gunther howled when hearing the teen's voice. *That* connection was one she hadn't figured out yet.

"Casper, what's up?"

"Where are you?"

"Heading toward Á La Mode to get a treat for Gunther."

"Good. I'll meet you there."

Chapter Four

Casper

Casper parked in the shade of the ice cream shop where her classmates congregated at the end of the day. Fellow students declared the homemade desserts part of a divine conspiracy to see each patron gain thirty pounds during the school year.

An abundance of energy and daily training negated it as a problem for her.

Four girls from her calculus class stood near one of the half-dozen picnic tables, engaged in a heated argument with local thugs. Minor squabbles reported on several occasions included minor scuffling but not severe enough to require medical care.

She was in Texas to do a job before searching for information about her family. This type of headache shouldn't be on her radar. However, one of the students present had extra-curricular contact with a local hardware store owner, found during her probing.

New school administration plus suspected illegal activities necessitated an in-depth look from an insider. She couldn't afford to let a possible suspect get hurt during a scuffle with the locals.

Sent to investigate ties between administration and gifted students, she needed a way into their social circle. Previous life experience ranked her low in knowledge of nail polish and hair products.

"Okay, Simon. Let's break this up without anyone needing a visit to the ER, okay? Everybody deserves one minor mistake without injury."

Her ability to communicate with the spirit realm had begun less than twenty-four hours after her beloved capuchin monkey was murdered in front of her.

As guardian of the amulet around her neck, she retained the ability to converse with and influence those in the spirit world. On more than one occasion, they interrupted her training, mealtime, and sleep. Spirits had little consideration for schedules of the living.

Ruffling of her hair swept longish bangs to the side before she opened her car door. His style of communication lent comfort.

"I love you too, Simon."

Show time. Considering the rabble and students involved, she'd have to plan her moves to keep her talents hidden, at the same time scaring the riffraff into leaving the students alone. If successful, it could earn her place in the current clique.

"Hey, guys. You all tried the honey jalapeno pickle ice cream? I hear it's phenomenal and worthy of our firstborns." Loud enough to carry over the small lot, her words focused all attention in her direction, as planned.

A pause in her step granted the right amount of startled appearance, feigned for effect. She made a sour face. "Don't tell me these are your new besties... I'm afraid I don't swing that low."

It was bound to happen sooner or later. A public confrontation with local gang members wasn't ideal, but she'd take the opportunity to set them straight and make sure students were off limits.

Anything that threatened her probing into illicit school activities needed to end decisively. A little one-on-one action would've been better, someplace out of vocal and sight range of others, but sometimes she had to take what life offered. She'd learned her lessons well, her favorite trainer a sling-shot-toting Frenchman with one hell of a right hook.

She sighed.

Four young men and two women, all dressed in dirty jeans and bearing the same colorful emblem on their jackets identified the local gang. Jackyls.

As one, six sneers turned her way. Four morphed into appreciation and a specific hunger she'd encountered and dealt with before.

Permanently.

If she'd caught up with one of the thugs before now, and without an audience, she could've left a lasting reminder of how dangerous it was to tangle with the unknown.

The girl with long stringy hair turned to the boy closest to her. On the back of her jacket was a stitched brown-and-white face, the animal's bushy tails and erect ears—smaller than a shepherd, larger than a fox—implied its genetics a mixture of both.

Since the wild animals' home grounds were Africa and Asia, Casper wondered how or if the knowledge had factored into the chosen mascot.

"Well, well. What do we have here? Fresh meat?" Short and wiry, the speaker raked her with his gaze, stopping on the return trip with a leer.

His small man-bun would make for a nice handhold in controlling his head during the coming scuffle.

"The only fresh meat you'll see is your tiny pecker in a commercial grinder if you don't leave my friends alone." Antagonizing the one designated boss was a strategic move.

A round of chuckles indicated energetic enthusiasm.

Once she beat the hell out of him, one of two things would occur. A, he'd call in reinforcements and try to take her by surprise at a later date. Or B, he'd leave her alone and give her a wide birth.

With a little help from her spirit friends, maybe she could push the odds toward the latter.

Wheels skidding on asphalt and a sharp bark indicated arrival of backup. Not that she'd ever turn it down, but she didn't need the responsibility for someone less experienced in hand-to-hand, no-holds-barred fighting.

Man-bun wasted no time in stalking forward.

She smiled and waited for him to approach. Having the extra room to move would allow her to teach a proper lesson outside of his buddies' or her fellow students' viewing range.

Gunther bolted past her to block her opponent's stalk.

"Hailey, call your dog. I've got this asshole, trust me. It's a lot easier than dealing with a gator. Really."

"Gunther, come." Hailey circumvented the stalker to block the other Jackyl's movement. "A shame these idiots don't know to back off."

On command, Gunther switched objectives and faced off with the remaining three intent on circling what they considered prey.

"Hold it right there, idiots. This is gonna be a fair fight." Hailey brushed the right side of her jacket to expose the gun on her hip. "Who'd like to be target practice?"

"Forget the older bitch. I want this one." Man-bun reached for Casper's right arm, but she ducked and swept his legs out from under him. He landed on his ass with one arm outstretched to break his fall.

The loud snap wasn't from chewing gum. A pained gasp exploded from his mouth, covered by a string of epithets. He was on his feet with his left forearm cradled against his chest in an instant.

"Well, that was easy. I didn't even work up a sweat. You sure you're not late for knitting class somewhere? Perhaps you could make yourself some padding for the next time you fall down and go boom."

"I'll teach you to spar with this, bitch." He grabbed his crotch with his good hand to signify the threat. The knife he then pulled appeared to be an extension of his fingers. "Time to teach you a thing or two. First is how to obey."

He thrust forward with his weapon.

She knocked his hand to the side and latched onto his wrist. Using his momentum to pull him forward and off balance provided the edge needed in dealing with his greater weight.

Stepping in with her left foot, she moved closer until their bodies made contact.

"Time for you to learn some manners, asshole. I was taught by the best." Phasing her left hand, she delved through the shirt over his left flank until reaching something squishy-solid.

Liver? Gallbladder?

Her schooling with Dr. Neah Channon included anatomy and physiology, but not what the organs *felt* like.

The scream in her ear reflected the effectiveness of her effort.

Before pulling back, she wiggled her fingers for good measure. "Let this be a lesson, moron. You don't mess with me. You don't mess with the GE students. It's an automatic death sentence. Got it?"

He stumbled back but didn't drop his weapon. His look of horror continued through ripping his shirt up and checking the wound.

Nothing but smooth skin showed. No blood. No bruise.

His expression betrayed the pain delivered.

"How'd you do that, bitch?" Instead of waiting for an answer, he rushed forward with his blade extended.

"Not a particularly bright one, I see," Hailey remarked, leaning against her truck with arms folded over her chest.

Keeping her opponent between herself and the gawkers, Casper phased her hand through his chest then down his abdomen. The next time she pulled back, she took a souvenir. A little blood went a long way.

Crimson coated her fingers up to her palm. "*Ew,* gross." Not wanting to dirty her own shirt, she wiped her hand on the filthy cotton covering his chest.

His lingering scream would be heard across the town.

Her opponent dropped to his arse and interlaced his fingers across his stomach, heedless of the wrist injury.

"What kind of freak are you?"

Casper stepped forward and leaned over him, watching him shrink from her proximity. No doubt he'd remember her whispered words for a long time to come.

"The kind you don't mess with and survive. And trust me on this, if you ever breathe a word of this to *anyone,* I will know. I will then walk into your house, through your walls, and gut you like the pig you are."

Straightening up, she rolled her shoulders and smiled. "Be seeing you around. Next time, I expect better manners, and if I visit you at your house, I expect an appropriate beverage and cookies. Any kind of chocolate will do."

Mere yards away, Hailey snickered. "I like the ones stuffed with crème."

Man-bun looked from Casper to Hailey. "Are you like her?"

"Wanna find out the hard way?" Hailey waggled her eyebrows for effect.

"No. No, ma'am. No, ma'am. We're good." Man-bun stood and again checked his abdomen; his shirt now tinged with a bloody smear. A glance at Casper's red-stained fingers increased his pallor.

"Cookies and chocolate," he said, gesturing wildly for his friends to get moving.

"Wait." Hailey intercepted the young man and held her hand out to stop his progress.

"What? I didn't do nothing." Man-bun took a defensive stance.

With a smile, Hailey held out her hand as if greeting him for the first time. "Look. No hard feelings. Let's end this on peaceful terms, shall we?" She kept her hand out, arched a brow, and waited.

Casper understood the gesture and approved. Anything gleaned through contact could help.

"Your eyes. Oh, shit. You're the witch everyone talks about."

"Not nice to disparage someone you've never met." Hailey thrust her hand out a little farther. "I suggest you take it."

With a tentative outreach, man-bun took the offered hand and pumped gently. Twice.

Hailey didn't let go, instead closed her eyes and tilted her head to the side.

"Um, can I have my hand back now?" The Jackyl tugged but didn't succeed in dislodging Hailey's grip.

Hailey made a low noise of disgust.

Gunther growled.

Man-bun froze.

After twenty seconds, Hailey released her grip and pulled back in disgust then shook her head. "You'll pay for that in the end. Believe me."

"Hell, boss." One of the Jackyl underlings took a few steps back. "Did you just get hexed?"

Hailey's grin lacked any semblance of pleasantry. "Have a good day, Frederick."

"Holy shit. She knows your real name. You are so dusted, man," said a second Jackyl, backing away from his leader.

"Let's get out of here." The self-proclaimed boss led the way to the far end of the lot where he'd parked. The others followed—at a distance.

Casper grinned after watching Hailey's talent at work. Her additional, "And don't forget the drinks. It's what any good host would do," preceded the lead thug's duck and cringe. She snorted, then nipped both teeth between her lips with Hailey's chuckle. "Well, it taught them a lesson, didn't it?"

Hailey just shook her head. "C'mon. Let's get our goodies and sit in my truck to talk."

"Hey, Casper. Where'd you learn to fight like that? And what in hell did you do to him?" The student whose face had been sheet-white during the confrontation now rushed forward with excitement lighting her eyes.

"Ah, my favorite uncle is a martial artist." Casper accepted the bottle of water and handkerchief from Hailey to clean her hand. "Listen, guys, I'll catch up with you all later." She nodded toward Hailey. "I've got some 'splaining to do."

She let the others assume Hailey was a cop, which made things easier and kept the police out of the situation since the Jackyls wouldn't dare make that call.

Gunther beat her to the order window and placed both paws on the counter. Instead of a reprimand, he received a scratch behind the ears along with, "Want the usual, fella? I got it ready while watching the show. Good boy to look out for those kids. Your treat's on me, today."

The wolf dog huffed and licked his lips.

Being the center of attention, he accepted his plastic bowl and took it to the side where asphalt met grass. He lapped it up in less time than it took Casper to get her sundae, not that she minded playing second fiddle to the dog. He was incredible, beautiful, and had a heart of gold, just like Simon.

The two had gotten off to a peculiar start due to Gunther's inability to see spirits unless Casper touched him. He now sensed when Simon was present and responded enthusiastically. At this point, filling his stomach took precedence over greeting a noncorporeal friend.

Once finished, he grabbed the plastic dish between his teeth and carried it to the trash can.

"Thank you," the server called out when serving the rest of the order.

Casper handed over Hailey's double-dip cone and opened the truck door to let him in. Sliding into the passenger seat, she said, "Well, that was exciting."

Hailey smiled. "Guess Frederick won't be bothering you ever again."

"Actually, I've found it can go either way. We'll have to wait and see, but I don't want them interfering with my deep dive into student life."

"I assume you have good security at your home?"

"The latest and greatest. Not even on the market yet. Plus, it's monitored offsite, as in constant monitoring." Casper wiped her mouth with the napkin provided.

"I won't ask, but I hope someday you'll tell me about it. So, what've you found out so far?"

"Several things. I got a call from my friend. The gun we retrieved was stolen from a disposal team en route for destruction. Kinda surprised it still had a serial number."

"How'd you find out so fast? I don't think even Leigh or Trenton have that intel yet."

"Um, connections. Anyway, it originally surfaced in a robbery up north. Somehow made its way south. It was confiscated by the feds, *but* stolen before it could be destroyed."

"Jeez, you're like a walking encyclopedia. So, you're talking federal alphabet type involvement in this?"

"Yep. And that's not all. We got a hit off the prints."

Hailey sucked in a quick breath. "How? That gun was in the belly of a gator."

"Not from the gun, per se, but from the bullets." Casper tweezed her phone from her back pocket. "Came back to one Babtiste Garnier."

"Oh, crap."

"What? You know the guy?"

"No, but I was hired just this morning to find him."

Specifics of the earlier conversation with the head of Upward Bound muddied investigative waters. "I wonder if Babtiste is working undercover, or perhaps maybe an informant? But then, why would he have a stolen gun, unless that was part of his cover? Maybe he's had it for quite some time."

Casper hated mysteries, preferring a straight-on approach to life's problems. "Maybe this Babtiste guy is working both sides of the fence. Or perhaps he forgot about the *ex* part of his gang member status."

Accepting Simon's soft patting of her cheek, she leaned her head back against the seat and closed her eyes. "I need to find some dead members of the gang, preferably ones willing to talk."

"What, you can force them?"

"*That* is never a good idea. Consequences and all that. If they died violently or have regrets, they usually share details." She'd learned that lesson the hard way. Spirits could lie as much as the living. Some carried their own agendas, others just wanted to be left alone.

"I got a call from Trenton." Hailey finished her cone and crumpled up her napkin.

"And? Was he in his usual grumpy state?"

Ignoring the comment, she replied, "He said the dead guy was Donald Fitzpatrick."

"We already knew that."

"He was a current ATF agent."

"No shit. What was he doing in the bayou early in the morning? And why would someone shoot him? Unless, they meant to hit Babtiste."

Hailey cocked her head to the side. "No, I think the shooter shot who he was aiming for. We just don't know why. Would've killed me if I hadn't ducked."

"Okay, we'll leave that be for now. I take it you got a vision with touching the sleaze now?"

"Yeah. Many."

"Can you sort through and order them?"

"No, at least not yet. It's kinda like bracing yourself before opening floodgates, then sorting through them after the fact. The order makes them open to interpretation, which I sometimes get wrong."

"So, what'd you learn? And by the way, I'm not sure which one of us instilled more fear in that prick."

Hailey chuckled. "Heightened emotion makes images a little difficult to sort. I did see that Frederick gave Babtiste the scar, sort of a parting gift when leaving the gang."

"What else?"

"Frederick killed two members of the gang who tried to leave last year. I don't think he knows of Babtiste's involvement with the bayou murder. Our boy Frederick does, however, want in on the gun trade. Quite badly."

"Any way to find evidence about the two prior murders?"

"Not that I know of—didn't have long enough contact. How about you? Making any inroads into the school investigation?"

"No, there's a kid in my physics class I'd like to know more about, but I've put it on the back burner for now. It's nothing that'll land me in an underground prison again."

"What? When?"

"Few months ago. Guess you escaped being hunted because of your family's reputation for Vodou. But there was a group imprisoning and experimenting on psychics. I got caught."

"Jesus, Casper."

"Hey. I survived when others didn't. The experience changed my life and my worldview." Highlights of the circumstances motivated her to help other psychics. "You should stay under the guise of occult religious practices for your own protection."

"Damn. You've lived three lifetimes already."

"I try to stay focused on the problem at hand, but when this is over, maybe I could introduce you to my classmate, you know, for a little insight?"

"Sure. Be glad to help."

Casper's world just got a whole lot more complicated. It was time to delve into ATF missions and one Donald Fitzpatrick. Her best friend's husband was a hacker with unparalleled talent. Rare were the firewalls that could stall Wyatt McGlauklin's hunt for information.

Chapter Five

Hailey

An armadillo leaping up in front of Hailey's truck forced her into a skidding stop. Seeing one of these mammals spring four to five feet in the air might startle potential predators into leaving them in peace but didn't reduce their numbers as road kill.

A deep sigh derived from more than sparing its life as she waited for it to reach the relative safety of the cord grass. The earlier conversation with Casper replayed in her thoughts.

Not only had the morning tallied more questions than answers, but Casper had proven again that she would continue to jeopardize her safety.

The Cliff Notes version of imprisonment in an underground facility smacked of big bucks, quasi-military, and far beyond the average civilian's reach in the legal system.

Not for the first time, Hailey wondered at the teenager's confidence, earned and based in reality. The nagging truth that other psychics existed left her unsettled and with the wary desire to connect with them. It also begged the question, what did her mother know of the psychic world?

She sighed. For now, it was time to deal with the problem at hand.

If someone blackmailed Babtiste into working with or for the Jackyls, then maybe he'd brought a shipment of guns in and was confronted by the ATF agent.

Charlotte declared with one hundred percent certainty her young man was clear of illegal activity. Yet, he was missing, and an ATF agent was dead.

Babtiste's prints were on the bullets. A setup?

She'd seen stranger things happen.

A call to Trenton incurred his ire along with more questions when she proved ahead of him in the investigation. After sputtering warnings to back off, he'd relented with a tidbit of information, revealing his intent to gain more in return. According to his superior, the ATF had an active investigation into gun smuggling in the Hamchet area.

End of story.

She hadn't expected help in that arena, not after spending the afternoon chasing down leads into Babtiste's disappearance. She was tired, hungry, and wanted to veg out in front of her computer with Gunther by her side.

Making a right onto her secluded street in the abandoned industrial park, she spotted a black BMW in front of her building. It stuck out like a turtle wearing diamonds.

Facing her direction, the vehicle had heavily tinted glass all around, except for the windshield. No one waited in the driver's seat.

Checking her phone, she hadn't missed any calls and didn't have any scheduled appointments. Her part-time receptionist was in class and drove an older model Honda.

Parking nose to nose with the other vehicle, she pocketed her keys. Gunther hopped out as soon as she slid off the seat.

A crawling sensation on her nape prompted her to slip her Hellcat .9mm in her back waistband as Gunther sniffed the black sedan then lifted his leg and let loose a stream on the rear tire. A snapshot of the license plate was standard—almost. Usually, she copied the driver's license of her clients.

No one stood near the glass wall inside the building on either floor. When she gave a tug of the business entrance door, it was locked.

Okay. One down, one to go.

"Gunther, let's go upstairs before we check the office." The building's secondary entrance positioned near the corner ran the entire width of the structure. From there, she accessed stairs leading to the second floor loft where she lived.

At the top of the steps, Gunther barked, sniffing and clawing at the seam around the door. Again, this one was locked.

When she turned the key and opened it, her furry companion bolted through as soon as space permitted his passage. His warning was clear to anyone inside.

Pushing the door wide, she palmed the gun at her back waist with her left hand. Whoever entered had unlocked the door, then locked it again once inside. Did they think she wouldn't notice the hundred-thousand-dollar car out front?

On the new couch Trenton insisted she have for when he visited, a stranger relaxed with one leg crossed over the other, ankle over knee. Gunther rushed forward and sniffed the outstretched hand. Ignoring the treat held in the palm, the wolf dog sniffed the arm, torso, and legs before sitting to gaze at the stranger's face.

"Brought something for you, fella. It's rude to visit without bringing a small token of appreciation."

A small cube of brown—something—resided in the open palm, waiting.

"Gunther, no."

"It's frozen cooked liver, a healthy snack that won't upset his stomach."

To her amazement, her four-footed companion again sniffed warily then accepted the treat before returning to inspect the stranger's expensive Italian shoes, then the suit likely costing more than her truck, before returning to his hand.

"Sorry, fella. Just one this time."

When satisfied, Gunther sat and looked back at Hailey as if to say, "He's okay for now, Mom. I've got this."

"Good evening." Tall even while sitting, the stranger's thick black hair held the vitality of youth. He had the lightest gray eyes she'd ever seen.

"Who the hell are you, and what are you doing in my loft?"

"My name is Dante Rossi, and I've come to offer my advice."

"Not in the market, but I do love collecting information."

"Ah, then we have something in common." Dante tentatively leaned forward to brush long, tanned fingers along Gunther's flank.

The wolf dog whined but accepted the petting. After a few seconds, he leaned into the stranger's caress.

"Such a good boy. You know when someone means your momma no harm, don't you?" Smooth and soft, the baritone eased the remnants of Gunther's obvious tension.

"How are you doing that? He never takes to strangers."

"Dogs have an innate sense about those they meet. Quite amazing actually."

"What do you want?" Hailey kept her left hand at her back waistband.

"To not receive lead from your Hellcat." A quirk of his right brow accentuated the slight scar slicing through it.

"And how do you know I'm not packing my Glock?"

"Because you left it on your nightstand. Nice quilt by the way. Did your mother make it?"

Handsome beyond all measure didn't grant rights of breaking and entering along with invasion of privacy.

"Yes." She felt compelled to answer honestly despite the sharp retort waiting to slash his obvious good humor.

"I've followed your blog. You have quite an eye for landscapes. I'm surprised you haven't gone pro, and to that end, if you'd ever like assistance, I know a guy." Gesturing to the chair opposite the sofa, he smiled. "Why don't you sit? I could pour you a glass of wine."

"I don't have any at the moment."

"You do now. It's cold, still corked, and quite good." Holding one hand out, palm up, he asked, "Would you like some?"

"You break into my house. You—"

"Technically, it's not a house, but I love what you've done with it."

"You turn my best friend into something I don't recognize. Then—"

"I assure you, he's the same. Once he got to know me, he realized I'm harmless. You should rely more on his instincts."

As if on cue, Gunther lay at the stranger's feet and rested his head on crossed paws.

Hailey snorted. "And you bring me wine...?"

"My mother raised me to have manners. Bringing the wine and other items was simply a matter of respect. I figured your fridge was bare."

He was too smooth, too polished, too self-assured. "If you think I'm gonna share a drink with a stranger who invades my privacy, we don't live in the same reality."

Arrogant to the point of being smug.

"Ah, but reality often shifts with different viewpoints, does it not? When you interviewed Armond Boyer, you thought him a flesh peddler, pervert, and scum, but not the snake who kidnapped and left you to die in the bayou. You were very resilient to flee with a twisted ankle, not to mention resourceful to survive the night. I've been curious as to how you contacted your federal agent for pickup. I'm also surprised to see he's found his own place. I thought you two were a couple."

Dear god, she didn't know which misinformation to disabuse him of first. "How'd you figure those details?"

"I make it my business to know, and I don't want to see you hurt. There is only so much I can do to shield you from those protecting their secrets. You should recuse yourself from the current case of the missing young man, Babtiste."

"Is that a threat?" Her raised voice instigated Gunther to rise to a sitting position, his gaze swiveling from Hailey to Dante.

"Not hardly. Though I haven't quite defined how you come by some of your information, I worry that too little will be just enough to get you in trouble—again. Tell me, are the rumors true? About your heritage?"

The absolute stillness of his frame and the intensity of his stare validated sincere curiosity. He was a predator at heart, skilled in manipulation and having the connections to complete a dossier on anyone in his sights.

She didn't like the spotlight.

"Depends on what rumors you're hearing." As much as she hated to resort to it, she needed to make physical contact to discover what secrets he held. Alienating him from the start was a bad idea.

"The ones that say you're into rituals and such. I didn't see any evidence of it."

"You mean you didn't find my stash of candles, chalk, and dead chicken skeletons?"

"The only skeletons I've found are the ones your mother kept from you."

Hailey sucked in a quick breath. Many of the details surrounding her father and unborn sister's death had remained out of official reports. Tamping down the anger and indignation with a mask of indifference required all her willpower.

"I think we've gotten off on the wrong foot. Why don't we start over? I'm Hailey Arquette." Holding out her hand, she stepped forward and pasted a sincere-ish smile on her face. If Dante became a problem, Gunther would rise to her defense.

In response, Dante crossed his arms over his chest, his look deadpan. "Really? And you don't need to hold onto your gun. Please, relax."

"Fine. Tell me how you're connected to the Gifted Elite school and gun smuggling." The first assumption was a shot in the dark but might make an important connection if answered. She took a seat in the wing chair, figuring she could retrieve her gun before he could stand and reach her.

"The first is private. The second, I don't smuggle guns."

"What do you do?"

"Solve problems."

"For who? Whose problems?"

"For those who employ me."

Well, this is getting nowhere fast.

"So, I'm a problem?"

"Not yet. No."

"And that's *not* a threat?"

"Again, no. I have not and will not bring you harm. Ever."

Yet he doesn't say he won't interfere in other ways.

"Who do you work for? A member of the school board?"

Dante sighed, pinching the bridge of his nose between thumb and forefinger. "You're not going to leave this alone, are you?"

"Not by a long shot."

"Then I've just made things worse."

"Who do you work for? Did you kill the ATF agent?"

Dante shook his head. "No, and no. I *have* killed before, but I was not involved with nor could I prevent Fitzpatrick's death in the bayou."

"Is Babtiste running guns for you or those who employ you?"

"Babtiste does not work for those moving weapons. As far as the Jackyls go, I suggest you not have another run-in with them. They have long memories and big egos, a bad combination."

"Well, you certainly don't look like a member of their gang, and for your information, they ran scared after our last confrontation." She'd intentionally made the connection with their leader to draw unnecessary attention away from Casper.

"Yes, one in which you dented his ego. It did not go unnoticed, and it will not be left... unaddressed. As far as the school, I would like to see the Jackyls and their dealings kept away from the students just as much as you do. Kids don't need guns or drugs as far as I'm concerned."

"But you're not the boss." She could tell that much.

"No, I'm not."

"You knew the ATF agent." The way he'd said the name—it meant something to him. Whether from regret or something else, she couldn't determine.

Gunther jumped to his feet seconds before thumping on the stairs alerted them to company. With tail wagging and quiet chuffs, the canine waited by the door.

It opened to admit Casper, who halted when seeing Dante stand. Her stance immediately went to defensive mode.

Yeah, he's got that mob vibe to him.

"Hello, Casper."

"Who the hell are you?"

"Dante, and it is good to finally meet you."

Casper looked to Hailey, then Dante, assessing. "The dog seems to accept you, doesn't mean I will. How do you know me? We've never met."

"I've read your file."

Hailey snorted. If ever there was a way to antagonize any teen, Dante just pushed all the right buttons.

"Yeah, I was adopted. Big deal."

"I mean the other one. It seems Major Clannahan has some very unique friends. I would love to meet them someday."

"The only thing you're likely to meet is my fist in your face, or a really pointy object up your ass." Three strides forward put Casper just outside of Dante's reach. Grasping the amulet around her neck, she smiled. "Help yourself, Simon."

Hailey heard it a split second before Dante startled and reared back. A long line of chittering sounded an awful lot like a monkey in a phase of extreme excitement.

"Who's Simon and what's he helping himself to?" A frown and scrunched nose converted Dante's smooth façade into a confusing mask. He waved his hand in front of his face as if batting an unseen insect from his field of view. His shoulders hunched and he looked around. "What the hell?"

A high-pitched screech forced Hailey to turn aside. Though unseen, Casper's ghostly friend suddenly made Dante quite unsettled.

Gunther barked, his excitement palpable. Hopping around Dante, he lowered his front shoulders to play-bow position before hopping up and doing the same on the other side.

"What the hell is happening?" Dante asked before rolling his shoulders.

"Hell could be just the beginning." Casper held her arm out. Her hand dipped for a brief second as if accepting a slight weight. She then bent it at the elbow and placed something unseen on her shoulder.

Hailey covered her smile and turned to the teen. "What brings you to see me, Casper?"

"Just wanted to touch base. Didn't realize you were having formal company."

"I didn't realize it either until I stepped into my loft."

"He threaten you? I saw his tag before coming up. Nice ride." Casper repeated the license plate number.

Dante narrowed his gaze at the teen. "Thanks, and you won't find anything, even with Wyatt at the keyboard."

Casper dropped back into a fighting stance, her right hand coming forward with a four-inch blade. "Why don't you save me the time digging? I will find out, you know. Everything you've done, seen, those you communicate with, and those who pay you—to do whatever it is you do."

Dante held up both hands to reveal no weapons. "I meant that as an introduction, not confrontation. And speaking of introductions, as I said, I'd like to meet some of your friends from Pennsylvania."

"Well, rejected. And the next time we meet, I'll know a lot more about your hunky ass. I don't trust—slick."

"From what I hear, you don't trust much of anybody. I have to admit I'm curious what talent got you into the school for the gifted."

"Has no one ever taught you lessons about curiosity? If not, I'm willing..." Casper tilted her head to the side, her gaze sizing up her opponent.

"Not here to fight. I guess it'd fall on dead ears to ask you to stop investigating the school students and staff. I heard you were more determined than any soul I'll ever meet, except maybe for this one." Dante nodded toward Hailey. "Look, please, just back off for a time."

"Funny you should mention the dead. Interesting to say the least." Casper sidestepped to allow Dante's circumventing trouble in his stride for the door.

As he brushed by, Hailey latched onto his hand when he paused to study Casper. She was prepared for him to yank back, but kept her hold for a split second longer. It was enough.

In her mind's eye, she saw Dante firing a gun, at night. The backdrop consisted of glass and brick buildings, a city street with cars lining both sides. She gasped, her eyes meeting his widened stare.

"You shouldn't have done that."

"Shouldn't find out who you are?" Hailey retorted.

"Look. I don't want to see either of you hurt. You're dealing with things beyond your scope or control." Again, Dante waved his hand as if shooing off an annoying insect.

"Back at ya, dude." Casper smiled openly, a challenge.

Dante merely shook his head and walked out, mumbling about good deeds not going unpunished.

When Casper started to speak, Hailey held up one hand. "I need to check the back fire escape to see if that's how he got in."

A minute later, she returned, shaking her head.

"No luck?" Casper had knelt to allow Gunther a nose-to-nose greeting with the unseen monkey on her shoulder. Soft doggy yips coincided with intermittent squeaks and signaled their audible interplay.

"Well, that was interesting. Who is tall, dark, and idiotic, anyway? Looks like a mob boss."

"I don't think he's a boss. Maybe a messenger of some kind? I got the feeling he's just as curious about us." Hailey moved to the kitchen. "Um, I'd offer you dinner, but I don't think there's any food worth eating, unless you'd like some chocolate sugary goodness."

"My favorite, despite my guardian's best efforts."

"Looked to me she's less of a guardian and more like an assistant. How is Sarah?"

"She's fine. Always asking about homework and what I've eaten. Quite annoying actually. Is that what parents do?"

Hailey smiled, thinking about her mother. "Pretty much." Cool air wafted across her face with the door's opening, along with the most heavenly scent. "Damn. There's, like, real food in here. And cheese. And wine."

"Red or white?"

"Neither for you." Hailey opened the Styrofoam takeout containers. "Oh, hell. He brought my favorite. How'd he know?"

"Might be poisoned."

"No, he didn't know you were coming. Looks like he intended to wine and dine me to soften the warning to back off. A bribe maybe?"

"So he delivers food with a warning? I don't like that. Or him." Despite Casper's stated objection, she drifted closer to see the offering, sticking her hand in the bag and taking her own survey. "Oh, hell yes. French bread po-boys from Bouchard's? This is great. What else is in there?"

And just like that, the younger woman's attention diverted to food.

"Well, he said he brought wine and cheese, so I guess we'll find some Cajun cheese. I love the roasted spicy stuff." Hailey plopped the bag on the table and retrieved the contents. "Okay. There's fried shrimp and soft-shell crabs here. Any preference?"

"All," Casper confirmed as she poured a cup of water from the tap while Hailey opened the wine. "He was slick, but do you think he's a killer?"

"I got a glimpse of him in a shootout."

"Against?"

"Don't know, but damned if I won't find out. I got the name and view of a street, but not the city." Hailey sat and took a sip of her wine. "What made *you* suspicious of the vehicle?"

"Too nice for the neighborhood."

"There is no neighborhood, just empty buildings." Hailey nodded in agreement. "So, tell me about Wyatt." It seemed Dante had an upper hand in the information department.

"Well, you know Wyatt's married to my best friend. And don't worry, you'll meet him someday, I'm sure. Just... not for a while."

"How're classes?"

Casper griped about school and then progressed to ask Hailey about her afternoon.

"I did find out something. There was a raid on the Jackyls by a task force I didn't even know about, which included Leigh. They confiscated a whole load of weapons. Get this, from an anonymous tip."

"Great. Now the gang's gonna think you and I are responsible. Did you thank your best friends for putting a target on each of our backs?"

"Trenton didn't know about our run-in at the ice cream shop at the time. But I'm sure by now he and Leigh are both up to date. I'll get an irate call as soon as the dust settles."

"Good thing he has his own place now. Does he have a key to your loft still?"

"Yeah, not that it matters." Trenton would have no difficulty obtaining a lock pick gun. Now, he wasn't the only one who could come and go without a trace.

"So, what's the plan? I, for one, want to know what Mr. Slick is up to."

"Something tells me he's gonna be a hard nut to crack." Hailey sipped her wine and thought about it. "I'll do some research tonight, see what I can dig up."

"I'll give Wyatt his tag number. Classes are short tomorrow. Next week, we have several half days."

"Really? I never got that. Things have changed."

"The time is designated to let students research their projects. Let's touch base in the morning. If we don't come up with an address for Dante by then, I've got other means of locating where he calls home."

As much as Hailey wanted to explore those means, they had other priorities. Dante was right, the Jackyls' leader would be planning to excise his pound of flesh from both herself and Casper.

Chapter Six

Hailey

Evenings of research required a computer, wine, and churro ice cream. Her fridge was most often empty, except for milk that may or may not contain a green skim on top, but she always maintained her stash of ice cream and doggy treats.

Leftovers from Dante's visit meant she didn't have to call for takeout.

The last rays of sun streamed down on the window seat before sliding toward the horizon and shadows joined forces to welcome the night. Gunther leaned against her flank and peered outside, his head resting on her shoulder.

Each tab she opened on her computer led to a dead end concerning Dante. His vehicle was registered to a corporation she couldn't locate. He'd given his full name, if in fact, it wasn't an alias, but he had no social media presence, no driver's license, and no criminal record. The last item surprised her the most.

It was a bitter pill to admit defeat, even temporarily.

Search results on the Jackyls, however, provided different results.

Street gangs maintained a presence in any large city. Hamchet, while small, was ideally located to nourish the illicit deals with myriad waterway escapes. News reports covered multiple clashes between gangs and students from both public and private sectors.

When she woke with her head leaning in the corner where nook met window, her laptop still on her thighs, she called it a night, taking Gunther out before going to bed.

Morning dawned early with Gunther's four-paw wake up.

Last night's dreams of gutted gators, arms chewed off dead bodies along with drugs and a slew of guns contributed to her restlessness. It didn't compare to the strangeness of a dead alligator talking with a seductive Italian accent.

It'd be a long time before she forgot Dante's handsome face, or the fact he'd killed in whatever line of duty that employed him.

On the upside, he'd brought enough food to supply leftovers for breakfast. That and strong coffee brought her fully awake as she contemplated her day of research, again sitting at her window seat.

She'd thought the timing of Trenton's call suspicious when her phone chirped a popular cop movie theme.

The smirk in his voice came through loud and clear when she admitted coming up empty regarding new leads to tug.

His tone would change on a dime if she described the stranger's visit. He'd demand every scrap of information and every detail, then reiterate the warning to back off the investigation before offering to stay with her until it all blew over. The latter wouldn't be so bad considering he was great company and they got along well.

The fact Casper had dropped by during Dante's visit would multiply Trenton's frustration radiating through the line. Not for the first time, she wondered about the extent of federal healthcare benefits.

In light of that, she kept Dante's visit to herself for the time being and let her friend focus on Casper.

"Hailey, that kid is trouble. Do not encourage her. I don't know what star she's orbiting to keep her history blocked from me, but I know it's not good."

"Hey, she's fine once you get to know her. Why don't we get together sometime? You'll see. You just have to come off... not like a cyclone."

The huff coming through the line said it all.

She had her work cut out for her. "Tell you what. Why don't you join us for dinner at Mom's tonight? She's making smoked turkey and ouille gumbo."

"Yeah, she invited me this morning. I'll be there."

It seemed even her mother had an agenda.

Trenton wanted Casper out of the picture. Her mom wanted to *guide* the motherless teen. Hailey wanted a partner accepted by all.

On prior occasions, Trenton invited himself to family dinners under the guise of *"Let's make sure Hailey stays out of trouble."* It was a sure sign her mother had gotten an earful and that a chastisement was in order.

For someone.

"Great. We'll see you there."

"*We?*"

"I invited Casper too." Hailey grinned as she hung up on a string of invectives that would make any sailor proud. She continued her research with a smile.

A little after twelve, her phone blurted out a familiar jingle.

"Hey, Casper. What's up?"

"*Wyatt and I came up empty on the digital search for the home of your visitor yesterday. It's driving him batshit crazy. It's so rare anything stumps him.*"

"Yeah, same here. But we'll figure it out."

"*Been there, done that. I got a little noncorporeal help.*"

"Excellent." Hailey figured she'd take the help from wherever it came. "How about I pick you up? We'll check it out before dinner tonight."

Inviting a prickly teen to dinner was a no-brainer. Cecile Arquette had a way about her and might be able to smooth the edges between Casper and Trenton. If Leigh came too, she'd enjoy the fireworks.

"Oh, and Trenton's been invited too, just FYI."

"*Great. I'm looking forward to this. Got a little something to leave for him. You know, show up and bring a gift.*"

If devious had a tone, it was Casper's.

Unlike the jeans and casual shirts worn on previous occasions, Casper strode out her front door in leathers and steel-toed boots, looking every bit the warrior Hailey suspected her to be. If not for the teen's ability to phase her body through any attack, Hailey would expect to see both blade and gun strapped to her side.

Casper stowed her knapsack on the rear seat before sliding onto the passenger seat and opening her phone's note section.

"What's in the pack?"

"Bare necessities." Casper grinned before adding, "Needed for every caper."

"Uh-huh. Before I forget, I just wanted to caution you. It'd be nice if you and Trenton could get along. He's really not so bad once you get to know him."

"Wonderful. Needling him is my favorite pastime. I'm sending Dante's address to your cell."

Hailey grinned with a side-glance of curiosity after viewing her cell phone, held in place over the vehicle's vent. "Wow, out in the middle of nowhere. How'd you dig that up?"

Casper chuckled. "Well... it seems the ATF agent knew your Italian stud better than we thought. Though the cagey bastard wouldn't give me more than an address. And even that cost me."

"What could a spirit possibly want?"

"My promise to stay away from the Jackyls."

"Hmm."

Like that's gonna happen.

Hailey sped over the narrow back roads wondering how that conversation had gone. It was most likely one-sided.

Casper sorted through her notes then sent them to Hailey's phone before looking up. "Hey, did you find the names of the two people killed by Frederick and his gang? It might help to talk to their families."

"Yes, I thought we could pay a visit to the victims' homes later."

"Or... we could just visit with them directly."

"They'll come to you after all this time? I haven't asked before because I didn't want to push."

"Sometimes, yes. It's time we shove Frederick right into a nice six-by-eight. I know someone else will take his place, but, gotta do our part."

Hailey slowed to take a right at a fork in the road. The home coming into view far exceeded her expectations.

The brick rancher appeared well-maintained, yet a little out of place. Fresh-cut grass tainted with the scent of onion merged with the marshy odor in the distance. A back porch, if it existed, would frame a perfect sunset.

Casper whistled low. "Bigger than I expected. What if he's married? When I fed Wyatt the address, he pulled up what he could. If there is any kind of security, it's private, not connected to any local company."

"I got the vibe he's either not married, or he's a player."

"A little sensual tension?" Casper asked with a waggle of her brows. "*Hmm*, as a distraction, maybe?"

"Don't know. Don't care. Not interested."

"I wouldn't be interested either if I had a *friend* like your fed. Though, I have to admit, there seemed to be equal hotness."

Casper slid out of the truck and held her hand up when Gunther started to follow. "No, boy. You stay. We'll leave the windows down and be back in a few minutes."

No cars in the gravel drive. No garage or outbuildings on what appeared to be a three-acre yard. Black shutters straddled mullioned windows covered in part by shades created a more formal look, continued with boxwoods lining the brick walkway.

"Well, if your Italian stud turns out to *not* be associated with organized crime, I guess I could take him off your hands," Casper murmured in striding up the steps and nodding to the swing on the covered porch. A small wrought-iron table beside it waited for a cool drink on a summer's eve. "Damn. This isn't him. It's all for show."

The frank assessment mirrored Hailey's thoughts. "No lights on inside, nothing moving."

"I don't see any video cameras." Casper pointed to each visible corner. "I'm not into waiting."

"I don't hear one, but what if he's got a dog?"

"Then I'll phase us through it and back out. No problem." She held out her hand expectantly.

"Okay. Let's see what we can find." Hailey took the hand and immediately had a different view. Understanding it was Casper's memory added a level of horror every time they did this.

In this instance, the teen sat on a cot in what appeared to be a jail cell, except it was an underground hi-tech, military-type facility.

Shaking off the image, she accepted the current, tamer reality of Dante's house.

The interior matched the formality of the exterior. They walked through the double doors with sidelights and into a grand living room lined with bookshelves on two walls.

"Let's clear each room before snooping." Casper urged her over the thick rug divided into geometric shapes of earthy hues that led to the far wall sectioning off the kitchen. Thick beveled glass topped the table with a wrought iron wine rack underneath.

Further exploration revealed three bedrooms and two bathrooms before returning to the living room.

"Let's see if he's the type to hide important stuff in books." Casper pulled out a volume by Robert Frost.

Hailey leaned in to read the title. "Hmm, you don't strike me as the poetry type."

"Trying to expand my horizons and all that."

It wasn't the silence that held Hailey in place. "Damn. Didn't expect him to be a reader. How educated do you think he is?"

Casper returned the book to its slot. "You think this might *all* be for show?"

"Wasn't around him long enough to form an opinion. Did he strike you as the type to read Shakespeare, Poe, and Michener? A little diverse, I'd say." Hailey perused the shelves while mentally reviewing Dante's visit.

"Not really. You like to read?"

"When I have time, I like photography journals and such. Leigh wishes I'd spend more time reading cookbooks."

Casper snorted and ambled around the corner. "Hey, take a closer look at this kitchen. This would make Wyatt jealous as hell."

"Wyatt's your computer genius."

"Yes, but like us all, he wears more than one hat. He's teaching us how to cook." Casper ran her fingers over the marble countertop comprising the massive kitchen island. "This guy must be one hell of a cook." As if compelled, she opened each drawer and cabinet. Plucking out a crystal glass, she flicked the goblet with her finger. "Money to burn."

It reeked of elegance and sophistication, but not home, which brought Casper's situation to mind. "Do you miss seeing your family now?"

Casper frowned. "I visit every weekend."

"From Texas to Pennsylvania? You must spend most of your time on the road or in the air," Hailey hedged knowing there was a secret nugget there, waiting and hoping her friend would share.

Casper shrugged and said, "Not as much as you think. You'll probably see it."

See what? "Let's move on. I want to go through his home office."

"Wyatt said if we found his computer, to stick this in and turn it on. He'd do the rest." Casper plucked a flash drive from the pocket of her leathers.

"Done this before, have you?"

"A time or two." Casper chortled.

A wide hall off the great room opened to four other rooms. The first was a guest bedroom in neutral colors with a padded headboard behind a queen-sized bed.

The second was a spacious spare bathroom with a soaking tub.

"*Hmm,* always wanted one of those." Hailey stepped inside to open the small closet. "Just spare towels and sheets."

The next door opened to the master bedroom. Here is where Dante made his mark. Rich mahogany furniture gleamed in the light streaming through double windows.

A deep navy-blue duvet covered the king-sized bed and complemented the pillow shams sporting playful foxes on the prowl.

Bedside lights, some type of elongated, colorful stone encased in clear material comprised the base and neck of the lamp sitting on the massive dresser. The split walk-in closet was bigger than Hailey's bedroom.

Casper strode to the bedside table where a matching lamp sat. A second after pulling open the drawer, she hopped back and snorted. "That son of a bitch!"

"What?" Hailey rushed over and nudged her partner in crime out of the way. "Holy shit. Well, doesn't that figure?"

Inside the drawer and facing up was a single piece of paper. Scrawled across the center was one line. Neat script.

Nice try, ladies, but you'll have to do better.

"He's got to have hidden cameras. Somewhere." Casper searched the room but found nothing. Undaunted, she headed for the en suite.

"You think he'd put cameras in his bathroom? That he's a pervert?"

"*No. Just being thorough. I'll find the damn things or eat raw tripe.*"

"Let's not get desperate." Hailey choked on her words. "For all we know he's listening to us now."

"*He's not going to best me. I won't get beaten at my own game.*" Anger filled Casper's muffled voice.

"So he figured we'd find him, but Casper, look around. Does this look lived in to you? I think we were right initially. This is all for show."

"*Trash cans are all empty and spotless. Every surface is almost sterile... Ha! Gotcha, prick.*"

"What'd ya find? Let's see."

For being a teen, Casper was observant as hell. Not one dish sat out of place, not one scrap of paper on any counter. No pictures of family or loved ones. Nothing of a personal nature anywhere. Yet the kid found a clue.

"Look at this. Found it in the drain." The teen returned and hooked a thumb over her shoulder at the master bath. "He left a comb in the cabinet and a few hairs in the drain. Hopefully, it'll supply adequate DNA samples." Casper retrieved a baggie and placed the evidence within, then shoved the evidence in her backpack.

"Fine, let's get this wrapped up. I don't want to be here when he returns, not that he likely keeps normal hours."

The last room checked occupied the back corner of the home. The office held the expected executive desk with a laptop sitting squarely in the middle.

"Now, this is odd. He knew we were coming, yet leaves this? If he thinks he can outmaneuver Wyatt on the keyboard, he's in for a rude awakening." Casper went directly to it and opened the lid. "If porn pops up on here, I'm just gonna take the damn thing with me."

"But your friend is in Pennsylvania. You're going to ship it? That'll take time, and might entail more risk."

Casper froze and met Hailey's stare. "Yeah, about that. Let's table that discussion for a more opportune time. For now, trust me." Within a minute, she had the computer booted up.

Hailey shoulder-surfed, frustrated but not surprised to see the screensaver.

"Aw, shit, Hailey. We've got our very own stalker."

The screensaver was a snapshot of Hailey and Casper during the showdown with Frederick.

"Looks like this was taken outside Á La Mode. Damned if there was anyone parked at that angle." Hailey thought back to the confrontation. The angle suggested the photo was taken from the road, but there'd been no one parked on the shoulder at the time, and no businesses were directly opposite.

"Could've been a drone stuck in a tree," Casper suggested. "We've done that before."

Surveillance equipment in Hailey's arsenal was still somewhat limited but due for an upgrade. "Speaking of which, if I had one, I'd set it up outside and keep an eye on *him*."

"No need. I'll have that covered in due time. I'm hoping a little DNA from the hair I got will give us a hit."

"Um, where exactly are you planning on sending the sample?"

Casper waggled her eyebrows and smiled. "Resources. Lots and lots of near-endless resources."

"Good. It's time to turn the tables on this guy." She hated it when someone got the upper hand. It was worse when he was all smooth talk and good looks.

Casper retrieved her phone and tapped out a text. A minute later, she shook her head. "Screw it. I'm not waiting." She closed the lid and stuck the laptop in her backpack. "Okay. We're good. Let's book."

It wasn't that Hailey minded leaving the house in her rearview, but theft had not been a part of her character. It made her wonder at what point her counterpart drew the line.

"You think he's not going to notice a missing laptop?" Hailey offered the mental nudge as they strode through the front door and into the bright sunshine.

"Shouldn't be spying on us. I want Wyatt to have full access. I can see it returned tomorrow."

"What if there's some kind of tracking software on it? It'll trace back to Wyatt."

"Nah, Wyatt's in the system as we speak. He'll clear anything out before it arrives on his doorstep."

The area was remote and quiet except for katydids and frogs. Trenton's warning to not involve Casper circled Hailey's thoughts once again. "This feels like the perfect setting for a hit man."

"Or a serial killer. Aren't they s'posed to be all charismatic?"

Casper opened the passenger door and paused. "Ya know, I was thinking last night. As much as I want to pursue Dante, for a whole lot of reasons, that moron from the Jackyls will be gunning for us. We need to get him off the street before we do anything else, and I think I've figured a way to do it. *Then* it'll be safer for us to delve into the ATF murder."

"I found the names along with pictures of both youths who tried to leave the gang last year." Hailey settled her phone in the cup holder and started the engine.

"Pictures are great, not that I've had many spirits lie about their identity. That sort of crap kinda falls away when you die, I guess. Tell ya what, let's go to my place. We can be sure there's no surveillance of any kind."

Hair prickling at her nape dictated Hailey stood on the verge of some extraordinary event. She felt a presence in the slight hum running through her veins and the soft feather-light brush across her cheek. Her grandmother would call it her guardian angel.

She pressed the accelerator a little harder.

Chapter Seven

Hailey

The ride back took forever but provided time for a little prodding.

"So, you're eighteen and working undercover at the GE school. How does Sarah fit in this, other than as a guardian on record?"

"*Hmm*, she tried the guardian thing for about five minutes. We've been on the same page ever since. I know she reports to both Clannahan and Nicholai, though. The hussy."

"Nicholai?"

"Head of the family. Keeps us all in line and oversees our training."

"Sounds very—military-ish." Hailey recognized certain traits common to both Trenton with his military bearing, and Casper, a teen wise beyond her years. It went without saying that Nicholai had military experience.

"Not really. At the time I met him, psychics were hunted. His strategies kept us alive."

"Nicholai more or less raised you?"

"After I left the foster system, yeah. There's quite a few of us now. We're not related by blood, but we're family."

"This Major Clannahan, how does Dante know about him? Think they're both ex-military?"

"Dunno. Clannahan is a tight-lipped bugger, but he's fair, and he's honest. I don't want to ask him about your Italian stud because if they're not tight, Clannahan will launch a full-scale investigation. He can be quite anal about safety."

"And that would tip Dante off. So, you respect your guardian but keep him at arm's length."

"Yeah, Clannahan said he'd help me figure out what happened to my parents when we get the school squared away. The new administration is clean on initial inspection, but there's definitely hinky stuff going on."

Squared away? That definitely smacks of a military background or upbringing.

"How old were you when Nicholai took you in?"

"Couple years. Don't know anything about my parents, just that they were in this area at one time."

"I'd like to help you search when the time comes. I have a few contacts here who could help." Hailey endured years of not knowing anything about her father. Helping Casper was simply the decent thing to do.

"I'd appreciate it."

"So, Wyatt...?"

"Married to Kiera, who saved my life the day we met. Both are friends, and mentors."

Hailey had just turned into the stately drive leading to Casper's home when the teen let out a snort.

"What's wrong?" At this point, not much would surprise her.

"See for yourself." Casper reached over and touched her hand.

"Oh shit." Hailey slammed the brakes with the scene coming to life. Instead of Casper's mansion, she saw a block facility surrounded by barbed wire. The mountain setting was desolate and eerie.

Physical contact with the teen revealed flashes of battle, but with a twist. Fire jettisoned from one man's fingers and lightning bolts flew from another man's hand. The fight ended with the collapse of a large block facility crumbling in on itself.

The scene switched to that of knives and swords, bolts of electricity thrown like darts, and animals of all types fighting against an enemy of insurmountable odds.

The surreal combat entailed the appearance of colored lights floating above those locked in the fight, then descending into men dressed in black with masks covering their faces.

"Looks like we won't have to wait long." Casper cleared her throat and nodded toward the house, removing her hand. "Sorry, I'm not used to working with someone who gets visions through touch. Shall we go?"

Broken contact disrupted the unfolding scene back to the southern mansion. "What? What do you mean? Wait for what?" She pressed on the accelerator gently this time.

The teen swiveled her head to meet Hailey's gaze and grinned. Instead of answering, she laid her hand on top of Hailey's forearm and then jutted her chin toward the house. "See for yourself."

"Shit!" Hailey swerved to miss hitting the boy standing hand in hand next to a teen girl. The two hadn't been there twenty seconds prior.

Tires ground to a halt, churning up lawn and dirt.

Casper steadied herself with the grab bar, using her other hand to brace herself against the seat. "Easy does it. You can't hurt them. Well, maybe their feelings, I guess, but not physically."

"I knew you saw them randomly, but damn. I wasn't ready for that." Hailey was out of the car in the next instant, looking around and not seeing anything of the two translucent visitors.

As soon as she'd lost contact with Casper, Hailey lost sight of the spirits. "Damn and double damn."

"Hey. Wanna park in the lot next to the other cars? Just a thought to save us a long walk. These guys aren't going anywhere."

Another lesson in patience awaited.

"Sorry about the lawn." Her mind spun through various scenarios concerning the spirit realm. Did spirits present themselves in whatever fashion they chose? At what point did they become cognizant? What rules of the physical world applied to them?

Is my dad's spirit still on this plane?

She'd never heard him, not like she'd heard the dead ATF agent.

"No problem." Once parked, Casper pointed to the house. "Look, Sarah doesn't know much about the stuff I'm into, so if she asks about your unusual driving tactics, just say you got stung by a bee or something."

"Sure." Excitement coursed through her veins like a race car taking off. There were so many questions, so many possibilities she'd waited for the right moment to explore.

Inside, Sarah greeted them in the foyer, frowning at Hailey when stepping closer. "Have a good time, ladies?"

If expecting to catch a whiff of liquor, she'd be disappointment.

Casper nodded before saying, "I've been invited to dinner with Hailey's mom, so if you want to take the rest of the afternoon and evening off, that's fine. I had the special at Bouchard's Café last night, and it was fabulous."

"Well, all right then. Call me if you need anything." Dressed in black slacks and white silk shirt, the guardian patted her blonde bob in place and looked around. "I'll just grab my purse and be off for an evening on the town."

Sarah left, returning a minute later with her purse under her arm.

"Are you packing?" Casper asked.

The guardian tapped her purse in answer. "Every time I leave the house." *So, more than a guardian.*

"Good. Be careful. The gang I told you about will be looking to make trouble. I've no idea how well connected they are."

Despite her petite stature and polished looks, a shrewdness lurked in the older woman's gaze. She held the confidence of one accustomed to taking care of herself.

Once the door closed, Casper led the way to the kitchen. "Let's grab a snack to eat while we talk to these guys."

"Are they inside now?"

"Yep." Casper's scowl lasered through the open space in the direction of the kitchen. "They're leaning over Sarah's freshly baked cake on the island." Casper gripped the amulet she wore in one hand and stabbed the air in that direction. "Listen up, you two. No shenanigans with my food, or I'll send your asses to the artic for a week."

Maybe dealing with spirits wasn't all kicks and giggles.

Casper sliced two pieces of chocolate cake and plopped them onto plates, offering one to Hailey. "There's bottled water in the fridge."

"Crap. Don't wanna step in their space. Where are they?" She stepped forward hesitantly to accept the dessert before opening the fridge.

"Don't worry. They're pretty nimble and don't like occupying the same space with the living. Unless they're trying to possess someone." Casper dropped down in a seat at the kitchen table. "Okay." She held out her left hand for Hailey to take. "Question away."

The touch of Casper's hand brought the couple back into view on the next blink. What surprised Hailey more was the monkey on Casper's shoulder, not noticed before but heard on various occasions. Its tail wrapped around her neck and one tiny hand rested on the crown of her head.

"Simon?"

In response, the monkey stood to its full eighteen-inch height and thrust both arms in the air with a loud squeal.

"Yes, Simon. She sees you, but we're a little busy right now."

Hailey shook her head and did her best to readjust her thinking. They had a job to do. Timing was crucial in avoiding a direct attack from local gang members.

The spirits both wore faded blue jeans and long-sleeved shirts that bore stains from their gruesome murder. Two deep stab wounds on the girl's torso had bled to her waistband. She'd been sitting at the time, judging by the flow over her thighs. Multiple shallow cuts signaled the torture that preceded her untimely death.

The young man, whose expression bore the pain of his companion's death, had identical wounds except for the long slice across his throat.

Their shapes were translucent with a slight outer glow that wavered like the air over asphalt on a hot Texas day.

"Um, hi. I take it you're Carla and Gurez?" Hailey asked.

Each nodded.

"*Can you get us justice?*" the young man asked, his voice reflecting nothing of the carnage his throat had suffered.

"*Can you tell our parents we tried to get away from them, to come home?*" Transparent tears rimmed with a golden hue tracked the girl's cheeks.

"Yes, and yes. But let's start with the basics." Hailey understood the grieving process, albeit from the north side of the grave. Sticking to priorities, she pared questions down and organized them according to priority.

"*Frederick stabbed us both. He'd knocked Gurez unconscious and tied him up.*" Carla sniffled and wiped at her face.

"*Then, he made me watch…*" Gurez looked away, unable or unwilling to meet her gaze under the onslaught of grief and guilt.

The details, though cathartic for them to share, were sickening. Each element of the crimes brought bile to Hailey's throat. When finished, they described the knife used. The same one Frederick used when attacking Casper.

Hailey took notes, doubting their voices would be heard on a recorder. "Hmm, it's been a year since this happened. That knife has to have been wiped clean at least a few times."

"*Huh, he sharpens it every week.*" Gurez looked away from Carla's gaze, shaking his head. "*There will be no justice.*"

"Oh, but there will be. It just won't happen in the conventional style," Casper assured them both.

Further details failed to direct them to specific evidence necessary for use in legal proceedings. Despite that, Casper's confidence never wavered. The couple left with hope lightening their ethereal steps.

"I need to physically touch Frederick again to get a glimpse of more past deeds. Who knows what else he's done?"

"We need to put him away for good," Casper agreed, having finished her cake with no outward sign of revulsion over the stories heard.

It was strange to see spirits walk through walls without hesitation or apparent thought, but hadn't Hailey done the same thing at Dante's house?

"Where do spirits go, when their unfinished business is concluded?"

"Don't know. Even the few I've gotten to know fairly well won't budge. Stingy as hell. Maybe they don't even know."

"Do your friends in Pennsylvania have the same ability?"

"No. Everyone's... different, except they all take great precautions to protect their anonymity."

"When I've touched your hand before, I got glimpses of you in battle, but there were panthers, bears, raccoons, foxes, men, and what looked like ninjas out of a movie. It was a nightmare."

"Yeah. That was a hard-won battle. It's also the day Simon died... protecting me." Casper hung her head then leaned into the monkey cooing softly.

"You've not had an easy life, I know. I hope you find peace here."

It was a hell of a thing to move across country to a new area, new lifestyle, with no friends in place, and start an investigation. At the age of eighteen. "About the computer..."

"Don't worry. Wyatt will have it by tonight."

The how was a mystery for another day.

"I get that our deceased ATF agent wanted us to find Dante's apartment, but did he say why or what outcome he expected?"

"No, just that they were connected. Again, spirits can be stingy with details. Just because they lack mass doesn't mean they're devoid of motivation or agendas." Casper tilted her head in thought. "I can't see any reason he'd put us in the middle of a firefight, not if he wants justice. Hence, I don't think Dante was the one who killed him, even if he is complicit in other crimes."

Hailey wondered for the thousandth time about the big picture and how she and Casper fit in it.

Chapter Eight

Casper

A quick call to her best friend armed Casper with what she hoped to be a proper token of appreciation when invited to dinner at a friend's house. Her school years, when attended, included survival and an ever-watchful eye over her shoulder.

From her backpack, she removed the bottle of Sauvignon Blanc. She didn't consume wine, beer, or drugs and wondered why anyone would.

She could however, wield a blade with precision, a much more useful skill that contributed to her continued existence. Few knew her best tactic consisted of bare-hand fighting. Those who learned generally died within minutes.

Hailey's invitation included the warning of Trenton's presence and to be on best behavior. The fed was hands down an overbearing tyrant. Handsome as hell, but in need of a muzzle.

"Simon, you'll help me keep my cool tonight, right?"

On her left shoulder, the spirit of her capuchin monkey anchored himself by wrapping his tail around her neck, the weight insignificant save the reminder of his support in all endeavors.

A concerted joint effort to smooth things over and sway the fed's sentiments toward her might help at some point. It was certainly better than his constant probing into her life. The latter provided amusement since the man was so persistent. It also frustrated Clannahan and Sarah.

The door opened before she knocked.

"Come in, Casper. I'm glad you could make it." Hailey's mother was tall and willowy with the same startling blue eyes as her daughter. A timeless sense of patience existed in her demeanor.

Stepping into a cozy and comfortable living space contrasted with the stark realities of her former homes. Even the warriors who'd adopted her favored practicality over aesthetics.

A large oak table separated an eat-in kitchen and cozy living room with a eucalyptus spearmint scent wafting from two fat candles, one on the table and one on the fireplace mantle. She recognized the scent from her friend's collection.

"Thank you, Mrs. Arquette."

"Please, call me Cecile. Come, dinner is almost ready." The matriarch eyed the bottle of wine with an arched brow while leading them to the kitchen. "Thank you. It's very... thoughtful."

"*Uh*, my friend said it goes best with most Cajun food, but I'm no connoisseur."

Behind her, the front door opened to admit Hailey and another woman, each chuckling.

"Hey, Casper. You're right on time." Hailey nudged her companion. "This is Leigh Briner, Trenton's sister."

"They come in packs? Does nature allow that?"

Leigh pursed her lips as if deciding on how to respond before her gaze flicked between Cecile and the bottle of wine just received.

Hailey snorted. "Forget it, Leigh. No cop mode tonight, and we're not going to contribute to juvenile delinquency."

Cecile looked at the door as if waiting for another guest. "Your boyfriend isn't coming?"

"Um, no. We, ah, kinda broke up. He got a job offer near Houston he couldn't turn down."

"Oh, sorry to hear that. I quite liked that young man." Cecile gestured for them all to make themselves comfortable.

"And you came by the bottle of wine how?" Trenton asked from the kitchen as he retrieved plates from a cabinet?"

"Bartered it for sex. Shame you weren't with me, Hailey. We could've gotten a six-pack of beer with it," Casper retorted without missing a beat.

Hailey sighed. "Which I could buy for myself since I'm of legal age."

Leigh stepped forward and held out her hand. "I think I'm gonna like you. Is that a northern accent I'm detecting?"

"Depends on how good a detective you are. I am, indeed, from Pennsylvania."

Before Trenton could antagonize Casper, Cecile ushered the small group to the table. "Let's all leave our troubles behind for now. Okay?"

Semi-formal eating amid polite company comprised a new experience for Casper. The group of warriors who'd taken her in after her adopted parents' murder were well-intentioned but rough-and-tumble types.

Dawning arrived with the impact of a two-ton wrecking ball when looking around at the seated guests. She was in way over her head. Either by luck or design, Hailey sat beside her with Trenton and Leigh across from them.

To her relief, Cecile began a conversation with talk relating to current events and Hailey's photography. With meager camera experience, Casper couldn't contribute to that discussion since her background generally involved how to avoid them. A topic that would certainly pique the fed's interest.

It didn't take long for the discussion to steer in the direction of the murdered ATF agent.

"That must've been an awful scene to come across," Cecile began. "You're so young."

"I wouldn't necessarily say that." Trenton narrowed his eyes over his drink. Fact-gathering tactics had ranged from indirect questions to innuendos.

Casper leveled a stare right back at him. "Well, I'm certainly not ready for iron supplements and a cane, although I do love a good walking stick, unless of course I gotta pull it out of someone's southern orifice first."

Trenton's mouth firmed into a straight line, his eyebrows a low slash over storm-gray eyes, a scathing retort bound tight within.

Casper was the fly he couldn't swat, the crooked picture he couldn't straighten, or the printer out of ink on the last page of a job. She smiled wider and touched her left shoulder, nodding slightly in Trenton's direction.

"Your parents obviously spared the rod with you," Trenton mentioned casually.

Leigh snickered. "Even I'd know to quit when I'm ahead, big brother."

On cue, Simon launched himself from her shoulder on a direct course for the object of his ire. Spirit form limited his interactions with the living, but when highly motivated, he could affect small objects.

The spoon in Trenton's hand flipped out of his fingers and onto the middle of the table, sending liquid into the candle's flame to sputter.

His look of shock seared itself into Casper's memory. To get her own pound of flesh, she said, "FYI, I never met my folks. Well, actually, I was born, so I obviously met my mother... then again, maybe I was the product of a C-section and didn't meet her at all. Who knows?"

Leigh dropped her spoon to her now empty bowl. "Ouch. Sorry for my brother's ah—" she waved a dismissive hand in Trenton's direction to convey her meaning. "Where did you grow up? In an orphanage, foster care?"

"I was in several foster homes then on my own before I was taken in by a group of folks who accepted strays. They turned out to be my kind of people. In effect, I've been very lucky."

"Your kind of people?" Trenton murmured with gaze narrowed. "As in lawless, entitled, and lacking boundaries?"

Cecile coughed delicately behind her hand. "Yes. Well, then. Trent, I think you owe our guest an apology."

The agent firmed his jaw then slid it side to side. "Sorry, kid. I should've known better." The apology held as much sincerity as a clerk at the Department of Motor Vehicles.

The audible grind of Trenton's teeth reminded Casper of one of her adopted uncles. If a slingshot emerged from beneath the table, Simon, now perched on Trenton's head, would intervene. As it was, the small primate pulled at the abundance of the fed's thick black hair, disrupting a few strands.

Trenton smoothed his fingers over his scalp, obviously feeling the tug.

Casper giggled. Beside her, Hailey snorted. She couldn't see the intended escapades, but she'd heard Simon's screeching, judging by the way she rubbed her ear.

"Would anyone care for some dessert?" Cecile's frown in Trenton's direction declared there'd be more said at a later time. From a cabinet, she withdrew plates and retrieved her fresh-made sweet potato pie.

Five people sat at the table.

Cecile returned with six plates.

"Ah, Mom?" Hailey frowned, wariness of how to broach the subject etched in her face. She nodded at the plates.

Cecile shrugged. "It is considered polite to offer food to *everyone* at your table, even if they don't display the proper manners." She barely skipped a beat before saying, "And animals don't belong *on* the table."

A thousand thoughts flew through Casper's mind at warp speed, ending with, *Oh, shit.* "You...?" was all she could muster around the softball-sized lump in her throat.

"Me what, dear?" Cecile smiled. "Not everything is as it appears on first blush. You of all people should know this."

Not a word was spoken. No one moved an inch.

"But they say you're into Vodou and all that stuff."

"As I said, dear. Not everything is as it appears, but we can talk later."

"O-kay." *Damn straight.*

Hailey hadn't mentioned her mother's psychic ability. Since it didn't always pass from parent to child, Casper assumed it'd skipped a generation.

"I have just one question first. Did you know my mother and father? They lived in Texas at one time, at least for a while. I don't know anything else about them. Just that I couldn't come down here until I came... of age."

True regret radiated from Cecile. "No, dear. I don't believe I ever did. And those are the sort of things I've kept abreast of over the years."

A slurry of thoughts ran through Casper's mind. If this family used religious hocus-pocus as cover for psychic talent, it'd explain why her parents had moved here. And if that were true, why hadn't Hailey's talent emerged sooner? Was she one of the late bloomers her Pennsylvania friends talked about?

Either way, these were people she didn't want to piss off. With her hand on the table and her fingers stretched out, she motioned for Simon to return.

The world just got a whole lot stranger.

"So, Hailey. I heard you had a visitor of the foreign accent variety." Cecile's subtlety definitely needed work.

"Yes. He didn't threaten me, and I had Gunther." Hailey shot a dirty look at her mother, who shook her head and held up both hands.

"I'm not telling you how I found out, dear. You know the Hamchet grapevine is alive and well. What I am curious to know is what exactly he wanted. I mean, a stranger showing up *in* your loft? That's ballsy."

"Okay, Mom. He wants me to butt out of the ATF murder investigation."

Trenton's jaw went slack. Shock warred with fury in his gaze. The expected tirade didn't emerge, but his hands fisted on the table.

Cecile nodded, but her frown signaled a parent's worry. "That sounds like excellent advice, even if it did come from a complete stranger. I'm glad he didn't mean you any harm."

"How come I didn't about know this?" Leigh slapped the table. "Someone breaks into your loft and you don't call me? What the hell?"

"I'm fine. It was just a conversation."

"And food. He brought the most delicious—" Casper let the rest of the words die on her tongue. She realized social etiquette was definitely not her thing after another glance at Trenton.

"You ate food, brought by a stranger, who'd broken into your loft?" The last of Trenton's words entered the higher decibel level. "What is wrong with you? Why didn't you call *me?*" Thunderclouds looked more inviting than the federal agent.

"We would have, but we figured you'd already eaten. And 'sides, he wasn't your type." Casper couldn't avoid poking the bear. It was too much fun.

"And what, he was *your* type?" Trenton yelled.

"Well, not exactly." Casper made a point of examining her fingernails in a casual manner. "He was a little old, but really, I wouldn't mind making an exception in this case. He was right fine looking."

"*Arrgh.*" Trenton scrubbed a hand across his eyes, clearly trying to erase some image from his mind.

"Unless, of course, Hailey, you want him. I hear men reach their peak in their twenties, and I think he's still in the range. Oughta grab him while the grabbing's good." Casper couldn't resist one last tug of the tail. If Trenton weren't such an overreaching bear, he might be a decent guy. She considered him a work in progress and worthy of the time, albeit for someone else.

Hailey rested her face in her hands. "Maybe this wasn't the best time for a get-together."

"Nonsense." Cecile pursed her lips in thought. "We'll get through this. We're all family here." The nod included Casper.

Casper's phone dinged with an incoming message. Pulling it from her pocket, she read the text.

"Well?" Hailey asked then looked over Casper's shoulder. "Oh. Oh, really? Your friend is quite the genius."

"What now?" Trenton deadpanned. "Does the Italian stud want to join us for dinner?"

"No, it's from my buddy, um, in Pennsylvania. He found a little background on Hailey's Italian stud."

Hailey groaned. "Oh, God. He's not my—anything."

Leigh shook her head. "And?"

Since Cecile seemed to be the most accepting, Casper directed the answer to her. "His computer was just for show. Nothing on it. However, he does share a tentative association with organized crime. There was a picture of him in Atlanta four years ago. Could've been coincidence."

"Uh-huh. I don't believe that for a second. Though I would certainly believe you'd commit B&E and steal a computer..." Trenton pulled out his phone to check his notes. "We have a dead ATF agent, gun smuggling, and now a stranger warns you off the case. Doesn't sound coincidental to me. I want every detail. I'll give you my number."

"Don't worry, fed. Believe me, I've already got it." Casper forwarded her notes. "And for the record, the *borrowed* computer will be returned."

After a brief pause, the rest of the evening devolved into friendly interrogation with questions fired from the two guests holding badges. Only with promises to Trenton and Cecile to be careful did Hailey avoid gaining a badged roommate.

Casper assured each she had more than adequate security. Leigh and Trenton appeared skeptical, until Cecile closed the subject with a yawn.

Chapter Nine

Hailey

Most teenagers of Hailey's acquaintance liked to sleep as long as possible before getting ready for school. Casper broke each stereotype that came to mind.

They met at the office bright and early, the teen carrying two bags in one hand and a coffee tray in the other. Frequent meals eaten on the run was another trait they shared.

Placing the drinks in the truck's cup holders, Casper opened a bag and offered a treat to Gunther. "Don't worry, boy. I'd never forget you."

In response, his cool nose nudged the teen's neck before accepting his peanut butter treat. A soft chittering acknowledged Gunther and Simon's greeting.

If not for Casper's insertion into her life, Hailey might've suspected a sharp mental decline responsible for hearing voices. Since her sister's warning saved her life in the bayou, she'd heard Simon's frequent lip smacking, just one of his friendly interactions with her wolf dog.

"So, did you and your mom enjoy a long talk after the rest of us left?" Casper sat in the passenger seat munching her breakfast. A serious case of side-eye betrayed her interest.

A twist of her lips belied the casual shrug. "Actually, we did. It shocked the hell out of me that she knew about Simon. Since my grandmother died, there's a few topics she avoids at all cost."

"She knew he was there. Doesn't mean she saw him. Monkey sounds are quite distinctive."

"Yeah, and as it turns out, Mom was a late bloomer in life too. We talked at length about Addy." The lump in Hailey's throat doubled when thinking about the sister she'd lost before ever knowing her.

"How much time has she spent talking with Addy? Must've made you feel like you've missed out."

"Actually, she's never had contact with her. Not sure why. Mom went into early labor and lost her child."

"Why no contact?"

"I suppose to spare Mom the grief. It's something we'll work on, if and when I talk to Addy again. Seems she only makes herself known when I'm in trouble."

"I can kinda understand that. I've only been dealing with spirits for a few months, but they tend to keep to themselves. Your sister probably hasn't had much in the way of companionship, learning what she can from observation."

"Can you, like, summon her?" Demanding her sister's attendance probably wasn't the smartest move, but Hailey realized the importance of family regardless of which side of the grave they inhabited.

"I could, but I've found that doesn't usually end well. It'd be better to encourage a natural relationship. There's so much I don't know. I'm learning as I go."

"Do they always appear as they did at the time of death?" Curiosity of the new dimension fascinated Hailey.

"No. They can appear at any age, shape, different clothing, whatever. I guess it's something they learn with time."

"Do they age?"

"I guess... if they want to, but they can also reverse it if they want to. Consider it all illusion. For all we know, she could've been modeling herself after you for years."

Hailey nodded her acceptance, glad for whatever knowledge gained. "Either way and despite our age difference, you and I will make a good team one day."

"One day?"

"Mom thinks you're seventeen, remember? Hence, in her eyes, you're still a kid." Hailey yielded to another vehicle at the stop sign before turning onto Cricket Road leading into town.

"Huh, I feel like I'm thirty going on arthritic and early dementia. I don't know how older folks cope. Sure gives me a new respect for my elders."

"What's making you feel old? You're a senior in high school." Hailey chuckled. If her teachers or fellow students suspected Casper's true nature, they'd likely run.

"Well, I've been on my own before, for a short time at least. But now I'm like, having to be responsible for others and making decisions that affect them. I don't like adulting much."

"Sarah is more of an assistant or an equal."

"Yeah. And we get along okay. She doesn't try and boss me around or anything, but when she goes out, I worry about her running into trouble she can't handle. She doesn't have any psychic talent."

"She carries a gun. Is she a decent shot? Would she hesitate?"

"She's almost as good as me. And no, I'm sure she'd shoot first then ask questions, even though we only met when I moved down here. Despite that, she doesn't have the advantage we have when we work."

"The psychic talent."

"Which your mom hides under the guise of religion. Smart lady. Do you have any other relatives?" A sliver of hope tinged Casper's tone.

"No. It's just Mom and me."

"I never thought I'd be part of a huge family, and don't get me wrong, there are drawbacks. Still, I love my guys in PA. I wouldn't have it any other way. We just... connected."

"Speaking of connections, I found one yesterday. A guy named Merrick Linther is a member of your school board and has had contact with our ex-gang member, Babtiste. Linther returned my call this morning just before you arrived."

"And?" Casper waited.

"Said they met at a gun show outside New Orleans. His picture popped up on Babtiste's social media." Hailey returned the wave from the driver of an oncoming car.

"Could be a coincidence," Casper suggested.

"Well, Charlotte at Upward Bound confirmed the Jackyls are into drugs and want to deal in the school. Do you think the connection stems from guns or drug smuggling? I'm thinking it could be either or none of the above."

"Don't know. Wyatt pulled up financials for all school board members and didn't see anything that warranted a closer look just yet. Could be they were just gun collectors."

"Babtiste was an ex-Jackyl and certainly not a student at the Gifted Elite. I can't see him being best buds with a member of the school board from a social standpoint. Nor from Charlotte's glowing description can I see him putting guns in the hands of the students any more than I can see the kids wanting them. They're not oriented the same as normal kids. Being a student there, you'd know that better than me."

"Well, for now, let's do this interview and get back so I can make it to class," Casper finished her breakfast and balled up the trash. "What do you know about this pair we're gonna meet?"

"A guy and his girl made contact with Charlotte at Upward Bound. They want out of gang life, but wanted to talk to me first."

"Why you?" Casper asked offering Gunther another treat.

"Said they wanted an impartial take on Charlotte and the way she runs the farm. Not sure if they know she has some type of leverage over the gang or not. She wouldn't share that secret."

"Charlotte must be pretty persuasive." Casper accepted Hailey's trash and smushed the bag into the door's storage compartment.

"She's a force to be reckoned with from what little I saw."

Through town and out the other side where an old strip mall battled the economy for survival, Hailey considered the puzzle pieces in play. Charlotte, the owner/manager of Upward Bound, swore Babtiste wouldn't involve himself with guns and drugs. Yet, Hailey wondered how difficult it'd be to leave good friends behind.

How much information this couple would be willing to share, and did they know of, or could they gather evidence for the leader's arrest?

"They picked a public out-of-the-way spot to meet. Either they're paranoid, or the Jackyls have some serious issues about gang members wanting to leave," Casper surmised.

"I imagine both. Frederick has killed deserters. Charlotte said they'd rather murder them than suffer their presence in town. Keep your wits about you. Everything I hear about this gang points to escalating violence. There's a cold war heating up on a daily basis. If we could manage to take Frederick of the picture, it would cool things off. At least for a while." Hailey turned onto the asphalt lot and parked near a discount home goods store.

A few morning shoppers were heading into the craft store boasting a half-off banner across the glass window.

"If Frederick learns of this meeting and comes after us, driving away won't be an option." Casper slid off the seat and waited for Gunther to follow.

"But to phase through an attack in public..." Again, Hailey wondered about her friend's training. No doubt there'd been quite a bit of it under different scenarios.

"Got a backup plan for that, too, trust me."

"I do. But I try to never walk into a situation without an exit strategy." Hailey itched to explore the details instigating Casper's grin.

Some day.

Two youths in torn clothes shifted back and forth beside a pair of bikes leaning against a lamppost.

The boy was likely sixteen or seventeen, wearing jeans and a tee. The girl appeared a little younger regardless of the many visible piercings. A belly ring peeked out between her cropped top and low-slung jeans. Each held the posture displayed by those hunted for sport, ready to bolt at the first sign of trouble.

Few vehicles meant light foot traffic and less obstacles offering cover for those intending to eavesdrop.

Hailey and Casper hopped out and rounded the hood.

"Thank you for meeting us here." The young man stepped forward with a wary step, tugging his girlfriend behind him.

"No problem. Charlotte said you wanted to talk and might have information on Babtiste?" Hailey figured both knew enough to put Frederick away for life. The question remained, what would entice them to open up versus divulging just enough to get what they wanted?

"I don't know where Babtiste is, but I can tell you he isn't working on behalf of the Jackyls." Shoulder-length hair pulled back in a low ponytail added a certain hardness to the young man's character.

The girl looked like she wanted to be anywhere other than where she stood. Long brown hair surfed the breeze as her gaze flicked around the lot, then between Casper and Hailey before doing another perimeter sweep.

It was no way to live.

"What about Frederick? Can you give us anything on him?" Casper met the girl's gaze before it slid away.

"Yeah. He's got a real nasty temper and very little restraint." She touched the bruise on her cheek, the movement speaking volumes.

It wasn't so much what they said as the way they continued to speak which confirmed the notion each had received some education. Perhaps they hadn't belonged to the gang for long.

Will that make it easier for them to leave?

"Sorry, guys. I forgot my manners. I'm Casper." Neither had offered their name. When Casper stuck her hand out, each took a half step back.

"You're one of the snotty Gifted Elite kids," the girl replied with sullen disapproval.

"I do attend the school, which makes me neither evil nor untrustworthy." Casper failed to retract her hand. In contrast, she took a half step forward to greet the girl personally. "Seems like you've been through a lot."

"What would you know about hardship?" With obvious reluctance, she shook the hand then retreated a half step.

"*Hmm*, see, unlike my best friend in Pennsylvania, I didn't grow up entirely on the streets. In reality, my time was considerably less after my first adopted parents died. When some asshat killed the second set, well, I decided I was better off on my own, which turned out to be a good thing. But I have learned that sometimes we make life harder than it has to be."

Finally, the girl's gaze rose to meet Casper's head-on. There existed a moment in time where each took the other's measure, judging for themselves the worthiness of what could be said. The first steps in a relationship were sometimes the hardest, but they could lead to a strong bond.

If it wasn't some type of setup.

Hailey took the hint and nodded to the boyfriend, moving several steps aside to allow the girls space for unmonitored conversation. "What can you tell me about Frederick?"

Scrunching his nose and casting a watchful eye over his companion, the boyfriend took a reluctant step away.

They could still hear snippets of the other conversation, and Hailey caught a fragment regarding the Lone Star Frontiersmen, the local chapter of a larger hate group.

"Rumor has it the Jackyls are trying to expand their business. Is that right?" Hailey drove right to the point where she saw at least two cultures intersecting. "Is Frederick challenging an organized crime faction making a move on the GE school?" It might be a wild theory, but was worth pursuing. If she could tie Frederick both to murder and the school, it could help Casper's investigation as well.

"There's been talk, but Frederick's all hush-hush about it. He's trying to make a deal where—oh, shit."

Hailey looked over her shoulder to see a car squealing into the lot. The red Chevy's driver conveyed arrogance and vengeance with one look. The passenger's nasty smile boded ill for anyone he crossed.

The pair who'd come on Babtiste's behalf now faced a dilemma. Indecision lasted for all of a half second as the girl faced off with Casper. Her low whispered, "Play along or die," held all the fear in her gaze.

"How dare you bring your trashy ass into our space. Go back to your snotty school for rich brats." Exaggerated hand movements accompanied the younger Jackyl's snort of derision.

"Hey," Casper shouted even louder, keeping up the charade they were forced to play. "You asshats think you own the town, but I'm telling you, the GE kids are gonna take it over, along with all your business. Tell your boss we'll be coming for him."

If ever someone issued a sideways challenge, Casper succeeded in spades. The girl thought fast on her feet and reacted accordingly.

"What's going on here?" The driver hopped out of the car and vaulted over the hood. "You uptown bitches need to learn your place. And I'm just the man to teach you."

Casper made a vague gesture toward the speaker's lower half. "Wrong. You clearly don't have the equipment for the job."

"I'll show you exactly what I've got before I deal with your witchy friend. We're gonna party all night long." The spring blade pulled from the driver's back pocket had a curved double edge.

"Ah, I see you need a lesson in blade combat. I happened to have learned from the best." Casper slipped a wicked-looking blade from her boot. It wasn't as long, but she handled it like she'd done so every day of her life. She probably had.

"So that's why you don't wear sneakers. Huh." Hailey grabbed Gunther's collar when he hopped out the window and lunged for the other Jackyl. "Dinner's not served yet, boy. They have to make a move on us to make it legal. Casper can handle herself against that dweeb."

"I've always taken care of myself. Look at the beauty I carry." Casper turned the blade to catch the sun's reflection. "No finger groves. Easy to grip. Can be used for slashing and stabbing, and it's stainless steel. It's never rusted despite all the blood it's seen."

The Jackyl's flicker of doubt bloomed into full-blown uncertainty during the running commentary. Her continued one-sided discussion referencing Southeast Asia's martial art style of Pencak Silat followed.

Her opponent visibly gulped then swatted at his ear. A jerk of his head sideways coincided with Simon's discordant scream.

"What's happening?" The driver dropped his blade and ducked, spinning in a three-sixty to check his perimeter.

"Simon, remember the rules. No physical damage." Casper snickered then held her non-dominant hand out. A slight dip signaled her unseen primate's hop before she touched her hand to her shoulder.

Hailey had an idea of the teen's training, and she damn well made a good showing. That plus Simon's intervention spooked the newest arrivals, enough for the driver's companion to pull him back.

"Damn witches and Vodou shit. This isn't over." The driver scooped up his knife. A flick of his wrist folded the blade back to safe position before he tucked it in his back waist. "I'll see you two when you least expect it."

"Hey, asshole. You know one of the differences between the living and the dead?" Casper didn't wait for an answer. "The dead don't sleep." A wide grin conveyed all that was necessary to send her opponent backing up without taking his eyes off his quarry.

A sharp look and nod sent the boy and his girlfriend scurrying to the car before sneering at Casper. "Your day will come, *puta*. It'll be here before you know it, for both of you."

Casper replaced her blade after the car drove off. "Well, that was vastly entertaining and a terrible waste of time."

"Not entirely." As soon as Hailey released Gunther's collar, the animal made a beeline for Casper. "Is it true spirits don't sleep? Where do they go when not with you?"

"Dunno. Cagey buggers won't share. Very stingy. Whether it's because of some unwritten law or something actually prevents it, I don't know." Casper slid her fingers under the amulet she wore and lifted it into view. "I've only had this a short while."

Casper turned her face to the side where Simon cooed. "Aw, buddy. I'm fine. They couldn't have hurt me whatever they tried. I've faced a hell of a lot scarier things than those little boys."

"Which I'd like to hear about someday. Really. What was that I heard about Lone Star Frontiersman?" Hailey asked.

"Ah, yes. It seems our gang leader Frederick has plans. I think he wants to fold into the larger organization and reap the benefits."

"Are we talking guns, drugs, or something else?" Hailey asked.

"Don't know. My conversation got rudely interrupted before the girl could tell me."

"I think it's safe to say those two kids are in trouble. I'll share with Leigh." Hailey snagged her phone from her pocket. If they couldn't get help for the two would-be informants soon, there'd be two more dead bodies found, or not found and forever missing.

"You gonna fill Trenton in on this too?" Casper hooked a thumb over her shoulder in the general direction of the mall.

"Yeah. He'll have more detailed information on the Frontiersman group."

"I wasn't able to get the girl's name, but I don't think she's having an easy time of it with the Jackyls. They obviously treat women like shit."

"Yeah, I got that vibe as well. Now, Frederick's trying to set up some kind of deal. We really need to shut him down before he makes the connection."

"Damn." Casper bent her head forward as Simon cooed softly.

"Yeah. I agree."

Chapter Ten

Hailey

Conversations with federal agents should never be taken lightly, even with friendship stemming from childhood. Nor should either be underestimated.

Trenton Briner was indeed a good friend, a good listener, dependable, and upstanding. He also had a mile-wide protective streak with no shutoff valve.

At times, he could be an overbearing curmudgeon if not handled with a delicate touch. Hailey needed the background he could provide, hence would have to choose her words carefully when describing her encounter with the Jackyls at the shopping center.

The phone conversation went as expected.

Not surprisingly, he'd asked if she'd taken a certain dark-haired teen along for the ride. Though Hailey had learned to navigate complex problems fairly well, she couldn't lie worth a damn.

It was time to invest in earplugs. She'd still hear normal, yet spare her eardrums from the worst of the federal agent's tirades.

An olive branch arrived with an offer to join him later for a working lunch at Bouchard's Café. In reality, he wanted another opportunity to reinforce the fact she should recuse herself from the investigation. He'd never lacked perseverance.

At least Gunther would enjoy the lunch.

After dropping Casper off, she drove to the farm for an update with Charlotte. Progress was slow in the beginning of most cases, picking up speed as pieces fell in place.

Most civilians didn't understand the way investigations worked, or the expected pace, but Charlotte had long since developed patience in working with ex-gang members.

By the time Hailey returned to her truck, she had a better sense about Upward Bound and their methods. The owner would keep her eyes out and welcome either of the pair from the shopping center wanting a new life.

With the farm's overhead sign in her rearview, she pulled onto the paved road and opened Gunther's window. "Well, boy, we've got a little time before we meet Trenton for lunch."

She hesitated when her phone rang, until realizing it wasn't Trenton's theme song. No doubt, he was busy pulling security footage and now had more ammunition to support his demand.

As soon as she swiped the phone, sniffling on the other end let her know some type of trouble had her in its sights.

"Hailey?"

One word spoken as a plea filled with hope. The girl who'd ridden off with the Jackyls earlier wasted no time in getting in touch.

"Yes."

"Charlotte gave me your number. I-I've gotten away from these assholes. I need help. Can you meet me, give me a ride to Upward Bound?"

"What about your boyfriend? Isn't he with you?"

"No. He's led them in another direction to give me time to escape."

"Have you called the police? Where are you?"

"I'll call the cops as soon as I'm safe. I'm in the alley behind Garden View apartments, behind the third dumpster."

It was indeed a sad day when someone hid behind trash for safety. Is that what the girl thought of herself? Hailey had seen hard days herself, the difference being she always had support in her corner—Trenton, Leigh, and her mother.

"Sure. Be there in fifteen." Swiping the screen, she felt a niggling doubt climbing her spine. She hadn't survived trips to hell and back without learning a thing or two.

Not wanting to pique Trenton's curiosity beyond tolerance, she sent a text telling him she might be a little late along with sketched details.

Why are meetings in the seedy parts of town?

The small complex consisted of two buildings separated from the alley by a chain link fence and a living green wall of holly. One discouraged peeping toms, the other meant to keep small children from wandering off. Hailey remained doubtful as to the effectiveness of either barrier.

Odors of spoiled food, oil, and things she wouldn't contemplate wafted from the mouth of the alley.

"Sorry, Gunther, I need the windows open so I can hear anything coming at us. This isn't exactly a high-class neighborhood." She felt sorry for the hard-working individuals who slaved away at their nine-to-fives but couldn't catch a break. It was all too common. Despite her breaks, she still lived paycheck to paycheck.

Something prickled at her nape, a feeling she couldn't ignore. The girl had sounded terrified yet sincere on the phone. She wanted out of the gang and away from danger. That much was clear. If her boyfriend paid the ultimate price for her freedom, she'd carry that guilt for the rest of her life.

Or, the call was a setup.

The lane was quiet, each small gate to the back of its designated apartment complex closed. Resident parking was located in the front.

Nightshift workers were tucked in to sleep and the dayshift wage earners had left hours prior. All was quiet except for the woodpecker tapping out his twenty beats per second on a nearby Texas ash.

The drive-thru alley exited on the far end onto a narrow road leading away from town. Road width denied the possibility of making a multi-point turn, so she'd approached from the higher traffic side to allow herself more paths of escape should the need arise.

With the apartment's backyards to the right and a barren field once intended for a playground to the left, her vehicle crawled forward. Cracked, heaved asphalt left chunks sliding into the gully and ensured lower speeds. It was more effective than any traffic camera or speed bump.

Five dumpsters positioned evenly along the apartment buildings would've provided space for residents to dispose of their trash if three hadn't been overflowing.

Hailey stopped beside the third dumpster and shoved the gear into park. Nothing stirred, not even a breeze to dry the perspiration popping up on her brow.

"This doesn't feel right, Gunther." Her friend Leigh had warned to heed her instincts, which now screamed.

Still, she couldn't abandon a young girl in dire need, plain and simple. She'd faced worse odds.

Sliding out of her truck, she again flicked her gaze to both ends of the alley. All was clear, no nearby traffic, no kids heard playing in the yards.

Midday sun denied the shadowed advance granting respite from September heat. She wiped her brow.

"Hi."

The familiar voice startled her into dropping her keys on the pavement. She caught movement from the corner of her eye in retrieving them.

Popping out from between the hedgerow and dumpster, the young Jackyl took a tentative step forward.

"Hey, I didn't catch your name earlier."

"They call me Teeny, kind of a joke to them."

Hailey stepped forward then halted at the sight greeting her. "Are you okay? What happened?"

Sharp holly leaves accounted for the myriad scratches on her arms and hands but didn't explain the rest. Blood spatters not present earlier adorned the tattered green top. Bright splotches of crimson under her eye and cheek would bloom into dark bruises in the coming days.

"Did your boyfriend get clear?"

Her gaze slid away as tears tracked her cheeks. "I-I don't know. I ran like he told me to."

"All right, then. Let's get you out of here and to the police station. We can file a report and—" The rest of Hailey's words dried in her throat with the sudden screech in her ear causing her to hunch her shoulders. She ducked the same time the crack of gunfire presented a new threat.

Teeny gasped and ducked, grabbing her left upper arm where a bullet ricocheted off the metal trash container and sliced through the outer edge of her bicep.

In the truck, Gunther barked, his gaze locked on the far end of the alley. Ears erect and forward with lips retracted, he declared his own warning in gleaming white canines. His muscles bunched in preparation to leap out the window.

"Gunther, stay. Down, boy." Her companion had saved her from trouble more than once, but couldn't stop a bullet from piercing flesh.

"I'm sorry. I had no choice," the teen blurted the rhetoric like a mantra, over and over.

"Shit. They were waiting for me."

At the far end of the alley, a familiar red Chevy turned into the alley and burned rubber, heading her way. The upper body leaning out the passenger window was also familiar. The gun in the Jackyls' hand, not so much.

At that distance, accuracy with a pistol went to hell. The shooter could've been aiming for either person.

Hailey grabbed Teeny by the hand and yanked her behind the truck for cover.

An instant flash seared a memory in her mind the second their hands joined. A blonde-haired boy and red-headed girl were tied to straight-backed chairs, each pair of eyes swollen closed. Each mouth missing teeth. Blood oozed from split lips and small cuts.

It was the pair of teens missing for over a year.

The vision continued. Before the boy, with fist raised high, Frederick stood. A physical caricature of contempt bordering on hatred marred a face ravaged by acne.

Teeny yanked her hand away, the connection lost.

"I'm sorry. I-I had to. They would've killed me." Two steps back took her away from cover and into the open. "I have to go back. They'll kill my boyfriend if I don't." With that, she turned and fled toward the oncoming vehicle.

The driver stopped twenty yards away, long enough to take in the passenger and for Hailey to see the intent written on the driver's face.

Torture. Murder.

There was no need to ask who ordered the ambush. Another shot pierced the glass of both her windshield and back window to sail within inches of her head. The closer they got, the more accurate their shots became.

She had nowhere to run that wouldn't endanger others. Her only chance to fight entailed making it to her truck. Her Hellcat with two spare mags lay in the glove compartment. Now, that wasn't an option.

The Jackyls now had two hostages. She needed to flee but didn't have a protected path.

Her first step left froze with the shrill, "*No!*" in her ear, followed by, "*Wait, Hailey. You've got backup here.*"

A heartbeat later, a second shot rang out from behind her, higher pitched. A rifle shot.

Her attention snapped back to the head of the alley.

Fifty yards away, a black sedan had stopped. The driver's side door was open and a man rested a rifle in the crook to steady his aim. All she could see of him was a full head of dark hair. But it was enough.

Dante? No. It can't be.

The shot wasn't meant for her. In fact, she heard it strike metal, but not her truck. Lifting her head just enough to see over the tailgate again and through the front windshield, she saw a hole in the Jackyls' windshield not present a second earlier.

In effect, she was in the middle of a shootout. If not for the curve in the road, Dante wouldn't have had a shot.

Another sharp crack from behind changed the Jackyls' intent from charge and kill to back up and run. The vehicle reversed from the alley and took the turn on two wheels.

A second later, it disappeared from sight.

"Well, that was interesting."

Local police would investigate the shots fired. Eventually. To explain *how* she'd known to duck would include a trip to a psychiatrist and then giving a statement about *who* countered the attack.

Neither was acceptable.

She'd had her suspicions about Dante that didn't jive with the night-in-shining-armor spectrum. Yet when he put away his rifle and offered a tip of his imaginary hat, she didn't know what to think.

A quick hand gesture urged her to leave before he backed his car into the intersection and sped off.

Shit. What just happened?

No sooner had she returned to the driver's side door, a squeal of tires jerked her attention in the opposite direction. Trenton's SUV barreled toward her and skidded to a stop.

"What have you done, now, Sparkles?"

"What makes you think I've done anything?" Despite the voiced bravado, Trenton would see the slight shake in her hand and hear the faint quiver in her words.

The next thought popping in her mind entailed, *How did Dante know where I am? Why did he intervene?*

"*He saved you. Isn't that enough?*" her sister's voice countered near her right ear.

"Got a report of gunshots in the area. I knew you'd be involved." Trenton strode forward, his gaze assessing.

"How'd you get here so quick? It just happened."

"I started this way when you texted." Running a hand through his hair, he scanned each end of the alley. "I, um, I put a tracker on your vehicle at your mom's house. Knew it would come in handy." Trenton wrapped his arms around her shoulders and held her tight. "How can I keep you safe when you continually go off on tangents?"

"*Arrgh.* I'm fine, Trent. I didn't see the shooter or the vehicle. I was busy taking cover." If Trenton suspected the lie, he didn't call her on it.

"Likely one of the Jackyls? But why'd they run? You're not holding your Hellcat." To prove his point, he retrieved her pistol and sniffed the barrel. "Not been fired recently."

"I dunno why they ran off. And I'm aware I have to give a statement."

"And get your windshield fixed." He knew the lie for what it was but didn't press his advantage.

Hailey sighed. It wasn't the first time her sister had saved her life. It was the first hope for a future conversation.

"*Addy?*" Speaking through her mind kept Trenton out of the loop. "*Why would Dante save me? Why would he care?*"

Stroking Gunther's head calmed her dog, but not her racing heart.

"*Things are not always what they appear to be, sis. You'll learn.*"

As the last words drifted through her mind, Hailey felt them fade. "Wait. Don't go. I have so many questions."

"*Now's not the time.*"

It wasn't until Trenton gave her a little shake she realized she'd spoken out loud.

"Sparkles, I'm not going anywhere. And what do you want to ask?"

"No. Not you." Ah, she couldn't keep things separate. "Crap." What she had was sensory overload. She'd seen one crime in a vision while taking part in another, then proceeded to talk with her spirit sister in front of Trenton.

"You need a break, Hailey."

"You're right."

The girl had obviously been a part of the ambush, but it didn't make her a willing participant. If the police got involved, the Jackyls would kill the girl. She was a witness.

Whatever she did next would have to be without Trenton's knowledge. That left a certain dark-haired, Italian-accented advertisement for hormones to help.

Can I really consider that as an option?

No, but if she could convince Leigh of the necessity, they could work out a plan together. A badge had to be involved at some point because the leader of the Jackyls wanted blood. Hailey's blood.

Frederick killed two people the prior year. The list was most likely much longer. He wouldn't be dumb enough to take Teeny any place the police would easily find. When looking for a killer, she had to think like one.

There has to be a better way.

"Okay, Trent. I'll meet you at the station in an hour. I want to go home. I need a little down time, alone, with Gunther."

"Okay, but don't make me come looking for you." Reluctance in his steady gaze when letting her go spoke volumes.

In the truck, she accepted Gunther's nuzzle and slurp along her cheek. "Yeah, boy. Thank heavens you weren't hurt. What d'ya say we go back to the loft and figure out a plan?"

Before making any calls, she wanted to get every remembered detail from her vision down on paper.

Trenton would have to wait his turn.

Frequent checks in her rearview assured she had no tail, not that she'd be hard to find. It all depended on how bad and how soon the Jackyls wanted her out of the picture.

Which brought Casper to mind. She was also a target now. At least she could phase her body and counter an attack—as long as she saw it coming.

Adrenaline washout left her drained and in need of a quiet refuge. With her part-time receptionist in class for the day, her building would be empty.

Perfect.

Another figurative shockwave rocked her body in turning onto her street.

Of course.

The same black BMW seen moments prior sat parked in front of her door. At least she'd be able to ask Dante a few questions. Whether he chose to answer them or not remained to be seen.

Gunther chuffed with excitement, his weight bouncing from foot to foot. As soon as she opened her door and slid out, he vaulted off the seat and raced to the front door, his tail wagging contorting the rest of his body.

Seriously? After one meeting, why?

She didn't bother to check her office, instead wondering if he'd brought food again. Being on the receiving end of target practice made her hungry.

Gunther pushed the door open as soon as she turned the knob.

Sure enough, he sat on her couch with one ankle crossed over the other knee and a dog treat in hand.

Gunther devoured the treat before she could set her keys in the tray. "Well, fancy meeting you here."

"I thought you were going to stay away from this. Are you suicidal?" Dante's casual tone belied the fierceness of his expression.

In lieu of answering, she went to the punch line. "Do you work for a crime syndicate?"

His eyes widened then narrowed. "You narrowly avoid death and that is your first question? I notice you didn't hang around for the police," he said in challenge.

"I left because I have questions for you and would like to ask them without an audience."

"I have no answers for you."

She stared him down.

After taking a deep breath, he relented. "Ask what you will. I'll answer what I can."

"You strike me as the kind of guy who doesn't miss."

"I didn't. I fired a warning shot. It worked. End of story."

"Would you have shot them if they didn't rabbit?"

His answer came in the form of a smile.

Okay, she tried a new tact. "Who is that girl? How's she important?"

"I've no idea to either of those questions."

Hailey was a decent judge of liars. Dante wasn't avoiding a deeper truth when he answered.

"Are you connected to the mob?" she pressed again.

"We are all connected, after a fashion. Take, for instance, your friend Casper. Who, by the way, I wish you'd talk some sense into." Dante pinched the bridge of his nose as if fending off a headache, a gesture common to both Leigh and Trenton.

Maybe I'm the problem.

"Casper has her own mind, her own talents, and her own way of doing things. I respect that, despite her age."

"Yes, talents. Lovely way of putting it. She's still a kid. This is one area where I agree with Trenton and Leigh."

"How do you know them?"

"Personally? I don't. I know *of* them. As far as Casper goes, she doesn't belong at the GE school. She's in over her head and it's difficult for me to protect her there."

"Aw, Dante. You have no idea." The remark occurred without thought and Hailey regretted the words the moment they left her mouth. She didn't want to perk his interest in the teen, especially considering who she suspected paid his salary.

"Your bosses are trying to move in on the school?"

Again, Dante narrowed his eyes before a mask slid into place. "You don't know what you're talking about."

"Talk has it that organized crime wants a part of the school's drug business, which puts them at odds with the Jackyls, already in the business. What I don't understand is how gun smuggling comes into play."

"You're not supposed to understand. Listen, if you need money. I—"

"No. Do not finish that sentence."

"How about we have something to eat?" Dante rose from the couch and sauntered over to the fridge, removing several cartons.

If he thought he could bribe her with food and good looks, he was wrong. She would, however, eat the food and admire the view.

"Sure. What do you know about the Lone Star Frontiersmen?" It struck her as both odd and comfortable to move about the kitchen with a man who was self-assured and handsome but made no demands. If not for recent events, he could exist squarely in the friend zone. Was he using her to get to Casper?

His interest in the teen didn't sit well.

Under different circumstances, she'd be more wary of a stranger popping into her apartment. Except, he had just saved her life.

"Hmm, the Frontiersmen are a well-organized group of small-minded radicals. And may I add, you should *absolutely* stay away from them."

"When did you have time to pick this up?" She gestured to the food. "And how did you find me in the alley?"

"I came here earlier. When I saw you were gone, well, let's just say I have my ways. I would think either your federal friend or Leigh would've put a bell around your neck by now, considering your penchant for finding trouble."

Hailey didn't intend to make this type of rendezvous a habit, but the food smelled divine.

Mysterious didn't come close to describing the man, but there was more to him than what appeared on the surface. "You've been watching me for a while. You knew about my clash with the GE teacher."

"I've kept loose tabs on you. Let's stick to the most important topic. The Jackyls will keep coming for you."

"Yeah, until I put Frederick away."

"Others have tried. And failed. Your badge friends will work harder on that now. Hopefully they'll find something before Frederick finds you. Again."

"Others who've come after me didn't have insider information." Frederick knew she was different in a big way. Would that make him retreat?

Dante paused then set this fork on his plate. His eyes narrowed as he leaned forward. "You keep tight to your secrets. Good. But understand this. No one is invulnerable. Everyone, and I do mean *everyone*, has a weakness. Arrogance can be the worst. Please keep a closer eye on your young friend."

If that equaled his sideways reference to psychic talent, he was among the very few who knew about them. "Is that a threat?" It didn't feel like one.

"No. It was a request to use caution. I'm trying to keep you alive through this foolish endeavor. As far as your teenage sidekick is concerned, anything said would be taken as a threat and lead to violence. It seems to be her go-to defense."

"Hence, you're going at her through me..."

"I mean to see you both safe."

"You've done a background check?" Hailey couldn't imagine him finding a whole lot in the way of details.

"What little I could collect. There's something very strange about that young lady, but the same could be said about you. The difference is, your family history is shrouded in the occult. She has no family history and no cover. I can't even find her birth record."

"She's looking for her folks too." Casper's goal of finding information about her biological parents had brought her to Texas. Dangling that carrot in front of her nose would lead to trouble.

Dante shrugged. His gaze took in the far wall where he pointed to a recent photo of panther kittens caught exiting their den. "Nice shot. How come you don't spend more time behind the lens?"

"I'm getting there."

Further discussion included her publication in a national online ezine, the proceeds paying for a new camera. When she brought the conversation around to the school for the gifted, the only comment she received entailed its importance to a specific, as yet unidentified, interest group.

Coupled with his possible ties to organized crime, it stood to reason the new group wanted influence and controlling interest with the school board with as much interaction with students as possible. Yet his interest with Casper hadn't led in that direction.

Yet.

Dante took a deep breath and let it out slowly before standing to go. "Look, I'm leaving for business, out of town. I'll be gone for a few days. Is there any chance—"

She didn't give him the opportunity to pitch another word of caution. "I'm not going to be sidelined by a pretty face. Sorry."

A half-grin and slight shrug acknowledged his confidence and affect. "Just be safe. Okay?"

All in all, she'd confirmed few details yet couldn't complain about the company.

Chapter Eleven

Hailey

A decent night's sleep often helped work out a problem, or at least find a new lead in whatever puzzle embroiled Hailey's world.

The only thing certain—she was worn down from Trenton's ass-chewing after her brush with the Jackyls' gunman.

Omitting Dante's involvement might bite her in the ass later, but for reasons she couldn't nail down, she didn't want to entangle her new acquaintance with the law.

Whatever embroiled Dante with the local faction of organized crime or the leading edge of a rival moving in didn't make him inherently evil. She wouldn't throw him under the bus until figuring out where he stood. He'd saved her life without taking one. That spoke of morality.

Not to be outdone, Leigh had descended on Hailey's loft after her evening shift in a cloud of righteous anger. Her search for the missing teens made inroads into the gang but yielded no results.

After a breakfast of her favorite chocolate cereal, she and Gunther made their way downstairs, where he went out back to do his business before they went into her office.

Classes were in session, so her part-time receptionist wouldn't arrive until after lunch. For all of Elizabeth's complaints regarding college courses, she never missed a class.

Once settled with a cup of iced chicory coffee, her computer went through its requisite beeps and chirps before the home screen replicated on her monitor.

Onscreen, Hailey sat between Leigh and Trenton, all with wide grins. Leigh had just won second place in the state championship finals for MMA, mixed martial arts. Continued sparring on a regular basis kept them both in shape.

Gunther circled in place two times before settling in the corner with his head resting on crossed paws. He'd grown restless having missed their afternoon run the prior day. She'd make up for it in the afternoon.

Logic dictated that something linked the Jackyls, GE school, and murdered ATF agent together. Babtiste's involvement was another mystery she couldn't solve, yet fit in there—somehow.

A knock at the front door reminded her she hadn't unlatched the bolt before retreating to her office.

"Stay here, boy. You scare the UPS drivers to death with your long black hair and blue eyes." A quick hand gesture settled him in place when rounding her desk.

Filtered light through floor-to-ceiling glass brightened the receptionist area and allowed her a view of the street, quiet and serene. A delivery van idled on the road's shoulder.

Flipping the lock's thumb knob, she paused before turning the door handle. Had she ordered anything recently? It wasn't unusual for Leigh to send packages here since she lived in an apartment and often couldn't take personal deliveries.

Backlighting shadowed the man's face standing on her doorstep. A wide-brimmed hat obscured the rest, his fingers flying over the screen of his phone as he tapped out a message. Judging by his demeanor, she figured him for a late teen.

It wasn't until she cleared her throat that he looked up.

And smiled.

It was the same clown who'd shot at her in the alley. "Shit."

One utterance brought Gunther racing from the office, his vocal response foreshadowing intent.

Short but wiry, the young man pulled his small-bore gun in such a way to remain hidden under his phone. Between the angle of his body and the large screen of his cell, the weapon avoided video capture by her security cameras.

"Tell your mutt to stay, or I'll shoot him. Can't miss this close."

He could get off a shot before she could swat the gun from his hands. She'd never moved as fast as Leigh.

Hailey whirled in time to snag Gunther's collar, pulling him close to her side. "There's surveillance all around this place that routes to an outside feed. You should smile."

Chin scruff didn't hide the scar running from temple to chin, but it did accentuate the white of his widening grin.

"Nice try, but I know where your cameras are. Now, leave your dog here and come with me." A dip of the barrel communicated impatience.

She had no choice.

"Gunther, stay." It took concentrated effort to hold her companion back and exit the building without him squeezing through.

"Why not just shoot me here? It's not like I know anything of use to you."

"Those aren't my orders, but yes, we know you didn't tell your fed toy anything pertinent about us." An exaggerated look around made his point. "Shame he's not here now. I've never done a fed before."

Hailey moved toward the cargo van, waiting for an opening to make her move. When he leaned around to slide it open, she'd nail his ass.

Her hopes died when a partner inside slid the door open while holding a .9mm pointed at her chest. A black mask covered his face. Crouching in the back, he waved her forward. "In you go, *puta*. We're taking a ride."

"I hope it's to Bouchard's. I love their boudin."

"No, we're relocating you to your permanent home." Masked man spread his hands apart, heedless of the barrel's direction, as if the answer was obvious.

A shove in the middle of her back forced her into the van and her arms forward to break the fall. Despite avoidance of a busted lip after striking the metal floorboard, she groaned. Something foul and sticky coated the floor.

Scruffy shoved her feet inside before he hopped in beside her.

The vehicle took off before the door slid shut.

She'd lied about the cameras. None led to an outside network. Considering the van and plates were likely stolen and scruffy wore a wide-brimmed hat, there'd be no lead for Trenton or Leigh to follow.

She hadn't heard any of Casper's ethereal friends lurking around her building. Nor had she heard her sister's voice.

Is she with Casper?

She'd have to deal with this mess alone.

Lifting her gaze provided a view of the road as the van careened around the corner without stopping, not that there was ever any traffic.

In the front seats, two men sat with their gazes scanning the road ahead. None of them spoke.

She couldn't get a good look at either before blinding pain coinciding with a solid crack to the back of her head narrowed her focus to the floor rushing up to greet her.

She didn't feel the contact between her cheek and corrugated metal.

Pain with an encore of confusion and disorientation instigated a low moan before she opened one eye. A steady throb ravaged her skull and rivaled the crash cymbal in a traditional drum kit.

One of the first things she noticed was a horrid stench, even before realizing she lay in near-total darkness—amid something slippery.

Her temporary bed consisted of myriad pebbles and various size sticks on what felt like a concrete floor.

Focus proved impossible for several long minutes. Slow breaths through her mouth helped mitigate the urge to empty her stomach. The smell was worse than anything she could remember.

At least everything outside her skull was quiet, like, tomb quiet. No bird song, not the slightest air current. Nothing.

She slid one hand over the back of her head to feel the sticky lump with a crusty substance forming a line to her jaw. Her fingers tangled in her hair before realizing she'd smeared whatever substance covered the floor over her scalp.

Wonderful.

Lying face down, she turned her head to see shadows of a moderate-sized, musty room. There existed another odor, much stronger with every breath, much worse.

Putrefaction.

"Where am I?" A small bar of dingy light streamed across her shoulders to showcase what looked like a long box beside her. "An open crate made of concrete?"

There was another one to her left. She estimated the length at eight feet long and two and a half feet high. It was difficult to tell with insufficient light and their elevation on slabs.

Shifting her position to sit drained what little blood was in her head to make her sway. A hand thrown out to each side kept her upright, but slid something gooey between her fingers.

Closed eyes and slow breaths through her mouth bypassed some of the stench.

The room appeared larger than first thought, maybe twenty-foot square.

"You're sitting between Damas Tisono and his wife. The others... well, they're kind of strewn here and there."

"Addy?"

"Yeah, sis. You're in a real pickle this time."

"Wait." Hailey looked around then recognized the boxes were crypts. "Oh, hell. I'm in a mausoleum?"

"Yep. We all are."

"Define *all.*"

"You remember hearing about the two kids missing for the past year?"

Hailey nodded.

"Well, they've been recently joined by Teeny and her boyfriend."

Hailey detected the change in direction of her sister's voice and swiveled on her butt, instantly sorry for the movement.

"You're lucky they didn't dump you in thicker fresh goo."

"Aw. Gross." Wiping her fingers on her jeans simply spread the odor. "I can't believe they stuck me in a mausoleum."

"Yeah. It's in the back of a private cemetery. They figured no one would find you. At least it's above ground."

"Any hope of walking out the door?"

"No. They rigged it with concrete block and some kind of rod. Walking out isn't an option."

"I'm surprised they didn't shoot me before closing the door."

"The one called Manuel was given that task. He was supposed to dump you and shoot, but one whiff of this place and he bailed."

"Great. Now all I have to do is find a way out." Hailey looked around. "Any suggestions?"

"*Look up, over here.*" Again the voice moved, this time toward the wall to her left.

Backtracking a murky swath of filtered light led her gaze to a small stained-glass window high in the wall.

"*Through there, but you should hurry. I think they're gonna bring someone else here.*"

"Babtiste?"

"*Not sure.*"

Hailey moved to stand, reaching for a crypt to steady herself. It was then she saw there was no top. "Why would any mortuary bury a body in a coffin without a top?"

"*It did have one... now, it doesn't.*"

A long sigh breezed through Hailey's mind before her sister's meaning slammed the breath from her chest. "Oh. Exploding casket syndrome? I've read about that."

"*When they dumped Teeny and her boyfriend in there and resealed it, well, decomposition, gasses, plus no room to expand equals kaboom. It's one thing to disrespect the living, but to do so to the dead is unforgiveable.*"

Hailey envisioned the scenario, every mortician's worst nightmare. "I've got to get out of here. Wish I had Casper's talent. I'd walk through the wall and be gone."

"*Oh, Casper. If I knew how to find her, I'd bring her here.*"

"How is it you found me?"

A long silence paused where Hailey imagined the spirit of her sister searched for the right words. "*I felt your pain; it drew me. Unfortunately, you wouldn't wake up. Not sure how we're connected from both sides of death, I just know we are.*"

"Can't you just go to Casper's house?"

"*Things don't work like that on this side. We don't have houses, streets, and stars to give us direction. Even time moves differently. I could get lost for months, or longer.*"

It was the frankest discussion of afterlife to date.

"*I was thinking, she'd make you a good partner despite still needing direction.*"

"Speaking of which, where exactly am I?" Hailey imagined her sister sliding through the wall, or just poking her head out to look.

"Too far in the sticks to walk out. I think you—"

"I don't think I can pull myself up to that window even if I had something to break it."

A subtle throat clearing from behind swiveled her attention on something long and cylindrical in the murky light. The inferred suggestion drove bile up her throat.

After purging her stomach on the already grotesque floor, she couldn't detect much difference in odors.

"Use the bone to break the glass? Really, did we not just reference respect?"

"You can't get justice for them if you don't survive, sis."

Loathe as she was to touch, much less use, either an arm or leg bone to break the window high in the wall, she sidled over like the skeleton would suddenly reassemble and animate for the sake of vengeance.

"They would want to help you any way they could."

"Where are they?"

"Dunno. Must have been killed elsewhere then dumped here."

"Does that mean they can't find their bodies?"

"Don't know. My circumstances are different."

Adjusting to low light levels allowed her to see vague shapes where filtered light didn't touch. Motivation for escape came as much from wanting distance to what she'd lain in as to getting justice for Teeny and her boyfriend.

Both caskets sat atop concrete blocks with roughly four feet between, yet they weren't centered in the room.

The reason for that became clear as her eyes continued to adjust while looking around. "That's a prayer chair in the corner."

"When someone wants to be close to their departed loved ones."

"Guess no one's been here for quite a while." Hailey preferred to never see it again.

Exploding casket syndrome didn't happen often, as best she knew, but she doubted this crypt would ever be used again by the Jackyls. Bones were strewn around the room, the top to each casket lying haphazardly against the wall.

"How long have I been in here?"

"Not sure, but the light is fading outside. I suggest you get out of here."

"Can you try to find Casper?"

"I—don't know how to navigate, but I can try."

Slipping twice in the liquid mass encouraged Hailey to walk slower and use caution. If she could relocate the wooden chair to the far wall, the back might be tall enough to help her out.

She didn't dare yell since she didn't know if someone waited on the other side. Never had she believed in evil other than in human form. No demons, no vicious spirits, no demented dead warriors hanging around graveyards. As a child, she remembered her mother's vagueness about the topic.

There're no such things as demons.

If she made no noise during her escape, they wouldn't give chase.

The chair was old, slat-backed, and covered in bits of blood and body parts. Still, it must've weighed fifty pounds. Either that or the head injury skewed her perceptions. By the time she manhandled it to the far wall, the sun had yielded to the face of encroaching darkness.

The bone she picked up felt slimy with thick strings attached at one end—bits of muscle and tendons, no doubt. Another round of retching ejected nothing but bile.

Any movement jeopardized her balance in attempting to stand on the chair.

Breaking glass sounded louder than the drumming in her head, now accompanied by an entire orchestra of percussion instruments. Small cuts incurred when using the bone to clear out the glass remnants didn't register as a current problem. Infections only affected those who survived.

She thought about the ongoing search for Teeny and the boy she'd risked her life to save, a selfless act ending in a horrific death. It wouldn't be the end of the murders if she didn't get Frederick off the streets.

Once word leaked that she was still alive, the Jackyls would double down to kill her, which brought to mind, how was she going to bring the Jackyl leader's deeds into the light? She needed another meeting, physical contact, preferably one she survived.

Using a strip torn from her shirt, she cleared the glass slivers from the lower sill. It was above her head but within reach.

Her first attempt to pull her body up and over the sill ended with her feet scrabbling for purchase against a wall slick with age and other things she didn't want to contemplate.

Her tennis shoes skidded on the chair's seat. The fall jarred her entire spine and renewed the nausea held at bay with a prayer.

After reclaiming her position on the chair, she braced her hands on the lower sill and hopped up so both feet rested on the chair's arms. It gained her six inches in height.

With attention to balance and the throbbing in her ears, she took all the weight on her arms and placed both feet on the chair's back.

Old wood creaked, but proved solid for use as a push-off. Her support would tumble sideways and leave her dangling if she used an unequal amount of force in her legs.

Pushing up in combination with pulling for all she was worth resulted in her upper body bursting into fresh air with the sill jabbing her waist.

Hanging half in and half out, she looked around and saw what appeared to be an abandoned farmhouse on a small knoll in the distance.

A classic landscape scene from a horror movie.

The path leading from it to a dirt road beyond revealed more weeds than dirt, though lack of light may have skewed her viewpoint.

The window was too small for her to do anything but push on the wall below her and squirm out headfirst. Her hazy mind estimated the distance to ground about eight feet.

Tuck and roll landing occurred as a by-product of sparring with Leigh and broke the momentum jarring her head. The movement brought to mind Casper's skirmish in the parking lot at Á La Mode.

The teen's confidence and reaction to the physical threat again indicated extensive training, both hand-to-hand and with weapons. Each time Casper confronted danger, her fighting stance occurred naturally and without apparent thought. Would she be prepared when the Jackyls came for her?

The air smelled better, the ground was drier, and the dizziness abated while she lay panting in the grass. Her eyes closed of their own accord.

Unless the Jackyls had more bodies to dispose of, she could rest for a few minutes.

When her aching muscles protested the prone position, she pushed to all fours and sat with her back against the brick mausoleum wall.

A rumbling purr in the distance grew louder with dust from a vehicle's passage creating a trail leading to the farmhouse. If the genre of the scene wasn't certain before, the ghostly structure against a darker sky made it clear.

What now?

She didn't have the strength to run, and probably couldn't even stand at this point.

Her fastest movement equaled a crawl as she made her way to the structure's side. It was then she saw the black Camaro swinging around the farmhouse and roaring down the hill.

Casper. She's all right.

The sports car skidded to a halt ten yards away with the teen hopping out as soon as the engine stopped.

"Hey, I hear someone call for an Uber?" Dressed in jeans and the boots she seemed to prefer, she radiated amusement and concern at the same time.

"I found Teeny and her boyfriend," was all Hailey could manage to say.

"Well, shit. Let's get you out of here, and into a shower."

"Gotta call Trenton in first." Hailey snorted. "He'll have a fit if I wash away evidence."

"Screw Trenton. Wait, that's actually a good idea. Might loosen him up a bit."

"No, thanks. Longtime friends. Help yourself."

"Nah, he's too old for me, but he's sure got it bad for you."

Hailey couldn't contemplate such thoughts with the throbbing in her head and stench clinging to her clothes. "I hope you have a towel or at least a plastic bag or something for me to sit on. I'm kind of gross."

"Always travel with a blanket in the trunk. My best friend taught me that."

"Sounds like a walking advertisement for preppers."

"In a way, yes. And you would be too if you'd faced what they have."

Again, that old soul aura settled around Casper like a blanket.

"Gunther."

"Don't worry. Simon's keeping him company. He's fine."
"Let's sit by your car and wait for the cavalry. Shall we?"
They were both in for a long night.

Chapter Twelve

Hailey

Ten minutes of Gunther's sniff testing and the wolf dog still wouldn't leave Hailey alone. Stepping into the shower, she breathed a sigh of relief after collecting her clothes for evidence. Whatever traces remained on her body would be lost. It wasn't like she'd scratched her kidnapper. She did have a fuzzy recognition of his face.

There wasn't enough water on the planet to make her feel clean again. The awful smell lodged in her hair, her nostrils, and embedded in each pore of her flesh.

Currently, Trenton waited in her kitchen, but Leigh marched right into the bathroom to start firing questions and recriminations without an audience.

It didn't take long for her friend's ire to lose steam in favor of guarded support.

When she stepped back through the door into the hallway, Trenton was there, wrapping his arms around her waist and resting his chin on her head. "What in hell were you thinking, Sparkles?"

"That I shouldn't answer the office door?"

"I mean in getting involved with this kind of case. These people are dangerous."

"Really? I hadn't noticed." It was too late to back out. The only way to the other side of normal was through the middle, which meant solving the case, or cases.

Whether the Jackyls thought she was after Frederick for past murders or finding their ex-member Babtiste didn't matter in the end. It all needed sorting and resolving.

She couldn't explain anything with her face smooshed against her friend's chest, but she didn't mind the deep rumble felt against her cheek. It lent comfort and a sense of normalcy.

Now that Trenton had moved back to Texas, her family felt complete. If only they would accept Casper as the same.

"We'd been looking for you all afternoon since you didn't answer your phone," Leigh added en route to the kitchen to spoon something from a casserole dish. "Your mom sent jambalaya, by the way, so sit down and eat before we take you around to the ER to get checked out."

"I'm pretty sure we shouldn't feed someone with a head injury until *after* they've been checked out," Trenton argued but released her when she stepped away.

"I haven't eaten all day. I've been through hell. And I'm not going *anywhere* until I've got food in my belly."

Eating at the table gave her something to do with her hands while her mind sorted recent events. Neither Trenton nor Leigh believed her story of how Casper "happened" to find her walking along the road.

Leigh had found her cell phone in the office, hence knew Hailey hadn't called for a ride. Not that she should've called a teenager after being assaulted and kidnapped.

"Look. I explained how Casper found me. Summoning her here is only going to antagonize the situation, Trent. You've already been called on the carpet enough where she's concerned."

"I don't care who or what she's connected to. She's going to answer for her actions. Showing up at a crime scene is just a little too coincidental. And I don't believe for a second she's only seventeen." Trenton's accusing glare demanded clarification.

Hailey couldn't give it.

It wasn't his FBI training that taught him to navigate Hailey's world. No, it was experience. He used Casper's limited involvement as an excuse to demand the teen's presence at the loft for an interview.

He hated unanswered riddles.

As soon as the younger woman walked through the door, Simon set up a round of screeches and chittering that made Hailey flinch. The fact she wore a dress caused Hailey to choke on her sweet tea. To her knowledge, Casper had never worn such a thing.

"What are you wearing?"

"You like? My dad sent it to me as an apology for being away so much." Casper raised her arms and twirled to flare the skirt. Form-fitting to the waist in the front, it had a flowing, blousy type back that added a casual flare—and probably hid a knife. Or two.

Hailey hadn't met Major Clannahan, referenced with respect and sometimes a little frustration. A cursory background check on his military service yielded nothing unusual, which made it more suspicious, given Casper's psychic talent and references to her adopted family.

"Looks great. What's the occasion?" Wise and savvy to a teen's subverted efforts, Leigh smiled and nodded. "I like the material. It'll be warm enough on your shoulders on a cool evening yet stylish. I should ask your Major Clannahan to shop for me."

"Why don't you have a seat, Casper?" Trenton pulled a chair out across from Hailey. The smile that didn't reach his eyes would not be missed by his interviewee.

Even as she grinned, a glint of mischievousness lit her gaze. The sparring match would now commence.

"Actually, I'm missing dinner. You mind?" An arched brow received a nod before moving to the island and dishing herself a bowl of jambalaya and inhaling the savory flavors with an appreciative nod. She took a seat beside Hailey and leaned over to bump shoulders. "You smell better."

"I feel better."

"Headache still?" Casper asked, dipping one shoulder and moving her opposite hand as if removing a slight weight to the table. She set her phone down and peered into Hailey's face, her concern evident.

"Yeah, I think it's gonna be with me for a while."

"I've got a friend who's," she paused and looked between Trenton and Leigh before finishing, "...a medic. I can guarantee he could help."

"Oh, yeah?" Trenton brightened and retrieved his cell. "What's his name and number? I can give him a quick call."

Casper merely stared. Mute.

Leigh chuckled. "Dude, you'll have to do better than that."

"I'm doing all right, thanks. Just need a good night's sleep and a plan to put Frederick away." Hailey bowed her head and smiled with the breezy touch along her cheek.

Thank you, Simon.

She recognized the primate's need to offer comfort and enjoyed the feather-light, ethereal contact.

"We've got a BOLO out for the Jackyl you recognized. Once we find him, we'll get the others. In reference to your headache, what you need is a trip to the ER." Tension in Trenton's shoulders and jaw coincided with his gaze narrowing on Casper.

"Good luck with that, fed man. Good luck." Casper's figurative thumbing her nose at Trenton was intentional and calculated, judging by the inflection in her tone.

"What do you know about Frederick?" Trenton fired back. "As I understand it, the GE school kids don't normally hang out with gang members during their free time. Yet you've had at least two interactions. One at the ice cream shop, the other at the shopping center."

"Don't know a thing about Frederick. I wasn't there with Hailey. Didn't see him."

Trenton didn't challenge her, instead sitting in his chair and leaning back while crossing one outstretched leg over the other at the ankles. Hailey saw the ploy as one used when he needed to take a step back and evaluate an opponent.

"So, what took you way out toward an abandoned farmhouse?" Trenton made a slight sucking sound between his teeth, his focus lasered on his prey.

"Well, Agent Dick. I wasn't looking for a place to party, that's for sure. Drugs are illegal. So is alcohol for someone my age." Casper's shoulders shook when Trenton snorted.

"You don't strike me as the party type of gal. I would imagine if I checked your phone, there'd be no calls pinging on nearby towers in that location."

"That would be illegal and an invasion of my privacy. Should I call a lawyer, or perhaps my father, Major Clannahan? I'm sure he'd be more than happy to speak with your agent in charge. Again."

The challenge was issued and raised.

Trenton shook his head. "No need. But I do have to get a statement from you regarding your involvement in Hailey's kidnapping. You know, since you *happened* to show up on a deserted road out in the middle of nowhere and rescue Hailey."

As if on cue, Casper picked up her phone and swiped the screen.

A second later, Trenton's phone beeped. When he opened the message, a low growl escaped his throat. "I never gave you my phone number and it's not the first time you've contacted my *private* line. Hacking *is* illegal."

"I gave it to her, Trenton. Figured if she's gonna hang around with me, she should have both of your numbers."

"Oh, I've had his number from the get-go. Would you like mine?" Casper giggled and stretched, puffing out her chest and stretching a seductive smile across her lips. "And I just sent you a copy of my signed statement."

Trenton scowled at the double entendre. "I've got yours too, kid. I see you were all prepared, huh? Spend much time in police stations?" Trenton asked, reading the document on his phone.

"No. But I know how the process works. I was thinking about going to college and majoring in criminal justice."

"So you'll know both sides of the law?"

Casper grinned. "My records are quite in order, I assure you. I could go to pretty much any campus I want."

"As long as they're hiring secretaries?" Trenton shook his head ever so slightly. He was losing the battle for control. "Or would your father see you enrolled?"

When Leigh's cell dinged and she looked at the message, she merely nodded to Casper. "Thanks. I'll put this in the case files."

Casper fisted one hand on the table. "I'm not stupid. I may not have had the advantage of a stable home life growing up, but I got my shit together now." A rise in volume ended with a level just below a shout.

"Enough, you two. Trenton, stop baiting her." Hailey swiveled to her youngest guest, intent on revealing an important insight. Despite worldly demeanor, Casper was still naïve with respect to various interrogation techniques. "He's testing you ten ways to Sunday. You have to learn to keep your cool. Otherwise, he'll strike with the big question when he sees you're off balance."

Casper closed her eyes and inhaled a slow deep breath before zeroing in on the federal agent. "What exactly is it you want to know, Agent Briner?"

"How is it you were out on that road, at that time, when Hailey needed you? And by the way, I'm betting we could match a boot print at the mausoleum to the pair I've seen you wear."

"I was there because my father is looking to acquire some properties, maybe a fixer-upper for me to work on in my spare time."

"You? With a hammer in your hand? The only way I see that happening is if you're preparing to use it. On someone's skull," Trenton shot back.

"*Hmm*, what an idea..." Casper tapped a finger on her chin as if deep in thought. "Know of any volunteers?"

"Couldn't say as yet. Not until we have forensics back on our victims at the mausoleum." Trenton arched a brow, waiting.

Casper snorted. "Good luck with that. It's not my style."

"I'd like to know more about *your* style," Trenton suggested.

"Ask the major. He'll tell you all you need to know."

"And that ends the conversation." Leigh tapped Trenton on the shoulder. "Leave her be. And for your own good, brother, don't ever have children."

Hailey avoided a trip to the ER with the promise to go if a night's sleep didn't help. Shooing her guests out, she had no doubt Trenton would be back and spend the night on her couch.

She woke early the next morning to Gunther's wet nose on her cheek.

"What's up, boy? It's awful early." Sweeping the covers back, she looked at her bedside clock. "Or maybe not."

Stepping into her jeans and pulling on a t-shirt, she noted the bruises from where she'd dropped from the window. They'd already started to darken and would take days to fade.

Her phone rang before she got out the door, the familiar jingle making her smile. "What's up, Casper? I'm just taking Gunther out for a walk."

"*We need to hoof it out to Upward Bound. Like, now. I'll pick you up in fifteen.*"

"What about classes?"

"*It's Saturday.*"

"Oh, yeah. All right. What's going on out there? Did Babtiste show up? Have you seen his spirit?"

"*No. Her name is Juliet.*"

Now she understood why she didn't hear Trenton in her kitchen. He was at a crime scene.

"What? Charlotte's assistant?"

"Yeah. And I'd advise you not to eat first."

"Gross, but okay. Come on over. I'll drive." She'd have just enough time for another shower. Extra hot with a side order of a stiff brush.

Gunther took his time romping around the yard then returned for a pack meeting. Tilting his head back, he let out a long soulful howl. Hailey paused in her musings to provide harmony in their morning ritual.

Whether from feeling abandoned the prior day or sniffing death all about her on return, her furry companion hadn't left her side until this morning.

When finished, he licked her face. There existed a certain freedom, a oneness not found anywhere else in nature, because Gunther responded in a way that let her know what he felt.

It was much easier to explain Gunther than her newest friend. Intuition dictated she and Casper would spend more time together, which necessitated some type of cover.

Casper's prior announcement of entering the law enforcement arena opened the door to an internship with a licensed private investigator. At least it looked decent on paper.

On the drive, Casper explained the circumstances around her early morning ethereal visitor, Juliet. To have spirits arrive and demand attention at any hour of the day would tax one's nerves, and maybe their sanity.

The insight offered Hailey another aspect of the young woman to consider and respect.

"This killer is smart. Unlike with your interaction facing the Jackyls, Juliet never saw his face. It was late at night when she went out to see what stirred up the horses."

"Did she hear anything unusual?" Hailey asked, pressing harder on the gas and wondering if Trenton would raise hell when seeing she wasn't alone.

Considering their previous confrontation with the Jackyls, he'd make sure to involve himself in anything connected. It hadn't helped that he'd made friends with Lieutenant Colson of the sheriff's department. *That* was a deliberate and calculated move.

The fact the two men shared a lot in common was a stroke of luck for the federal agent. Trenton wanted an *in* on cases that were technically outside federal purview, and Colson garnered favor with Leigh's brother.

"No. She was making evening rounds, feeding the horses, when someone shot her. Never saw it coming."

"Damn. We're gaining dead bodies without pinning down suspects. Not good."

When they pulled up the long drive, Casper sighed. "Figured your boy would be here."

"He's not—never mind. Listen, we'll say we're on our way to shop for boxing gloves, but I needed to stop and give a progress report on Babtiste."

"At least I'm dressed the part. Kinda. But if Trenton asks to take a boot impression, I'm gonna put this size nine-and-a-half up his ass."

Hailey parked beside Leigh's SUV. "Looks like it's all-hands-on-deck. You know Leigh, but not the other detective, Lieutenant Colson. He's a bit of a hard-ass and by the book, but he's fair and can usually see reason."

"*Hmm*, so half like Trenton but reasonable. Sounds like he might be likable. Oh, look at that, will ya?"

"What?" Hailey paused with her fingers on the door handle.

"Look how Leigh and Colson are standing. Then check out Trenton's scowl." Casper snorted. "Well, I know what fires to light now. Is Trenton protective of his sister?"

"Yeah. Very," Hailey replied with a groan. She could see the fireworks now.

"This isn't gonna be so bad after all."

Hailey had seen the working relationship between Leigh and her supervisor weave stronger than a casual rapport. So far there'd been no difficulty between the two men, either personally or with jurisdictional disputes. It looked like things might change.

Gunther hopped out to greet his counterpart before Hailey could tell him no, greeting Charlotte's golden with a play bow. After being stuck in the loft most of the prior day, he deserved the physical outlet.

"Casper, why don't you wait here by the car and see if you can draw Juliet to you? Maybe she'll be able to tell you something else." There was no way Hailey wanted her protégé closer to the beehive of activity.

Trenton redirected his irritation the moment Hailey stepped within earshot. "Are you out of your freaking mind?" His gaze shot to Casper, his meaning clear.

"Why? What's happening? Casper and I were on our way into Hamchet, but I stopped to speak with Charlotte for a minute."

The owner of Upward Bound sat on the porch with her eyes squeezed shut against all the activity around her.

Splotches of dead grass ringed a fifty-gallon drum at the base of the steps, its lid to the side. Forensic techs were busy scooping out liquid into smaller containers for transport.

"Why is it you and your irritating sidekick appear at every crime scene?" Trenton swatted at something beside his head.

Hailey bit the inside of her cheek to keep from smiling at the sound of Simon screeching in front of her. It didn't take psychic intelligence to know the primate was doing his best to wreak havoc with the federal agent. From what she could see, a lock of Trenton's hair stood up in a non-existent breeze until fingers roughly combed it back in place.

"Hey, this is my client, and I'm here to speak with her."

"Not until we have her statement."

"C'mon, Trent. She'll tell me more than you. I assume you want to solve this?" Hailey waved her hand in the general direction of the porch. "Whatever it is."

As she watched, Charlotte rose from her chair, then automated movement took her into the house, the screen door bouncing on her heel.

"This is a murder scene. Charlotte's assistant was shot. The killer stuffed her in the drum with what appears to be chemicals used in cleaning the barn."

"To degrade any evidence. You think it was the Jackyls?"

"That'd be my first guess." Trenton again combed fingers roughly through his hair as Leigh ambled over.

Lieutenant Colson oversaw the tech proceedings but kept an eye on both visitors.

"I hear you two are going shopping? Make sure to take plenty of crypto currency." Leigh thrust her chin out, a habit to keep the slight grin off her face.

"Please, no grave jokes. I understand dark humor at gruesome sights, but really?"

"Too soon?" Leigh wrapped an arm around her shoulders. "Sorry. I know you're here to see Charlotte. We'll get to the bottom of this."

"I know," Hailey pulled away, "...but I still stink." With a backward glance to see Casper nodding her head, Hailey climbed the steps knowing when they left they'd have up-to-date information.

Hailey stepped into a typical farmhouse kitchen built decades prior. Rustic furniture and neutral colors encouraged a peaceful atmosphere.

Charlotte sat at a rough-hewn table and waved the trio to sit. Trenton and Leigh took seats across from the homeowner to allow Hailey to sit closer to their subject.

"I'm so sorry, Charlotte. You've known Juliet for a long time, yes?"

"She was the first to leave that damn gang. Been with me ever since."

"Did she have any other enemies?" Hailey retrieved some paper towels to use as tissues and mopping tears.

"Other than the thugs plaguing our existence? Not that I know about. She was one of the sweetest girls, always with a ready smile, loved by everyone she met."

Except for the person who killed her.

"Can we see her room?" Leigh asked, already standing.

Charlotte nodded and led them up the stairs, explaining Juliet's duties, hobbies, and recent activities.

"Did she have a boyfriend, or had she started seeing someone recently?" Hailey asked, waiting outside the bedroom with Charlotte while Trenton and Leigh went in to look around.

"No. She wasn't seeing anyone that I know of."

"About last night, did—"

"I didn't hear anything. We were late getting back to take care of the horses. Juliet said she'd feed up so I could lay down. I had a migraine and took medication. I guess I... slept through her terror." Covering her face with her hands, she cried.

Once downstairs again, Hailey sat with Charlotte until her emotions were under control. "Do you want me to stay the night, Charlotte?" Hailey stood once more after receiving a small shake, uneasy about leaving the homeowner alone.

"No!" Both Trenton and Leigh snapped at the same time.

Charlotte waved her hand. "I'll be fine. I have my dad's old shotgun I inherited when he passed. I'll be more alert from now on."

As Hailey opened the screen door to leave, she glanced back to see a lock of Trenton's hair standing straight up again.

A minute later, she felt the brush of ephemeral fingers against her cheek while descending the steps. "*Hi, Simon.*"

Casper was in the truck waiting, her fingers flying over her cell phone's keyboard.

"Find out anything interesting? And by the way, I think Simon has a permanent grudge against Trenton."

"Wyatt is still digging into Frederick's past. He found prior arrests, but nothing ever sticks. There're at least eight suspected murders credited to him."

"It's time we deal with Frederick, get him off the street for good." Hailey backed out of her parking space and followed the winding road to the entrance.

"We're gonna have to separate him from his lowlife friends to question him, then find his souvenirs. I've got a list of suspected victims. We find his stash, we prove he's a serial killer."

"Shouldn't be too hard to do," Hailey picked up speed on the highway. "I've got an idea."

"I'm trained to fight, not investigate. You question, I'll take notes. Oh, and one more thing, the DNA we got from Dante's drain has no match in any database. Can't find any record of him in a shooting, city street or otherwise."

"So we know next to nothing about him." Hailey sighed. "At least he's not a convicted killer."

Chapter Thirteen

Casper

The weight of responsibility for a teammate's safety fell squarely on Casper's shoulders now that she considered herself part of a team of two. Not for the first time, she understood what Kiera endured when leading others on missions.

Under normal circumstances, and if alone, she'd waltz into Frederick's home, find the evidence needed, then call the authorities. She could phase her way through any booby traps and be out in time for her next meal.

The resolve to stay focused and get the job done remained forefront in her thoughts. Her penchant for getting distracted had decreased with practice, and her observational skills had improved, which lessened her vulnerability.

Without her Pennsylvania team for backup, everything changed. A side-glance at Hailey revealed her new friend equally deep in thoughts as she drove.

A conversation with the spirit of Hailey's sister yielded a goldmine of information. Not only was Addy able to form a loose connection with two of the murdered gang members, she'd also offered insight into Hailey's future.

It bugged the hell out of her when the spirit wouldn't divulge more—like how she knew this, was it fact or intuition? Perhaps if alive, Addy would've been a seer.

According to the spirit, Hailey would be powerful. To date, only a fraction of her abilities had manifested.

Cool wind blew in through the open window, reminiscent of years prior when her adopted parents drove her to school, back before men with guns wanted to study then kill her.

Watching the raw land pass by her window, she wondered if her life would ever feel normal again, or if the current situation comprised the newest version.

"You're awful quiet, Hailey. Having second thoughts?"

"About calling out and taunting a serial killer? Heavens no. Do it all the time." Her gaze remained locked on the road despite the sarcasm and grin.

"At least I'm not cracking jokes about crypts and corpses. I'm wondering if Leigh is ever gonna let that go." Casper didn't have the heart to reference her partner's near-death experience again. It hit too close to home.

"Because you've seen death, too. Up close and personal. You're young, but in experience, much older than anyone I know."

"More than you could ever imagine. There's a whole other world most people never see. In the past year, we've taken down an organization who imprisoned psychically talented kids after killing their parents, and that's just the tip of the iceberg. There were three facilities we raided and released those who'd been poked and prodded, some to death."

"What? Is that what I saw when I touched you?"

"Yeah, we've fought assassins, mercenaries with and without talent, and a psychopath bent on enslaving mankind."

"I guess every culture has their share of nuts."

"Along the way, we got help from shifters and those from the spirit realm. So, yeah, I guess I have seen a lot, but I'm ready to settle down, at least for a while. I want to learn about my roots. I know my parents are dead, and I'm guessing have moved on. I can't call them to me because I don't have a name or even a mental picture of them. But it's possible I have other family."

"You've seen much in the way of death and terror, but you did what you had to do. You survived."

"I was held captive for a short while, a victim of my own arrogance. Because of that, someone else died. I hadn't known her long, but she gave her life for mine. It's something that stays with you."

"So, you irritate Trenton..."

"It's my way of blowing off steam, and it's fun. I couldn't do it as much with my teammates."

"Why not?"

"They'd retaliate using psychic talent. You'll understand someday."

They fell into a companionable silence down the lonely highway, their destination prearranged with Clannahan's help. Scant traffic meant less collateral damage if their situation took a southern turn.

Casper checked her phone for messages. "Okay, Wyatt's tracked Frederick's cell to the warehouse where we're supposed to meet."

"And you lured him out with a mere phone call?" Hailey chuckled. "Nice work."

"I plucked his ego. He and his morons have swung and missed each time they've come at us. He has to come or lose face as leader of assholes."

"You sure they can find the place?"

"Yeah, you'll understand when you see it."

"Glad it's owned by your foster dad, Major Clannahan."

"Yeah, this way we'll have eyes in each of the two warehouses." Casper holstered her phone and reviewed their plan.

"I don't believe for a second he'll come alone." Hailey slowed to turn onto a secondary road, Station Lane.

"Wyatt says there's four known associates with him, but they're in the adjacent warehouse."

"Are you sure our new spirit friend can pull this off?"

"I think Donald Fitzpatrick is damned motivated, and yes. Possession isn't a difficult thing, unless someone has a natural shield. There's no way all five of these bastards are immune."

"Has Fitzpatrick given you any other tidbits of info?"

"No, but he sees this as the only road to justice. He's still not saying much, feeding us only as much as he thinks is necessary. We went over the plan, and he's squared away."

"What else has he told you?"

"Said he was working undercover and had brokered a deal with someone, someone he didn't name. Just like we suspected, the guns were designated for delivery to a faction with organized crime connections."

"Damn. Wish he'd tell us who ordered them or who was he supposed to deliver to, as in specifically?" Hailey asked, taking her eyes off the road long enough to consider Casper's response.

"He didn't know. He was introduced recently enough to be low man on the totem pole. Which brings to mind, either side might have made him for a fed and killed him for it. That much he did tell me."

"Double damn. I can't help wondering how Dante fits into all this. Why would he save my life? If he wore a badge, he would've gone after them, instead of retreating. At the very least, he would've passed the information up the chain if he was also working as an undercover operative."

"You said Trenton got a tip about smuggling…" Casper held her hand out the window, her fingers undulating as if riding a wave.

"Yes, but it was a female informant, one they haven't been able to trace. Considering the last part, I wonder if this informant has anything to do with the GE school. Not many can hide from Trenton."

Casper shrugged. "Well, I'll be glad to get Frederick off the streets. How long will you need physical contact to see pertinent memories?"

"Depends. I'd think less than three to four minutes."

"Okay, let's go over the questions I need to ask. Oh, before I forget, you should know, Addy wanted in on this. I told her it wasn't a good idea." Casper had learned firsthand how distractions led to death.

"Agreed." Hailey checked the navigation screen on her phone. "Looks like our destination is just up ahead."

"Clannahan has always supplied us with whatever we needed. I think he's a bit nervous what with me striking out, well, not on my own, but without my usual team. Things are different now since you and I have formed a new team."

"How's it going with the investigation into the school board member?"

"I've sidelined that until we're straight here."

"Well, then, it's showtime. You ready to phase us?"

"Yep. I'll slide out your side in case they have a sniper waiting."

"Frederick's not going to shoot at us until he hears about the evidence we've collected."

"Which is nonexistent." Casper snorted. "And, Hailey? One more thing to keep in mind. We do have backup if we need it. It's not something I'll explain, but if I tell you to take a step forward, even if there's someone standing two inches in front of you, do it. I'm asking you to trust me over your five senses."

"Got it. Oh, hell, Casper. Really?" Hailey eyed the bright yellow banner over the warehouse's roll-up door with bold lettering stating: *Welcome, Thugs-r-Us!* "That's… um, definitely calling them out." Hailey parked in front of the first warehouse beside an old Chevy four door.

"I wanted to make sure they didn't miss it."

Gray corrugated metal sides with faded color and smudged dirt belied newish construction. A small vent in the gable end allowed air exchange and would help cool the interior.

Knee-high switchgrass denied the possibility of regular maintenance. However, evenness of the blades pointed to the fact someone went to the trouble to make the property appear unkempt. The second structure beside it was a carbon copy.

"How'd you come to pick this location? The sign says Albright Storage, but it looks abandoned."

"Its location is close enough for others to help me if needed, but far enough away to not look connected. Suffice it to say, there's surveillance to the nines in and around it. The major's a little overprotective at times."

"You don't call him Dad. He doesn't feel like that to you, does he?"

"No, not at all. We haven't known him that long. Nicholai was the one who took me in and feels more like what I think a dad would. He's pulled our entire group of psychics together and made us a family.

We met the major through one of his friends. Nicholai has trained us and directed our missions. He can be bossy, but I don't mind. He's given me purpose, made me part of a team, regardless of the distance separating us."

"Your family is in Pennsylvania, and the major is gone so much. Who manages this?"

"My guardian supervises. She's on the other end of these." Casper slipped two ear mics from her shirt pocket and handed one to Hailey.

"You really are connected, aren't you?"

"Yep. Let's put this asshole behind bars, or in the ground, whichever is appropriate." Casper inserted her ear bud and murmured, "Sarah? Sitrep."

"Got you loud and clear. Hailey?"

"Here and ready to get this done."

"Okay. You've got three gang members in the adjacent warehouse and one between the two. Scan shows everybody's armed with what looks like .9mm weapons. I've got facial rec on all except the one between structures. Wyatt et al are watching the feed also. They'll help if needed."

"Alrighty then. Sounds like fun." Casper slid out of the truck and paced beside Hailey to the personal door on the closest corner of the closest building.

The oversized rollup door used for vehicles was closed and the grass around it undisturbed. Without windows, they had no direct view of the interior.

"Okay, Frederick has pulled a pistol from his back waist. He has another one on his ankle."

"Thanks, Sarah. It's go time." Casper nodded at Hailey's larger hand holding her own and grinned. "Think he'll get the wrong idea? Nicholai always says to use any distraction available."

"Who knows? But you're really not my type."

"Because I'm not tall and dark with an Italian accent?"

"Dante doesn't strike my fancy that way. Plus, you're seven years my junior."

Casper snorted, but added, "Colin, my boyfriend, is still in Pennsylvania trying to decide which direction he wants his life to take. His brother and only family left want to stay north. I'm thinking he's gonna stay there too."

"Ah, I hope it works out for you. Maybe he just needs a reminder, a visit with you." As with prior connections, Hailey's mind flooded with visions. This time, they centered around a teenage boy with brown hair and bright hazel eyes. "You miss him."

"Yeah, but he's got to follow his own path. I hope it leads him down here." Casper reached for the door. "Let me touch all objects first as I can phase everything but my hand. I'll unphase your fingers when you grab hold of Frederick."

"How are we going to get him to hold still for this?" Hailey's brow creased, her head tilted to the side, listening before Casper opened the door.

"Leave that to me. It's one of my specialties."

Chapter Fourteen

Hailey

Any casual observer would note Casper's training as intense, her directions clear and succinct, her focus consistent. This wasn't her first op.

Between her talent and orphan status, she had little in common with normal teenagers. It made Hailey wonder if the teen had ever gone out to a movie with friends or played on a sports team in school? She was strong, agile, and if not mistaken, could kick the ass of most men she crossed.

Ear mics, maintaining warehouses for show, surveillance equipment even Hailey couldn't detect. It all added up to money, maybe military, but definitely extensive training.

"Hailey, got your head in the game? Distractions are deadly."

"Yeah, I'm ready."

The door opened under Casper's fingers. Well-oiled hinges denied betrayal of passage.

The interior was open-spanned and void of any item bigger than a speck of dust, which would've been highlighted via the abundance of strong lights set on thick rafters twenty feet above.

"Ah, *putas*, so nice of you to leave your door open. I was hoping you wouldn't keep me waiting. Nice place your papa has. I think I'll take it over and use if for storage between transports." Frederick stood in the middle of the space holding his gun pointed at the newcomers.

"We both appreciate punctuality. Anything else is simply rude," Casper replied as she held Hailey's hand and strode forward like she didn't have a care in the world.

"Where is the evidence you claimed to have?"

"It'll be right up here in a few minutes," Hailey said with a tight grin and tap to her temple.

"Along with the bullet I put in there for company." Frederick aimed at Hailey and pulled the trigger.

The sound was deafening, reverberating off the walls.

When he realized he'd missed, he fired again.

And again.

After six shots, he aimed at Casper and fired three more rounds.

"Wow, what a moron." Casper stopped one foot in front of their quarry and rested her right hand on her hip. "You really don't learn, do you?"

"What the fuck are you?"

"Your day of reckoning," Hailey replied in reaching her hand out.

Frederick took a quick backstep and inhaled deep. "Ah, hell no. You wouldn't back off with a Vodou doll or gator head in your truck, and wouldn't die when we tossed a gargoyle off the roof at you. I'm damned sure not gonna touch that." He eyed her hand as one might view a mythical troll.

"But the gargoyle and totem were months ago. Why, then?"

"Because you were nosing around our drug trade. You should've minded your own business while you had the chance."

"Sage advice, asshole." Before Frederick could call his companions for help, Casper shoved her phased hand into his chest and watched his eyes widen in fear and pain. His back arched on a guttural and strangled scream. Crimson-tinged cheeks paled then turned pasty.

"Listen up, jackass. I've got hold of your right lung. If you move, you die. If you try to scream, you die. Nod if you understand."

Choking sounds erupted from a face contorted in agony. The nod resembled that of a bobblehead figure.

"Okay, Hailey. Do your thing. This guy isn't going anywhere."

It took a second to accept what her young partner had done.

Yep, she stuck her hand in the bastard's chest and is holding onto his lung. Wow.

It was also obvious she'd performed similar services on prior occasions. Hailey's thoughts flashed back to visions of battle. She was never certain of why specific visions came to her and others didn't. They seemed to center around what her target thought about at the time.

"Now, Frederick," Casper said in the manner of speaking to a belligerent child. "This is how it's going to go. I'm going to ask questions. I really don't give a damn whether you answer me or not, the result will be the same. However, if you give me trouble, as in any type at all, I will start removing your internal organs, one at a time."

"I'd say by the looks of his ashen cheeks, his blood pressure is dropping. Might want to ease up just a skosh, partner."

"Yeah, he really is a candy ass. Most people tolerate it just fine until I start pulling out bits and pieces." Casper made a low noise of disgust. "Take a breath, you big baby."

A sudden deep inhalation produced a whistling sound from their predator turned prey. Wild eyes, nares flaring, and sweat dripping down his face declared his state of being.

Touching him was repulsive enough, yet the dirt acquired could be washed off. Soaking up his memories was altogether different. Hailey felt ill-prepared for the sick images that were sure to come. She nodded when ready.

Casper held Hailey's right hand snug. The teen's other hand was buried deep inside of Frederick. With their captive held steady and enduring the ultimate distraction, he'd have no hope of keeping a clear mind. Any question asked would result in a slew of flashbacks, especially if his sadistic streak ran as deep as suspected.

"First question, asshole, and we'll start with something easy. How many people have you killed? I don't want them in alphabetical order, or even chronological order necessarily. I just want a sum total if you can count that high."

Hailey closed her eyes and concentrated when the profusion of killings flitted through her thoughts.

"He enjoys killing. Gets off on terror and pleading." It took all her effort to sort through the various settings and victims. "Seventeen as clear as I can count."

"So, you've been a busy boy." Casper's voice sounded a little strained.

Probably from keeping herself in check.

"Second question. What type of souvenirs do you keep, and where are they?"

Gasping sounds reminiscent of a fish out of water, magnified by a hundred, precluded the killer from speaking.

"Ohmygod." Hailey snatched her hand back and wiped her fingers on her jeans, knowing they'd never again be clean. "I've seen faces, first names, and what we need to finish this. Damn. Not sure I can keep them all straight. We'll need DNA to clarify."

Casper nodded and turned her attention back to the gang leader, his breath coming in short pants. "Okay, Frederick, did you have anything to do with the ATF agent's murder?"

A thin mewl was the only sound escaping Frederick's throat.

Hailey touched the Jackyl's hand but didn't have to wait. "*Argh*," She groaned. "He didn't kill our ATF agent. I've got what we need. Let's get out of here."

Casper took a step back and withdrew her hand, without removing flesh or organ. Crimson slicked her palm. Her smile wasn't one meant for calming others. "Okay, Donald. Hop in and have a ball."

Frederick fell gasping to his knees with both hands wrapped around his neck.

"*Been waiting for this. I'll find you if there's anything else you should know.*"

"Hey, man, remember one thing. If you kill him, he won't get to rot in jail, like, forever. You wouldn't want to miss a minute of that, would you?" Casper chided. "Think of all the fun you could have for years to come."

In the next instant, the gang leader's hands dropped to his sides then thrust out wide to keep his balance in hopping to his feet. His mouth contorted into a silent scream when one leg thrust out parallel to the spotless cement floor and made big circular motions in the air.

"Well, then. Have some fun, why don't you? When you're finished, you know where we'll be." Casper shrugged as if the end result were a foregone conclusion.

Hailey felt the minor shift in air currents when the personnel door opened. "About time you guys joined the party. What took you so long?"

Wearing ripped jeans, a wife-beater t-shirt, and a braided bandana around his head, the husky man drew his gun. "What've you done to him? This is more of your Vodou shit." Fear overshadowed surprise or anger in the older man's gaze.

"I'd advise against you pulling the trigger, but then again, my ideas aren't always the best," Casper sing-songed the last part. It was the only warning she gave.

It took a second to understand the younger woman's meaning. It became clear when Hailey swiveled her head to glance over her shoulder at Frederick.

Bandana raised his gun and shot at Casper, who stood in a direct path between him and his leader.

The bullet passed through her and knocked Frederick to his back with a cry of pain.

"Bet that hurts like a bitch. Shot by your own man to boot." Hailey shook her head in mock disgust then turned her attention to the newest threat. "I'd tend to my boss if I were you. He's gonna be a little pissed off."

Hailey paced her partner's steps, watching the gunman's jaw drop in disbelief. It'd occurred that they might have trouble escaping.

Casper could keep them phased, but could she control it long enough for them to sit in and drive a car while bullets speared through the windows?

Seeing the end result of Donald's possession, she knew they'd have at least one ally.

"While you're at it, tell your posse to stay the hell away from us." When alongside the would-be killer, Casper wiped the expression of rage from his face by reaching inside his abdomen. Though gruesome, the simple act would ensure submission.

His scream echoed off the metal walls when she decided to poke around. Twisting her arm one way then the other, it was as if she tried to correlate what she felt with classroom anatomy lessons.

It took a minute.

"Oh, have you had an appendectomy? Gee, I didn't know the Jackyls medical plan covered such things."

She withdrew her hand before the door opened again, this time emitting three more gang members. "Ah, more bumfodder."

"What?" Bandana doubled over with his hands on his knees. "Are you?"

"She called you toilet paper." Hailey snickered. "Good assessment. Now, Frederick, tell your goons to back off before they get hurt."

Frederick's mouth opened to emit a gurgling reminiscent of a toddler learning to speak. "Back off, guys. Let the ladies go."

It might have been the change in the way he addressed them or the near purple color of his face, but his cohorts kept their guns in their waistbands.

Each stepped to the side when Hailey gestured for them to do so. Disbelieving gazes bounced between their leader and obvious second in command, one a dark twisted mask, the other pasty white, both in obvious pain.

The last to enter appeared younger than his companions. Either one or all three brought an odor the likes of which belonged in the swamp.

Hailey waved her free hand in front of her face. "Damn. Whatever you all are wearing is the best vag repellent on the market. Water isn't just for drinking, in case you're wondering."

Casper paused in her step. "You wanna take a crack at them too?"

"No. Not now. My mind is flooded with torture and death. I've had enough for the moment."

The last of those who'd entered had a scar running from right temple to cheek, which still bore the puckered red of a fresh wound. He obviously decided it was a better idea to shoot instead of following orders.

If it equaled his way of gaining recognition or advancing in the pecking order, he'd soon learn differently.

His first shots passed through Hailey and ricocheted off the side wall. Either not learning from his mistake or not understanding what transpired, he shot again, this time at Casper, who shook her head.

"Idiot." The bullet passed through her abdomen and embedded in the second in command's stomach.

With jaw dropped and a disbelieving scowl turning to rage, he kept shooting until the lowlife next to him shoved at the barrel.

Four more shots had passed through Casper's body from hip to ankle and ricocheted off the cement floor. The last one tore through her boot.

Hailey hadn't seen it deflect at an angle.

Casper's grimace of pain and low growl declared the strike a direct hit. She didn't have time to react before the spirit possessing Frederick's body raised his gun and fired at the errant bastard.

Blood leaked from between the young man's fingers clutched to his leg. "Fuck. That hurts," he exclaimed as he dropped to his knees.

"When I give an order, follow it." Not only did Frederick's voice come with a new speech pattern and unique cadence, it arrived with a distinctive northern accent.

Hailey switched her grip to wrap around Casper's shoulders. Not wanting to reveal the dirtbag's success, she urged them forward. "Let's finish this." She tipped her head toward the door.

"Thanks, Donald," Casper's harsh words were delivered with a hitch she couldn't cover.

"If you'll keep the rest of them here, it would be much appreciated. Feel free to shoot anyone who tries to follow us. We'll call EMS from the car." Hailey smiled sweetly then helped her partner out.

Once in the vehicle, they both drew deep breaths.

"Sarah, can you make a call and tell Mountain I'd like a word with him? I'll be home in twenty, no, make that an hour."

"Sure you don't want him to come to you, Casper?"

"No. I can wait. I'm gonna go with Hailey to collect some souvenirs and then come home."

"All right. Oh, I just got a message. They've watched and he's on his way. He'll be waiting."

Hailey wondered about what she'd heard and her partner's mode of transportation. This *Mountain* watched the scene unfold while in Pennsylvania, yet was due to arrive in Texas within the hour.

"Let's not give them the chance to follow." Hailey fired four shots into Frederick's tires to ensure the coming time frame wouldn't be interrupted. "What happened back there? How can there be a bloody boot trail from the warehouse into the truck?"

"Well," Casper breathed hard before answering, "...the prick shot me in the foot. I bleed like anyone else."

The younger woman closed her eyes and slowed her respiration. "See, if I phased all of our bodies, we would drop below ground level and not be able to get out. I phase everything but the soles of our feet. That's the weakness of phasing."

"Damn. Let's get you to the hospital."

"No. We've got a stop to make. Frederick's house, I presume? Then, I'll go home. There's a plan set in motion for this type of event. And believe me, it's not the worst thing that's happened to me."

"Hell. Are you sure?"

"Yeah. Let's get our stories straight for when you take the evidence to the police. Those assholes back there are gonna have all kinds of crazy-ass tales. I can mitigate some of it, but I can't erase what the cops are gonna hear, even if they don't believe it."

"All right, but well, okay, then. What about the blood you left behind? That could validate some of what they say."

"Don't worry, I'll have that covered."

A thousand questions circulated Hailey's mind, each like a little kid in school with a hand waving in the air to gain the teacher's attention.

Priorities.

According to his memories, Frederick kept an assortment of jewelry, glasses, and even a rabbit's foot in a locked box at the back of his closet. Arrogance and stupidity wove together to lend a hand in his downfall.

Casper removed her boot and assessed the wound. "It hurts like a bitch." Looking in the back seat, she grabbed a dog towel used for Gunther. "Mind if I use this?"

"No problem. I'll stop—"

"No. Keep going. I got this. No need to take longer than necessary."

Hailey stepped on the gas but kept an eye on the proceedings. A string of cussing ended with a hiss while her partner applied pressure to the wound. "Look. About going to the station, I can say I went alone."

"No. I'll be fine. It's better to stick as close to the truth as possible. The only permanent wounds suffered came from their own men. We're in the clear."

"There's aspirin in the glove compartment."

Casper rummaged through napkins, straws, and several protein bars before finding the tablets. Shaking two from the bottle, she dry-swallowed them. "Thanks."

The rest of the ride included details about what she learned from touching Frederick. Torture and murder via unique methods sealed the leader's status as a sadist.

The neighborhood she rolled through was quiet with more houses appearing abandoned than occupied. If gang members lived on the street and were home, they'd see who parked along the road.

Together, she and Casper strode into Frederick's empty house, surprised by its cleanliness. With gloves, she found the leader's stash of souvenirs and selected a few items that would prove more distinguishable or be more likely to contain their owner's DNA.

"I don't want to take everything. This is enough. We'll let the police execute a search warrant and get the rest." Hailey watched Casper limp.

Despite her grimace, she didn't give voice to her pain, nor did she leave a bloody trail.

If not for her partner's pride, she'd offer a piggy-back ride to the truck.

By the time they stopped in front of Casper's home, two people waited at the front step. A blonde dressed in black leathers smiled and nodded.

The other was a man who was quite possibly the largest person Hailey had ever seen. Straight black hair, dark eyes, and skin tone common to Native Americans signaled his heritage. Worry stamped its signature on both their brows.

Neither waited for her to shut off the engine after parking.

The door opened and the male smiled slightly. "Hello, Hailey. Thank you for bringing her home." Turning to Casper, he said, "How bad?"

"Foot. It's no big deal, but thanks for coming." Apparently used to the protective nature of her teammates, Casper didn't complain when he scooped her up and pivoted to stride up the steps.

"Hi, I'm Kiera." The blonde was about Hailey's age and held her hand out in greeting. "Thanks for bringing her home. She'll be fine. Are you injured?"

Hailey shook the hand briefly. Glimpses of a six-foot diameter circle appeared in a vision. Grayish light radiated to the interior and blocked the view like fog. She shook her head when Kiera dropped her hand and smiled.

"Huh. Bet that'll make you wonder. Glad you're on our side."

Straight to the point and respectful all in one. Hailey liked her instantly. "Um, hi. I'm Hailey. No, I'm not hurt, and I'm sorry about Casper. I didn't know about her vulnerability."

"Don't sweat it. It's not something she'd advertise."

"I'd like to at least see her inside."

"Don't worry about Squirt. Ouray will take care of things. She'll be right as rain in a few. How 'bout I have her call you in a half hour or so? I assume you're heading to the police station?"

"You're part of the family she's not talking much about."

Kiera smiled. "Don't worry. She's a little reserved in getting to know folks. Give her time."

With that, Kiera shut the door and pivoted to go into the house.

"Well, that was interesting." Hailey started her truck and touched the button for her Bluetooth. When the line connected, the first thing she heard was a sigh.

"What trouble have you found now, Hailey? Tell me you had nothing to do with the call EMS just received." Leigh, her best friend, always had her back even when she got in over her head.

"Trouble? No way. But I do have something to give you that's gonna make your day. Meet me at the station."

Knowing the coming interviews would tie her up for hours, Hailey didn't have time to review the conversation with Kiera or her partner.

She couldn't consider the operation a complete success, not when Casper had a bullet hole in her foot. On the positive side, Frederick and his top lieutenants would soon be out of the picture.

Chapter Fifteen

Hailey

Hailey sat at the conference table, thankful to avoid one of the interrogation rooms. Leigh involving Trenton shouldn't have come as a surprise any more than him quietly blowing a gasket when presented with evidence against Frederick.

Colson and Trenton had been asking the same questions, albeit in different formats, for an hour.

It'd grown tiresome after twenty minutes.

"Look, I wrote my statement, signed it, and delivered evidence, which by now you should've verified by finding the rest of Frederick's stash."

Lieutenant Waylen Colson pursed his lips as he stared at the written statement in his hands. "Yes, I see, and I've read it. I just don't believe it. Not after what I've heard from the others."

"Maybe he'd believe my foot up his ass." Addy had joined the interview at the start but remained quiet—for about five minutes.

Hailey's initial startle response when first hearing her sister's voice drew a puzzled frown from Colson and a new wariness from Trenton. It'd soon become clear Addy didn't like Colson, at all. Trenton's status remained iffy.

Physical evidence of Addy's behavior yielded Colson's frequent need to brush the lock of blond hair that stood up straight from the crown of his head. Rubbing his left ear might or might not have resulted from the spirit's attempt to deliver a wet willy.

"You find something amusing?" Colson stared hard.

"No. Not at all." Hailey bit the inside of her lip to keep the smile off her face. She failed when a giggle erupted.

Behind Colson, Leigh stood with her back leaning against the wall, no doubt to keep her smile hidden. She'd remained quiet throughout the duration except to clarify key points.

On the other hand, Trenton sat at the end of the table, keeping his distance and a watchful eye on the proceedings.

"Why did you drop Miss Decuir at her house? Since she was with you during the confrontation and at Frederick's house, why not bring her here?" Trenton tapped the table to gain Hailey's attention. "You know we have to interview her too. We'll also need to get a written statement from her for the record."

"She said something about washing her hair?" Hailey retorted, thinking of nothing better to say. "She's a teenager. We all know how they can be."

"According to Frederick, now in the hospital along with one of his gang, your junior partner was shot. We found a trail of blood leading to what we assume was your truck. Yet, when a uniform went to her house, she wasn't there. Neither was her car." Trenton studied her face, ever watchful for a telltale sign of deceit. "Does she need medical care?"

"No." At least, she hoped not. "As far as any blood, well, I don't know. Her father does own the place. Maybe she stepped on a nail at one point. We haven't had any rain for a while…"

"They're bluffing, sis. That blood was cleaned up. Trust me."

"I do." Hailey realized she'd answered her sister out loud instead of thinking her answer.

"You do what?" Trenton asked. "You need medical care?" He leaned forward to stand, halted with Hailey's arm thrust out.

"No. Sorry." She couldn't explain, nor did she care to try.

Still leaning against the mirror, Leigh cleared her throat.

Behind the federal agent, the door opened to admit Casper, dressed in a short sleeve button-down shirt and jeans covering the tops of her steel-toed boots. Unlike the ones worn earlier, these had no dust on the tops. In fact, they looked brand new.

"Hi, guys. Miss me?" Casper strode in and patted Trenton on the head. Instead of taking the seat beside Hailey where Colson pointed, she sat cattycorner to the federal agent.

"Where have you been?" Colson sat back in his chair, a little wary of the teen. He'd earned the hesitation after Major Clannahan had reportedly engaged in a brief but decisive conversation with the captain on a prior occasion.

"Oh, I stopped for a couple of candy bars. I hate missing meals, especially the big brunch with my family." Casper retrieved two chocolate bars from her shirt pocket and tossed one to Hailey. "Thought you could use one. I'm told the civility factor is sometimes missing in these kinds of situations."

"You don't have family," Trenton replied with an arched brow.

"Family doesn't have to mean blood relatives, fed. You of all people should know this."

"What he's trying to say is this." Leigh stepped forward to stand between Trenton and Casper. "We were concerned for your well-being after Frederick claimed his man shot you."

"Do I look like I've been shot?" Casper sat up in her chair and opened her arms wide. "I'm right as rain." With a come-hither look at Trenton, she added, "Who knows, so much has happened lately. Maybe you should search me, Trent."

Emphasizing Hailey's shortened version of his name instigated a frown on the federal agent. With a gaze betraying the slow burn within, Trenton fisted both hands under his chin and closed his eyes.

"Well, if you change your mind, I'm open to suggestion," the teen taunted.

"No need for that. Trust me," Trenton replied.

"Give me one reason why I should." The conversation took a sudden turn with the subtext.

"Because I'm trying to look out for you, in spite of yourself and whatever fantasies you're harboring about a thrilling detective career. If Hailey had any sense, she'd disabuse you of the notion."

Casper stood and bent until within inches of his face. "Trust me, cop. I have no fantasies, at least not about guns and badges. Don't particularly care about either. However, I'm old enough to know where I wanna set my sights."

She remained in his space for a half minute while her words sank in, then straightened.

Trenton remained mute, his calm façade unshaken. Crossing his arms over his chest along with a deep sigh was his only response.

Against the wall again, Leigh snickered.

Colson merely shook his head.

"Now, back to the incident before we were so rudely interrupted." Trenton pointed to Casper's foot. "How 'bout showing me your right foot. Think there'll be blood on the sole we'll match with that found at the scene?"

"You don't have a warrant, can't get one, and shouldn't bother trying." Casper tapped the table in front of Trenton and smiled wide as she sat. "'Sides, you didn't find my blood at the scene."

"Got something to hide?" Trenton leaned forward, his gaze latching onto prey.

"Not at all." A shrill war cry echoed off the small room's block walls to register Simon's objection.

Casper giggled.

Leigh snorted. Although Hailey's friends couldn't hear the primate's fury, they witnessed the results when Trenton repeated the gesture of scrubbing a hand over his right cheek and nape.

Undaunted, Trenton continued. "I'd like to see your right foot."

"Fine. I'll let you undress me." In response, Casper swung her boot up and thumped it down on the tabletop, grinning the entire time. "Get an eyeful."

"Ah, Trenton. You might not want to continue with this line of questioning. The girl said she's fine. You've seen she's not limping." Colson adjusted his shirt collar as if it'd become suddenly tight.

Trenton leaned forward and hardened his jaw. "Take the boot off, kid. And the sock. I want to see your foot."

Leigh held both hands out and shook her head. "Not a good idea, big brother."

"Actually, I think I strained my back this morning, you know, calisthenics in the shower." Gesturing to her boot, she added, "Knock yourself out."

Trenton wasted no time in unlacing the strings, his hands efficient and methodical. Instead of setting it on the floor, he examined top and bottom both visually and with his fingers, going so far as to shove his hand inside.

"I'm sure every teenager has more than one pair of tennis shoes, er, I mean boots. Some meant for going to fancy parties, dances, or kicking ass," Trenton murmured when not finding anything amiss. "This looks brand new."

After removing the sock, he tossed it on the boot. Lifting her foot higher, he again examined it closely. "Damn, they all said it was your right foot. I see a red spot, but no sure sign of injury."

Instead of asking, he picked up her other foot, removed the boot, and checked both top and sole for signs of injury. "Double damn. Doesn't mean there isn't something strange occurring here." The federal agent made a low noise in his throat, his gaze assessing Casper's stomach. "Did you incur any *other* injuries during your confrontation?"

"Ah, now it gets interesting. Care to continue your search?" Casper stood and slid the top button of her shirt through its hole.

Trenton reared back as if she'd slapped him.

"That won't be necessary." Colson slid his chair back and stood. "I think we're done here."

"No. We're not. Not by a long shot." Trenton met the teen's glare with one of his own.

"Listen, fed. A, we didn't run into any trouble. We merely asked Frederick for information, and he gave it."

"Just like that? No fuss, no problems? This after his man took a shot at Hailey in an alleyway?" Trenton asked with obvious scorn. "He told you where he lived, where he kept evidence that would convict him of murder, and then let you waltz out of a warehouse, unharmed? A unit I haven't been able to confirm ownership of, by the way."

Casper continued in a mock-saccharin tone, "Yep. Just like that. And B, before you interrupted me, I wanted to tell you that I sent you my written and signed statement. It's on your phone."

Trenton snatched up his cell and cursed after reading a message. "Look, kid. You've got no business hanging around with a private investigator. And she," pointing to Hailey, "...has no business sticking her nose in gang life. It's going to get one or the other of you killed. Got it?"

Casper plopped her foot back on the table. "You gonna do the honors? It's the least you could do."

Trenton ignored her but shot a glare at his sister Leigh who continued to chuckle.

Undaunted, Casper shrugged before shoving her feet back into socks and boots.

"You both are approaching this like it's some kind of game, a child's puzzle to solve. This is no game and not the type of incident either of you should be involved in," Trenton reiterated.

"Well," Casper placed the back of her hand against her forehead with an exaggerated sigh, "...what I've got is a complaint to make, should the need arise." An exaggerated swivel of her head signaled her search for something high in each corner. "I see there're no cameras here, which should make my next statement more interesting."

"And that is?" Colson asked, his tone wary. He'd taken his cue from Leigh and distanced himself from the conversation between the federal agent and Casper.

"The one where Trenton demanded I remove clothing. When I said I couldn't, he did it himself." Casper adjusted the hem of her jeans over her boots and stood. "I'm going to explain to *Daddy* how you undressed and then touched me."

Wild horses couldn't move faster than Trenton. His chair scuttled over as he windmilled his arms to remain vertical after shoving backward.

"I-I did no such thing!"

Against the wall, Leigh snorted. "Now, you've done it."

Colson held his hands up and backed away.

Casper giggled and turned to Hailey. "I'm hungry. Affairs always make me that way. Shall we go get something to eat?" Her left arm dipped then bent.

Hailey heard Simon's *scree* of victory as they sauntered toward the door.

Not one to give up, Trenton matched her step and held one hand out to halt her progress. "Listen, kid. I've known your type before. I'm just trying to see you don't get hurt. And that is because I care... for a *kid*."

A strange expression overtook Trenton's face, almost one of wonder. He touched his cheek and closed his eyes before ducking his head slightly.

Simon's gentle coo trailed Casper out the door.

"Well, that was interesting." Hailey hopped into her truck, glad when Casper slid in from the other side. "Where's your car?"

"I got a ride from a friend. Listen, the reason I was late—I found Babtiste. Well, I know where he is. Either way, we need to go talk to him. He's injured."

"By who?"

"Don't know. But we need to get to him before anyone else finds him."

"Where is he?"

"There's a shack behind the old Welton place. You know where that is?"

The fact Casper didn't know meant she hadn't spoken at length with the young man who still drew breath.

"Yeah, I do. A lot of low land out that way. How'd you find him?"

"He's kept in contact with one of the Jackyls." Casper held up one hand to forestall questions. "Before you ask, I don't know who he's talking with or why. I just know there's a connection of some kind."

"Let me guess. Your hacker buddy?"

"Yeah. Wyatt's quite talented. We need to stop by my house. Before we go out there. Sarah's packed a first aid kit along with food." Casper indicated for Hailey to turn left out of the parking lot.

"Okay. By the way, I liked your friend this morning. Kiera. She seems like a good soul." Hailey threw out the bait, hoping for at least a small nibble.

"She most definitely is. So is Ouray, AKA Mountain. The best in fact. More on them later."

The flat road led them out of town and along miles of wild grasses interspersed with fewer homes the farther they drove.

They arrived at their destination just as the sun announced temporary retirement and slipped below the horizon. It wasn't ideal timing to approach an injured, hunted man but waiting wasn't an option.

Long shadows stretched from the remains of an old house ravaged by time and years of storms. Partial walls offered refuge from heat during the day and cool winds at night. In defiance to nature, a brick fireplace stood among the rubble, its presence a testament to the mason who set each piece.

Casper pointed to the shed behind it. "He's in there, but he's not alone."

Hailey parked behind the tallest of the crumbled walls and shut off the engine. It made enough noise to alert Babtiste to their presence. "I hope he can clear up at least parts of this mystery."

A quick jab turned off her headlights as Hailey opened her door.

Pampas grass marked the overgrown path leading to the small shed, still standing. At least until the last of the sagging roof gave up the fight with the next stiff wind.

Casper joined her in front of the hood and ambled beside her through knee-high weeds. "Let's link up. Just in case."

"You think this is a trap?" Hailey accepted, this time not assaulted with visions of vicious battles or underground prisons.

Instead, she witnessed a large gathering of people in the backyard of a mansion. Kiera and the one dubbed Mountain were present, each smiling with their arm around their partner. A man she recognized as Clannahan from a picture in Casper's house stood at the head of a picnic table with a glass raised in one hand.

The vision vanished as quickly as it'd appeared. Hailey shook her head.

"Don't know what Babtiste has in mind, but better to be prepared. Just because Frederick is out of our hair doesn't mean whoever shot our ATF agent isn't now trying to tie off loose ends."

Hailey pocketed her keys while studying the structure. Old and weathered, the vertical wood siding should've fallen decades ago. Holes from woodpeckers and several broken boards would offer all manner of vermin a little protection from nature.

Things in life rarely panned out in the manner one expected, which made her wonder what would happen in the coming minutes. The door was closed, but not latched due to its angle in the frame.

Before they reached it, rusty hinges squeaked to admit a lighter cast of shadows inside.

She expected a haggard, injured Babtiste to step out. Instead, a gangly-looking young teen emerged, her long hair stringy and her expressive brown eyes too large in her oval face.

She looked familiar, seen in one of Hailey's visions, the recipient of a brutal beating.

"Ah, hi?" Indecision warred with determination until the stranger jutted out her chin. "You're the ones working with Charlotte?"

"Yes, hi." Casper stepped forward. "I'm Casper, and this is my friend Hailey." Indicated with a head tilt. "We're here to help. Look, I know Babtiste is in there, and he's hurt."

"How do you know—" The youngster stared at Hailey, her jaw dropping slightly. "You're the Vodou lady's daughter." A hint of awe carried the soft voice forward.

"*Her name's Daphne.*" Addy's voice sounded right next to Hailey's ear.

"Your name is Daphne, right? And yes, that is what people say about me. What they might not offer is how I try to help others."

"I've heard that, but not from Frederick or his sadist friends."

"Frederick is no longer in the picture. Neither are his lieutenants," Casper assured the younger teen. "They've been arrested."

"That doesn't make us safe. One of Frederick's men was ordered to bring Babtiste down, dead or alive. They won't stop searching until they find him."

"Which one?" The sooner Hailey closed this case, the sooner Trenton would ease the pressure on Casper.

"I-I don't know. I just know it was one of the Jackyls."

"I'm glad Babtiste has a friend to look after him. Everyone needs a friend at times. Do you mind if we take a peek at him? We've come to help." Casper pointed to Hailey's truck. "There's a first-aid kid in my backpack. If you'll let us in, we'll see to him. There's also some food in there."

Trust equaled a slow-built bridge constructed with time, effort, and materials. Time, they didn't have. Effort came at a premium depending on the severity of the injured man's wounds, and materials, well, they had food and bandages in short supply.

Casper followed Hailey and Daphne into the shack after darting back to the truck to retrieve her pack.

The interior wasn't as desperate as the outside suggested. Barren of furniture, it did lack signs of current rodent infestation.

A soft light glowed from the flashlight resting in the hand of a man lying on his left side. Sweat bathed the flushed skin of his face and neck, his eyes dimmed with fever.

"Babtiste, what happened? How bad is the wound?" Hailey knelt on one side and gently repositioned him on his back. "Let's take a look."

"Not deep. It's a through and through shot, but I think infection is setting in."

Casper opened her bag and produced a package of gauze, iodine, and alcohol. Medical adhesive tape soon followed.

Hailey finished unzipping the pack to reveal the rest. "You brought antibiotics?" She picked up the bottle labeled with a long generic name, unsure how to pronounce it. "Ah. You are prepared."

"He hasn't eaten today." Daphne hovered near her friend's head. "You said you brought food?"

Hailey retrieved several wrapped sandwiches and handed them to the girl. Two bottles of water soon followed as she watched Casper tend to the wound. Extensive training was evident with confident movements.

Casper held her hand out to block the girl's food delivery to the wounded man, shaking her head. "Wait until we're finished before you eat."

"How'd you know we were here? And before you ask, I'm not turning myself in. I didn't kill Charlotte's assistant, nor the dirty ATF agent."

Casper tapped him on the shoulder to gain his full attention. "First of all, we're not asking you to turn yourself in. Second, we'll help you, but we need information to do that. If you didn't shoot the ATF agent or at Hailey in the bayou, you must know who did. Finding the shooter will clear your name. Got it?"

"Let's start at the beginning, Babtiste. Tell us what happened at the meet," Hailey began in a low soothing tone.

"I was sent to the bayou to pick up a package."

"You mean meet someone to collect a load of guns," Hailey clarified. "Who sent you?"

"I thought at first it was Frederick, but the voice was robotic. They set it up over the phone. Said if I didn't pick up the guns and deliver them to the derelict house on Baker's Ave that he'd kill Charlotte."

"So, the killer knew of your connection to Upward Bound. That's certainly public knowledge." Hailey held a plastic bag to accept the bloody gauze deposited by Casper.

"Yes. He blackmailed me."

"Did he have an accent?" Hailey held her breath, praying he didn't say, *"Yes, Italian."*

"No, I don't think so, but the voice was also a little muffled, so, maybe."

Daphne brushed hair from Babtiste's forehead in a soft, comforting gesture. "Frederick has been trying to get into the gun trade for a couple years. He wants to squeeze out the local mob wannabe."

Hailey took a chance in exposing a secret. "The ATF agent was working undercover. He wasn't dirty."

Daphne inhaled sharply. "Did someone find out and kill him for it?" Holding one hand on her stomach, she held the other over her mouth. "Oh, God. I've been listening in on Frederick's conversations. He was expecting to get guns at some point, but whoever threatened Babtiste also found out about the shipment and tried to steal them. Right?"

"I assume so, but we won't know until we find the shooter."

Babtiste frowned, the crows feet around his eyes deepening to create darker shadows. "I was told to be quick. The shipment was paid for but there might be others coming for them too. It sounds like the agent set up his own mini sting to bag both me, Frederick's courier, and the mob's guy sent to collect."

"If that were true, why wasn't there a ton of ATF agents present to back the play?"

"Because," Babtiste looked stricken, "...I intercepted him before the designated rendezvous point. I was supposed to approach at Mitt's Bayou, but I figured I could catch him easier up the river. It gave me a better vantage point and more avenues of escape if things went south."

"That explains a lot." Hailey nodded. "You beat everybody to the punch. Well, everybody except the shooter. Tell me, do you think someone followed the agent? Is that how he was killed before anyone else was aware?"

"They likely keep their operations hush-hush," Casper replied. "I know someone I can ask, but he might not answer."

Hailey helped apply a bandage. "Since there's no bullet to retrieve, we won't have that piece of evidence."

Which doesn't mean there's not internal damage that needs attention, especially if he's got a nicked bowel.

"Where were you when you got shot, Babtiste?"

"I was trying to sneak back to check on Charlotte, but someone was watching the place. I had a boat nearby and slipped away."

"So, maybe not the same shooter who nailed the ATF agent. Did this happen Friday night, the night Charlotte's assistant was killed?"

"Yeah. They must've known I'd go back." Babtiste shook his head. "This is nothing but a mess. My best shot at survival is to leave the area." His questioning gaze slid to Daphne, who nodded.

"No, that's where you're wrong. If you run, you'll be hunted by both the government and whoever wants to shut you up, permanently," Casper warned.

"Listen. I have no place to start looking. No alibi, and no one to help. I won't risk Daphne's life. She's been feeding me information about Frederick as she can, but she's heading north to her folks' home, if they'll take her back."

"Since no one else knows you're here, give us a day. I'll bring you food, whatever you need," Hailey advised, hoping she could wrap things up before Trenton found and interrupted her plan. She hadn't removed the tracker he'd placed on her truck but made it a high priority.

"I have a place they can stay. Give me a minute to get the ball rolling. There is a condition to this, however. No phones go with you, no going outside once you're there. You'll be safe and looked after, just no communication with anyone else." Casper retrieved her phone and tapped out a message. "It'll be ready in an hour."

"Casper?"

"It's fine. There's a house twenty miles from here, rented by my father's corporation. It's not fancy, but it'll do."

Hailey collected the trash and used the flashlight to make sure they didn't leave pertinent or identifying items behind. "Considering the circumstances, Daphne—"

"I'm going home. I can't go back to the Jackyls. They'll know I betrayed them." Reaching out, she took Babtiste's hand.

Deep affection shined from his dark eyes. "Go to your parents. Since the gang never knew where you came from, you should be safe. I'll come for you when I'm clear." Babtiste moved to sit, holding one hand on his flank.

"If we can track down the owner of the house where you were supposed to deliver the guns, we'll have a strong lead, something to work with." Casper zipped up her pack and slung it over her shoulder. "I happen to have a friend who can hack deed records."

Hailey cringed with the thought of further embroiling Casper in borrowed trouble. She'd already been hurt once. "Let's get you two in the truck."

Chapter Sixteen

Hailey

The first explosion equated to a small boom. Percussions felt in the chest from Roman candles, bottle rockets, and brocades flaring to life followed. Assorted variations of fireworks took full advantage of the black sky and broadcast their contrasting colors over the community baseball field at the edge of town.

Hailey felt each thunderous detonation as she stood with her mother and watched townsfolk mingling with those of Upward Bound. Charlotte had spared no expense with the celebration. The visual display was scheduled to last twenty minutes.

Sizzles, pops, and cannonades punctuated conversations of Upward Bound's first annual festival coordinated with the community fair. Artisans displayed homemade crafts, painted canvases depicting key points in history, and tables filled with sugary and Cajun delicacies offered slices of yesteryear.

"Hailey, hiding a fugitive will bring you nothing but trouble." Cecile Arquette offered a praline brownie to her daughter.

"Mom, Babtiste isn't a fugitive. No one has confirmed his presence at any crime scene. The only one who could, isn't talking, at least not to anyone with a pulse."

Cecile smiled. "I'm so proud of you, coming into your own."

"Why didn't you tell me about your connection with plants when I started having visions with touch? Your talent is phenomenal. And how did you know about Simon if you can't hear or see spirits?"

The fact her mother could, at some level, communicate with anything using photosynthesis still blew Hailey's mind. She took a bite of the offered brownie and hummed her appreciation.

"Simple, dear. The other day when you two stopped by, Gunther was romping around the backyard with someone or some *thing*. When Casper made a motion with her arm and shoulder to disengage with it, well, she certainly wouldn't have been carrying a person. And cats couldn't jump the way indicated. So…"

"Simon is a capuchin monkey."

"Oh, how unusual, but back to my point. I've never discussed talents before because I didn't know how your ability would evolve. Now that I do, I worry more. This job of yours, well, it scares me, sweetheart. It's dangerous. From what I hear—"

"You hear everything that happens in this town."

"You're tangling with the Jackyls. Honey, they'll kill for much less reason than someone sticking their nose where it doesn't belong."

"Actually, we've taken their key players off the board."

"We, as in you and Casper? This isn't a game, and Casper is too young to understand her own mortality. Are you really going to take her on as your partner?"

"Unofficially for now, yes. And trust me, she has more skill and talent than anyone we've met."

"With spirits," Cecile confirmed.

"Tip of the iceberg, Mom."

Gunther rubbed against Hailey's thigh, a slight whine rumbling in his chest. Looking around, she saw nothing amiss.

"Dear, unlike you, I get a sense of spirits, though I can't see or hear them. You're very lucky to be able to hold frank conversations."

Her mother didn't ask about her deceased husband, something which had to weigh on her mind. "Mom, I'm sorry I didn't get to talk with Dad before he moved on to, well, wherever they go."

Cecile wrapped an arm around her daughter's waist. "Everything is as it was meant to be, dear. I'm glad your father and I were together for as long as we had. I still feel blessed."

Gunther chuffed and whined at her side before bolting forward to greet the tall, familiar man approaching.

"Oh, my. Who do we have here?" Cecile gave Hailey a knowing smile and her waist a light squeeze as she polished off the rest of her brownie.

Dante crouched to offer Gunther a treat with one hand, stroking his chest with the other. "Hello there, boy. Nice to see you in such good spirits."

Only after a proper greeting did he stand to acknowledge Hailey and her mother.

"Well, I see Hailey's companion approves of you. I'm Cecile Arquette." Holding out her hand, she offered a smile. "You should grab a snack while you're here." She pointed to the left outfield where vendors had set up tables of assorted local cuisine.

"*Hmm,* tempting. As far as Gunther," Dante gave the dog's head a final pat, "...he's a great judge of character." An arched brow in Hailey's direction conveyed the rest, *"Even if his handler isn't."*

"What are you doing here?" Hailey had no intention of letting good looks and a smooth façade get under her skin.

"He's checking to make sure they don't use partially hydrogenated vegetable oil in cooking. You are the fat police, right?" Casper stuffed a last bit of cotton candy in her mouth then offered her sticky hand to Dante as she stepped up beside him.

Dante kept his hands at his sides and stared, his shoulders shaking slightly.

"Oh, where are my manners?" Tossing the now-empty cone in the nearby trash can, Casper held out both hands in front of Hailey, nodding to the water bottle in her hand. "You mind?"

It was Cecile who poured water into Casper's waiting hands. "Here you go, dear, and how are your classes going?"

Casper washed her hands, shifting one shoulder to keep her backpack in place. "Honestly, they either bore me to death or the teachers talk over my head. Those people are a bit strange, and I think one might be a pervert."

"Then it's a good thing you have help." Cecile smiled and offered a napkin from her purse to dry the teen's hands.

From a distance, conversations paused like a wave falling over the crowd. The result was that nearby conversations became more distinct.

"What I'd like—" Casper stopped talking, turning her head to stare at empty space beside Dante. A second later, her eyes grew wide and her jaw dropped. "Hailey?"

In the distance but growing louder, small engines approached. It took Hailey a minute to work out from which direction the threat derived.

"Yeah, I heard." Turning to her mother, she urged her forward. "We gotta leave, Mom. Now."

"Sounds like drones heading our way." Dante rolled his shoulders as one would in preparation to fight. "I don't think that's a good thing."

Shrill screams from the designated food court spurred more of the same until the discordant alarm devolved into growing pandemonium.

Lights scattered strategically over the grounds went dark, but not before Hailey saw what appeared to be isolated smoke pockets. "What's going on?"

"Trouble. In spades," Casper supplied and pivoted to scan her perimeter. "We gotta get everyone out of here. Take Dante to the equipment shed. It's closer than your car and out of the path of mass stampede." Her first step paused with a particularly loud bang. "I'll get Cecile to a safe spot."

"We should stay together." Dante grabbed Hailey's forearm over her sleeve, tugging her to evade a frantic woman's race toward the parking lot.

Hailey understood Casper's desire to protect both her secrets and Cecile.

"We're all more than the sum of our parts. I need you to trust me, Cecile." Casper shoved Dante toward the shed and led Cecile toward the right outfield.

"Damn it!" Dante hesitated, then urged Hailey away from the attempted mass exodus.

"Dante, no. Trust them. Casper's right. We've got to deal with this situation, and we can't do it worrying about my mother." Hailey nearly yanked Dante off his feet when he hedged.

In the distance, gunshots rang out over the growing mass hysteria. The panicked crowd moved as one toward perceived safety, the parking lot beyond home plate.

It was clear someone made an effort to herd them in that direction. Gurgled cries and angry shouts defined growing desperation.

The first vehicles roared to life. Tires spewed dirt, grass clumps, and small rocks in the haste to leave.

Metal shrieked in protest with the first of what Hailey guessed would be many small fender benders. In the midst of chaos, the fireworks display ceased.

Cries of those seeking shelter coincided with angry shouts of others, clipped and impatient.

Dust kicked up, mixing with whatever the drones released, creating a haze over the mob. Three teen girls knocked a young mother to the ground trying to pick up her child. The man next to her hauled them both up and tugged them onward.

Past the center field fence and extending to the right, temperature-controlled storage compartments would offer Cecile protection. Casper took an exaggerated and rounded route that bypassed the general stampede.

An unmistakable crack distinguished itself as separate from any of the previous airborne noises. Hamchet's computerized fireworks display didn't compare to the distinct sound of gunfire.

Terrified residents were herded like frightened animals toward the parking lot. Fences separating metal bleachers behind home plate and dugouts on either side created a bottleneck where those trampled had no escape.

Noise from the drones increased in volume.

One drone would issue the sound equivalent to a single excited beehive and could be ignored. A half-dozen produced an entirely different effect.

Metal nightmares flew overhead in a single pass, the engines growing quieter until swooping back for another pass. Moonlight gleamed off the blades to add to the eerie atmosphere.

Hailey saw in a car's headlights what appeared to be white smoke trailing behind the lead engine. As she ran with Dante, she asked, "Was the lead drone smoking, catching fire?"

"No." Dante gripped her arm tight and yanked her hard sideways to avoid trampling by foot traffic. "They're dropping some kind of drug."

He shoved a bandana against her face. "Hold it there and get to that shed. I've got to find your mom and that harebrained kid." Again, he kept her upright when with an outstretched hand.

"No." Hailey set her stance and yanked Dante back using her lower center of gravity to best advantage. "Dante. Trust me. No. She'll be fine." In seeing Casper lead Cecile away, Hailey knew her partner would phase Cecile through any threat.

In their haste to flee and little more than intermittent moon glow to guide them, festival patrons shoved and knocked each other down for the hope of their vehicle's relative safety.

Hailey lost her balance when a man shoved her hard and kept going. Dante's arm might as well have been made of steel.

Though her mother would be safe, she might demand answers as to how Casper maneuvered her through the crowd without injury.

Casper could handle it, and Cecile would have that much more confidence in her daughter's partnership.

Hailey stumbled over a low spot where chalked base lines intersected at first base. Beyond that, fallen dew slickened the grass leading to their destination.

"Casper will be back in a minute, Dante." It spoke volumes that he trusted her judgment. It didn't mean he wouldn't question her to the nth degree.

The shed housing sports equipment was solidly built but small. And locked.

"Damn it. We need something to break the lock." Hailey looked around for a rock large enough to use against the padlock.

"Move, I got it," Dante said as he retrieved a handgun from an ankle holster.

One shot obliterated the lock. Lucky that it coincided with a staccato burst on the other side of the field. He replaced his gun and opened the door.

"C'mon. Inside. I need to make a call." Dante nudged her in first then followed.

"Because you don't think the local police are aware of an attack of this magnitude?" Hailey asked, retrieving her cell to use its flashlight app.

She knew from experience the three plastic tubs where she sat held all manner of bases, gloves, and sports paraphernalia. She listened to Dante, thinking it an excellent opportunity to eavesdrop, until he spoke in Italian.

Great.

When he disconnected the call and turned, she saw rage. "Who'd you call?"

"Doesn't matter. Look. You stay here, and I'll come back for you. Do not leave the shed. Okay?"

"No. If you leave, I'll follow." It was all she could think of to buy time. Whatever was happening outside, they didn't have the firepower between them to counter it.

Hasty decisions led to disaster. Whatever plan Casper had up her sleeve, she'd get Cecile out of firing range first, to the self-storage compartments. Even in the midst of protecting others, she multi-tasked and kept her secrets.

The Store had opened two years prior with the promise of more jobs coming to Hamchet. Most units were empty and waiting.

Two wings of twenty compartments each attached perpendicularly to a longer side comprised the horseshoe shaped structure. Another string of units divided its parking lot in half.

She and Casper had proven they worked well together, but Hailey had no clue what they faced or how they'd deal with Dante. Meantime, and until her partner arrived, she'd cull a few answers. Judging by the look in Dante's eye, he knew a lot.

"Dante, explain how you're mixed up in this."

"I... can't."

"Can't or won't?"

"Doesn't matter."

"Are you working for the ATF, the mob, or another agency?" Striking at the root of her frustration with the man addressed multiple problems. Not that she'd shy away from danger, but she did work within the limits of the law, at least within the spirit for which it stood.

Dante advanced until towering over her. "Don't you think you've put yourself in enough danger? Why look for more?"

There existed no menace in his tone, just annoyance and irritation as he raked a hand through his hair.

"I can handle myself."

"Look. I need to find your mom and your idiot partner, then figure out what craziness has befallen this town. I can't concentrate if I'm concerned about you. That damn kid is going to get them both killed."

The shed's opening door spared her answer.

Dante turned and rushed forward, stopping when Casper held out her hand.

"Easy there, tiger. We're on the same team." Striding in, she ignored him in favor of taking a seat beside Hailey.

"Is Mom safe? What's happening out there?" Hailey watched as Casper pulled a laptop from her backpack.

"Cecile's safe and Gunther's with her in one of the storage units. But we've got a situation developing." The lid to her computer brightened to brilliant blue before a capuchin monkey took shape on the screen.

"How many are shot?" Dante asked. An air of menace enveloped him in a way not noticed prior.

This was the coiled animal ready to spring, caged fury ready to explode, narrowed on a specific target at a moment's notice.

"No one that I could tell. It's apparently all for effect. That was just to get the ball rolling and clear the general public. These guys are organized and have a definite plan." Steady tapping on the keyboard ended with a private messaging service coming online.

"Hey, kiddo. Figured it wouldn't take long for you to find trouble. Need my wife to come over and help?"

"Nah, thanks, Wyatt. Hailey and I can handle this."

"If you think you can corral this wild child, please, join us, whoever you are." Dante held up his hands in silent supplication.

"What exactly is *this?*" The voice on the other end sounded as calm as he did confident.

"Gang members are holding a few kids from Upward Bound hostage. They've got armed drones in the air to keep cops at a distance. They've also dispersed a few drugs via air." Casper waved a hand in front of the camera. "Hey, Kiera."

"Hey, yourself. So, why haven't you gone and gotten them out?" Kiera asked. The blonde stood behind a dark-haired man whose fingers fairly flew over his keyboard.

"Not alone here. Dante, say hi." Casper held her arm out to prevent the Italian from viewing her screen.

"Hi, Kiera. Would love to meet you sometime." Dante's voice came out a smooth rumble, soft and self-assured.

A rumble of a different kind emanated through the messaging app.

"Oh, Wyatt. He doesn't mean anything by it. He's just being friendly." Kiera patted Wyatt on the shoulder. "Tell me, can you spoof the drones flying around the field?"

"Sure, but it would go a lot faster if you'd brought one in for me."

Casper snorted. "Gee, I have to do like, everything. I'll be right back." Closing the lid, she handed the computer to Hailey with a warning. "No peeking, got it?"

"Sure." Hailey grinned. They both knew it'd be the first thing she did. She watched her partner stand and adjust her back pack.

The moment Casper started to move, Dante blocked her path. Hailey recognized the Italian as an expert who knew how to play the game. The suits he wore couldn't disguise the dangerous predator underneath.

"No. If anyone's going out there, it's gonna be me." He'd used the same tone previously, trying to dissuade Hailey from investigating guns and murder.

Casper snorted. "Listen up, meathead. I don't have time for this." She threw a solid sucker punch to his gut that doubled him over then strolled out the door before he recovered.

A light clinking signaled the broken lock back on its staple, an effective lock to anyone inside.

"Dante, please listen and hear me. Those gangbangers are just trying to clear the field now. I need you to trust me. Casper will be fine."

"What aren't you telling me? Is she mixed up with them?"

"What? Good lord, no. Not at all."

"Then, how is that going to protect her from a bullet? I didn't notice metal armor, though she sure as hell doesn't punch like a girl."

She couldn't tell him the teen could phase through any threat. She also couldn't tell him Casper had exceptional fighting skills and likely carried a gun in her pack. She couldn't tell him anything that wouldn't increase his suspicion.

"You heard her replace the lock. We're stuck here for a moment." Instead of continuing the argument, she opened the laptop, shaking her head when Dante sat beside her.

Dante growled low in his throat. "Okay, sometimes you learn more by listening. I just don't want innocent kids hurt. I don't want Casper hurt either." He made the distinction clear, if not his suspicion.

"She'll be fine. Again, I'm asking you to trust me."

"That kid doesn't realize how bullets tearing through flesh is painful even if not lethal."

Hailey shrugged. "Give her a few minutes. Let's see what we have here." She knew Wyatt was the family's keyboard genius, but hadn't yet met him.

The screen was dark.

Moving her fingers on the mouse pad didn't waken the program. "Figures."

"Am I the only one bothered by the fact your mother is missing and there's a kid out there playing super-agent?"

Outside, a grinding noise followed three gunshots in quick succession. It didn't come as a surprise that Casper carried a gun, but she'd have to hide it before explaining its presence to the authorities.

Casper's muffled guffaw came next. *"Assholes. I'll be with you in a few minutes."*

"Sounds like she got what she was after." Hailey didn't bother closing the laptop, instead went about talking as if she could see those on the other end of the connection.

"Kiera? Is she okay out there?"

"She's fine. Probably stopped to get something to eat. That kid is always stuffing her face."

"At what point should we worry?" Dante asked, again leaning over Hailey to view the screen. Still blank.

A moment of silence ensued where Hailey imagined a muted conversation took place on the other end.

"When she's quiet—and not eating," Wyatt's disembodied voice replied from the black screen.

Outside was quiet. Too quiet. The mass exodus from the grounds took with it the noise created by hundreds of frightened men, women, and children.

Apocalyptic foreboding stretched out until Hailey shivered. Instinct dictated her present companion had no hand in crafting current events. It didn't mean he wasn't involved, even if indirectly.

Distant sirens blasted the arrival of police vehicles. If this turned into a drawn-out hostage situation, Hamchet sheriff's department had no experience unless their newest rising star, Lieutenant Colson, proved the exception.

More shots were fired.

"Enough of this shit." Dante stood and removed his jacket, handing it to Hailey then facing the door.

"Not without me, you don't." She had no intention of sitting back while others risked their lives.

Whether from experience or simple logic, Dante placed his first kick close to the knob. The door exploded outward to reveal Casper present and extending her hand.

"Well, what a gentleman, opens doors and everything. Maybe you *are* a keeper." Casper waggled her eyebrows at Hailey, the meaning clear.

"Jeez, I forgot what teenage hormones were like." Hailey eyed the busted drone held out like a prize.

"Well, thank you for opening the door for me, but really, I'm much too young for the likes of you. More's the pity." She strode by Dante, whose jaw closed with a teenage index finger under his chin.

"Who was shooting that close?" The Italian accent became a little thicker when stressed.

"Police versus drone standoff." Casper shrugged like it was expected.

In taking her seat again, Casper asked, "Did they keep you entertained?"

"Yeah, I like the Italian accent," Kiera replied then murmured something to her companion.

"Dante Rossi isn't his real name from what I'm finding. Shame he didn't touch the keyboard. He drives a BMW, is six-foot-two, and has a scar over his right eye. Decent bank account," Wyatt continued his spiel of details.

Hailey covered her chuckle with a fisted hand, more difficult with Dante's look of disbelief.

"He likes to be thorough, so he'll dig into every aspect of your life." Casper connected the damaged drone to her laptop with a USB cord from her backpack. Once done, she asked, "Got it, Wyatt?"

"Yeah, give me a minute. As soon as I've spoofed the others, I'll run them over the field to check the situation."

"Okay, but keep the police at bay until I retrieve someone. I need a few minutes. I'll let you know."

"Right, then, go ahead and figure out your plan while I keep the gang busy. It looks like they're trying to hustle a woman and three kids out the far end of the field."

"Can you block their exit with the drones and hold them still until I'm finished? I'd like to get at least one of them. We need answers on a shipment of stolen guns." Casper stowed her computer then stood to face Dante.

"Look, I know you're all macho and shit, but this isn't your bag of expertise. It is, however, mine. I need to go to work now, so sit tight or I'll put your lights out."

"I'm not gonna sit here while you go out and face," Dante spread his arm wide, "...whatever is out there."

Casper grumbled in her chest. "Fine. I'll retrieve Cecile then Hailey and I can circle through the woods to the parking lot. You go tell the police they have a hostage situation but with a man on the inside. That way they won't come in with guns blazing and hit the hostages."

Hailey spotted the lie even if Dante didn't.

Not waiting for a reply, Casper grabbed Hailey's hand and tugged her through the exit. Field lights were still off, but moonlight defined the tree line on the east side.

"Will your Italian stud do like he's told?" Casper asked, edging them northeast toward the shadows of the storage units.

"He's not my... anything. But, yes, I think he will. Seems odd, though, doesn't it? We are heading for the storage units, yes?"

"Think he's got some kind of ability? And yes, Cecile is in the second unit closest on the forest side." Casper kept hold of Hailey's hand, matching her pace.

"And?" Hailey waited, wondering if Casper had revealed her ability to Cecile or picked a lock.

"I didn't have to phase her. Picking locks is one of my, um, lesser talents." Filtered light gleamed off white teeth when she smiled.

"You came prepared for everything tonight." Hailey tapped her partner's backpack, wondering if she'd kept or ditched the gun.

"I had a noncorporeal warning. Lucky for us, we now have a spy within the Jackyls' gang."

"Who?"

"One of the murdered kids who tried to leave the life behind."

Low-growing jasmine had long since lost their blooms, but the glossy green leaves defined the edges of the park where asphalt led to the storage units. Heavily forested land stood on two sides, the third taken up by a service road leading to a larger business park.

As expected, Cecile waited inside the unit, sitting on an old dresser and petting Gunther.

"Well, then. It's clear to go?" Dusting her jeans off after standing, she looked expectantly at first Hailey, then Casper.

Casper retrieved her phone and swiped the screen. "Guys? Sitrep."

A conversation Hailey couldn't hear didn't warrant concern. She instead turned her attention to her mother. "You okay?"

"I'm fine, and wholeheartedly approve of your new friend and partner."

That drew Casper's attention and a wide grin. When she disconnected the call, a heavy sigh escaped. "They're holding Charlotte and some of her kids in exchange for—guess what?"

"They're demanding the location of a gun shipment? But how'd your backup know that?" Hailey asked.

"Drones have video and audio. The local gang spared no expense." Casper returned her phone to her pocket.

"They'll kill Charlotte for spite," Hailey assured them. "With Babtiste missing, they'll think he has the guns."

"But he doesn't. He doesn't even know who does." Casper looked at Hailey, then Cecile. "I need to go in and get them. Cecile, would you stay here if asked?"

"No, dear, but I will stay out of sight. I can help." Her mother had always been fearless. Standing and striding to the personnel door, she asked, "Are you two ready?"

DECEPTIVE SILENCE

When did she decide to go Jessica Fletcher?

Chapter Seventeen

Trenton

Trenton's SUV skidded to a halt on the parking lot where crumbling asphalt met grass shoulder. With his badge held up, he bypassed sheriff's deputies taping off a perimeter behind the home plate fence.

I knew it was bad timing to try and visit my folks.

That wild teenager plus Hailey equaled trouble. Every. Damn. Time.

It wasn't the fact the kid hated authority that made her wild. He could see the recklessness swimming in her gaze each time they'd met, the same as it did with Jaxon, his younger brother.

"What's the situation?" He'd been back in Hamchet long enough to reacquaint himself with the locals and earn their respect. Now wasn't the time for pleasantries.

Lt. Colson stood in conversation with the sheriff and a state trooper. The circumstances were dire enough for all-hands-on-deck.

He'd gotten word from Father Ryan of an unknown but developing situation involving guns, the festival, and mass hysteria. That knowledge dictated both Hailey and her sidekick must be present.

Colson acknowledged his approach with a nod. "We don't have enough details to move, but it appears local gang members have taken the owner of Upward Bound and a few of their members hostage."

"What do they want?" Trenton eyed the man standing off to the side who wore slacks, a button-down shirt, and deep concern as his gaze swept the field. He wasn't a deputy, wasn't associated with any department according to Trenton's record searches, yet stood among the officers as if he belonged. His air of confidence instilled the need for further inquiries.

"They want their leader and lieutenants released from county lockup." Colson pinned an area map against the hood of a patrol car with his hands spread. A slight breeze folded the top half up at a right angle before he weighed it down with his flashlight. "They're using drones for surveillance and to drop what we suspect are drugs. Our sniper can take them out if they approach us."

The forecast had promised clear skies and no wind. At least they'd be able to see anything coming at them.

An itch Trenton couldn't define stirred uneasiness in the back of his mind. Maybe it was the timing of murders, missing guns, and Jackyl arrests.

"Letting killers go isn't gonna happen. We've got them all dead to rights on multiple charges." Trenton caught his sister's eye after she lowered a set of night binoculars. "What?"

"We've got an extra man on that detail in case their buddies decide on an unfriendly visit." Colson studied the layout of the field and forest. "Is this fog rolling in? How? There's no vegetation on the field. The ground is bone dry and too damned warm."

Trenton had his suspicions but shrugged then exchanged it for a more pertinent question. "Have you seen Hailey and Casper?"

"No." Colson switched focus from Trenton to Leigh. "Did they come tonight? You two are normally joined at the hip."

"Dante here," Leigh gestured to the non-official bystander, "...says Hailey is in the shed on the first base side last he saw her. Cecile is with her." Static from the radio at her waist blurted a brief report about officers positioned in the surrounding woods.

"If there's trouble, Hailey will find the middle of it." Dante replied but offered nothing further.

Damn it, Hailey. Where are you? Not for the first time, Trenton wondered if his childhood friend would ever settle down. Considering she'd taken a mouthy wild-child under her wing, chances were slim at best.

"And?" Trenton asked the obvious without another word. He knew Dante lied about something, but not what.

"We can't get to them, Trent. Not yet. Not with weaponized drones making passes, and they've got more hidden. As long as the women stay inside, they should be safe." Trenton's sister turned the squelch down on her radio.

"How do you know more are hidden?" He didn't recognize the local gang was so well-equipped or any members that intelligent.

The local sheriff greeted Trenton with a handshake. "We tried to circle through the woods and approach from behind. The officers couldn't even tell where the shots originated from, not in the dark. They've either got snipers or drones spread around. We do know that much. Our men are staying in place, for now."

"You're conferring with state SWAT?"

"Yeah, but as you can see, we're in the middle of nowhere. It's gonna take time."

Trenton turned his attention to Dante. "Where were you when all this started? And why's a guy like you hanging around the Arquette women?"

Dante flicked dust from his shirt. "I was speaking with Hailey and Cecile, both safe in the shed. I find them both quite fascinating actually."

Trenton studied the smooth operator for the presence of a lie. His speech, like his movements were well-controlled. Practiced but not perfect.

"Then set your sights elsewhere, like maybe the swamps. I'm sure you'll find your equal there."

Dante continued as if Trenton hadn't spoken. "We were standing near the pitcher's mound when all hell broke loose. It turned into an instant stampede. Hailey and Cecile had a better chance of avoiding injury by taking shelter in the shed and not getting caught in the bottleneck."

"And you left them there? What kind of asshole—" Trenton stalked forward, cut off by Colson.

"I left to assess the situation. Jackyls have set up a base in the left outfield side."

"Hey, Trent. Kicking his ass won't help the women. I'll go out as soon as it's safe." Leigh tugged her brother's arm.

"Fine." Trenton directed his attention back to the Italian. "Tell me, was there a mouthy black-haired teen with them?" He exhaled slowly. If the pair were together, there was no limit to what mayhem would happen next.

Dante stared hard at the federal agent as if making a decision then looked away. "Not sure. I was busy making sure Cecile and Hailey didn't get trampled."

And what kind of attachment is forming there?

He didn't approve of the association. The newcomer was too smooth, like an upgrade from Hailey's last disastrous relationship.

The slick bastard was holding something back. The question was, was it pertinent to the current circumstances?

As the eldest of the Briner siblings, Trenton had long since fine-tuned his bullshit meter. That same skill translated to his working relationships over time. Dante either outright lied or held onto key information.

A staccato burst of weapons fire redirected all gazes to the outfield.

"Lieutenant, they now have either drones or snipers covering each angle of approach to the woods. We're not able to surround them." Leigh indicated on the map the approximate origin of the shots, then held one finger up while continuing to listen to the report coming over her radio.

"How close can our men get? What radius can they block off?" Colson asked. "Considering the height and angles used so far, it's likely they're using drones, number unknown.

"Looks like they've set a radius from first to third base, extending outward toward the river bend. Which means we can't get to Hailey and Cecile until this standoff is over." Leigh tugged at the collar of her shirt.

"Looks like the Jackyls plan on getting out of this in one piece." Colson studied his map, tapping several locations. "They could be planning on pickup by vehicle here or," his finger trailed around the river's bend, "...escape by waterway over here. We don't have the manpower to monitor that large of an area, at least not fast enough. We have to nail them in place."

"Can you get a department drone over for a looksee?" Trenton clenched his fist in frustration. A member of his makeshift family in Pennsylvania designed drones for every circumstance. If only he'd brought a few when leaving—a situation he'd soon correct.

"Shot down before it got within thirty yards. We can't even retrieve it," Leigh replied, then briefly held her radio at arm's length, staring as if it would bite. "Who the hell is this?"

A minute passed as enlightenment arrived.

Shit.

"Let me guess. They've got one of your radios. Is there a man down?" A decidedly sinking feeling rooted Trenton to the spot.

"They're demanding Frederick's release." Leigh checked in with each officer in the field. "Our men are accounted for, but there're plenty of apps and sites that let people listen to police radios. To talk to us, they've either stolen one from another department or hacked through using a computer. They could be outsourcing tech skills."

"Spread the word. We're going to cell phones," Colson ordered. It was common enough practice when an officer didn't want sensitive information on the airwaves.

Rural departments interacted differently than their larger suburban counterparts. Smaller divisions harbored informal relationships where phone usage rivaled radios for non-urgent conditions. It wasn't a difficult or time-consuming switch.

The sheriff appraised two arriving troopers of the situation, one with his K9 at his side. All were ready for the next move, whatever should occur.

These people have no idea what Hailey and Casper can do. Hell, Trenton didn't even know all the details. They'd all heard the rumors, but he doubted any other than he and Leigh knew even partial truths.

Hailey had become more reserved since meeting Casper, a trait he intended to change. He missed the close comradery of his best friend. If he had to make peace with the kid, so be it. A necessary evil to protect them both.

"What fresh evil is this?" Trenton eyed a larger wave of fog rolling toward them, a creep factor as yet unknown stealing up his spine. "You're right, Colson. This isn't natural." Respect for the Arquette women got an upgrade, but challenging street thugs with guns while unarmed was the product of a deranged mind.

If insanity were contagious, he prayed fate would spare him.

Damn! If Cecile is in the mix and helping cover Hailey and Casper's next move, the shit's about to hit the fan.

Hailey didn't know her limitations, and the kid was at the age she still felt invincible. It was a recipe for disaster.

Chapter Eighteen

Casper

This wasn't the team Casper trained beside for hours every day. Hailey and Gunther weren't family, wouldn't anticipate her actions as quickly, nor did they understand her talents and how she'd use them. Tonight's response was a half-assed attempt to right a wrong. It was dangerous.

In effect, they weren't quite family yet.

Tomorrow, she'd have to give serious thought to offering more detailed explanations and demonstrations of her abilities. There was no reason to hold back. Commitment to a partner was long overdue.

Hailey held an incredible talent, and if the spirits were correct, held the potential for a lot more. It was time to become a cohesive unit.

The odds they faced could be a lot worse. Casper could feel responsible for more innocent lives.

Oh, wait. I am *responsible for more. Charlotte and her associates from Upward Bound.*

On the plus side, she didn't figure any of the Jackyls could slow time, throw bolts of electricity, or shoot fire from their hands. *Every downside has an upside, according to Nicholai.*

With Wyatt's assurance that all the drones were under his control and several more would arrive within minutes, the area was secure.

Her backpack equated to a military personnel's go bag and contained most everything needed for an op—if only two were involved.

Casper's handing Hailey an ear mic with an apologetic, "Sorry, I only have two," earned a knowing nod from her current partner's mother.

"Don't worry, dear. I'll stay here and provide support while you both figure a way to sort out these young ruffians."

Hailey and Casper made their way through the woods with Wyatt keeping watch via drone and ensuring the Jackyls couldn't flee. In the same vein, a swat team couldn't approach.

She smiled at Hailey, understanding how her partner's mother would help. Prior words reiterated in her mind. Cecile links with plants.

The large wave of fog moving in provided good concealment.

From the right field side, they stood on a small rise, as much as such things occurred in the area, and surveyed the opposite field where overturned tables obscured the view of prisoners and gunmen alike.

Casper retrieved her phone, wondering if she should call in backup. "Wyatt? What's the police presence situation?"

"I've got them in a holding pattern, at least for now. The problem is, I can't shield you from sight without Kiera's help."

"Noted, but there's enough fog to help with that."

"Remember, concealment isn't the same as cover."

"Got it, let me know if snipers are getting ready to make a move."

"I've fired warning shots to keep them in place. Also, I have three reinforced quadcopters, the latest in tech, image stabilization, industrial engines, and agile as hell for their size on site. Compact machine guns aren't light, but these things are great."

Jeez. Give a man a toy...

"Good. We'll take it from there. Oh, is Trenton among the cops?"

"Yeah. So is your man Dante. Looks like trouble's brewing on the horizon."

A text to Trenton would stifle the swat team's firing a bullet to split their skulls. It also might instigate a stroke. Casper nixed the idea. Hailey should do it.

"Okay, Hailey. Wanna send your fed a text and let him know you'll handle this then turn off your phone?" Casper imagined the steam pouring from Trenton's ears after reading such a message. "We'll leave your mom here as overwatch with my ear mic since you and I'll be together."

The elder Arquette accepted the token to her safety with a calm nod.

"We've got fifty yards between the Jackyls' stronghold and the tree line on the third base side. They've overturned tables around them so they can duck down to avoid snipers." Casper studied the layout. They didn't have a lot to work with.

"They know police won't risk hitting a hostage," Cecile advised.

"We'll need a diversion to remain unseen by the police. Any ideas?" Short of donning a balaclava, Casper had nada.

Hailey grinned in turning to her mother. "Can you enhance the fog you're creating for us? Send it toward the pitcher's mound?"

"Huh." Casper studied the grounds and nodded approval. "We do make a good team."

"I can, certainly. I can guarantee plenty of fog. What I can't do is stop a bullet or change its trajectory. Please keep that in mind." Cecile hugged her daughter tight then did the unexpected.

Reflex caused Casper to phase her body when Hailey's mother stepped forward with arms outstretched. Solidification occurred a split second before contact.

"Young woman, you may not be my flesh and blood, but I feel like I've already adopted you. So, please, stay safe."

Gobsmacked, Casper couldn't move or form a coherent thought, much less an appropriate answer, so she nodded and smiled.

"Gunther, protect Mom," Hailey said as she steered them around Drummond maples whose leaves would soon turn to rich, bold shades of red.

Once out of view, Casper took Hailey's hand and said, "I like your mom. Kinda makes me wish I'd had one growing up."

"Never got close to any foster women?"

"Nah, but there's a woman in PA who feels like what I think a mom should. Reminds me a lot of Cecile."

"Don't tell her that. She'll pull on the motherhood cloak and you'll never be free," Hailey murmured. "Despite whatever we use as a distraction, there's a lot of open ground to cover. I don't want Charlotte or her associates, much less the rest of the Jackyls, to discover your secret."

"Wyatt has control of the drones. He'll turn several on the Jackyls to keep them contained, but he won't risk shooting a civilian. I just hope the dirtballs keep their cool. That covers half our problem." Casper paused then said, "I like your mom's psychic talent. We need to have some frank discussions later."

"You're right, yes. She can link, for lack of a better word, with plant life, anything that uses photosynthesis. She can also sense spirits, but not like I can. She can't communicate with them on any level."

"Okay. Is she, like, gonna make the trees walk on their roots and bat those assholes like baseballs?"

Hailey chortled softly. "No. Nothing like that, but she'll probably take advantage of the bushes on that side of the field and create more fog."

"How does she create fog in a natural manner?" Of all the strange psychic talents Casper had encountered, this wasn't among them.

"Several ways. Radiation fog is created as the surface temps cool and moist air near the ground forms. It's the type that makes driving hazardous. Advection fog is also from condensation but created from the horizontal movement of warm moist air over a cooler surface. Mom'll use bushes and tree limbs in the woods to create the gradient in air currents."

"Cops are gonna have a field day with that one." Casper rolled one shoulder and touched the amulet at her neck. "You ready, Simon? We're probably gonna need your help."

"Any other noncorporeals around?"

"Yeah." Casper nodded to the spot behind Hailey. "Our ATF agent is looking for a little action, even if it isn't the right target."

"Looks like we have all the backup we need." Hailey swiveled her head. "Donald, I'm sorry your life was cut short, especially in that manner and in the swamp. However, we're looking for a zero body count here. Okay?"

"*Fine, but you'd be better off giving that advice to your sister.*"

"Addy's here?" Hailey paused in her next step, stopping where limbs from a pine tree passed through her chest and abdomen.

"*Yeah, sis. I'm here.*"

"Sorry, Hailey. I didn't say anything. I was afraid you'd get distracted."

"Damn, if Mom only knew. She'd give her eye teeth to be able to talk to you, Addy." Hailey shook her head as if to clear it.

Casper thought about it.

Maybe I should arrange that. She'd spent her life under the radar and wanted to be certain her decision was a solid one. Trust took time to earn, tested under duress and difficult situations. Tonight was an excellent example.

"How will the cops explain tonight's fiasco?"

"Don't sweat it. Mom is rumored to be a Vodou priestess descended from La Belle Fontaine. Police will attribute anything strange tonight to her and me. We're used to it."

"In that case," Casper phased them through a group of American elms and a fallen tree, "...maybe I'll find my own way home and let you deal with the cops? One more mishap, and the major's gonna make a trip to Texas. I really don't want him breathing down my neck."

"They don't think you can handle yourself?"

"It's more like growing pains. We've always worked as a cohesive unit, and he sees me as isolated down here. I haven't told him about your abilities, and I won't until you give me the green light. Though when we captured Frederick, we gave them something to work with."

"The major sounds a bit overprotective," Hailey surmised. "I understand that, but it can make life tough."

"Kind of like your non-boyfriends Trenton and Dante. Of the two, I'm not sure which I'd choose. Trenton reeks of testosterone and all that male goodness, but your Italian stud, I've got to wonder what he's got under the hood. Shame they're both so old. What are they, like, thirty?"

Hailey groaned. "Trenton and I are friends. Yes, he's thirty. Dante is... difficult to explain, but not boyfriend material, that's for sure. I can't figure out if he's working for the mob or the feds. I'd like to keep him on the fringes until I figure it out."

"Wyatt hasn't got a bead on him. Yet. As soon as he does, I'll let ya know."

"Wyatt's monitoring activity down here?"

"Yeah. Since I've been questioned at the station, he'll monitor everything."

By unspoken agreement, each delved into their own thoughts as they circled wide and slipped through the woods adjacent to left field. Air currents picked up with the movement of surrounding bushes and carried leafy debris in their wake.

Brief glimpses of the field showed thickening fog.

Ongoing assessment occurred through training and experience. Part of that included wondering about the PI's field training, and how she'd react in various situations. So far, she'd proven herself steady, resourceful, and not one to freeze during a crisis.

Fog on the third base side was lighter but growing thicker. "Their use of tables to stay hidden will require assessment on the fly." It used to be Casper's standard MO.

Nothing like trial by fire.

"I counted three men with guns earlier, and a head full of brown curls just above one table. That's Charlotte, and she'll keep the kids close." Hailey pointed toward the field. "The fog cover is good, lower to the ground, but I see two gunmen standing now. They might see us if we're not crouched low enough."

"Then we'll stay low."

As if on cue, two drones flew overhead and into the open. Unlike the one she'd shot down earlier, these were military-style quadcopters carrying machine guns. Each flew low enough to the ground to obscure details of their payload.

Wyatt wouldn't risk taking a shot and hurting a civilian, but he'd draw their attention.

"Where'd those come from? They don't look like the one you brought into the shed." Hailey stared as the larger engines passed.

"Um, that would be my backup. Kiera and Wyatt are showing off. *Those* are the latest in military applications, equipped with both audio and visual feeds to accompany the extra firepower." Casper advanced to the edge of the tree line and watched from behind a stout maple trunk.

"But—your backup is in Pennsylvania...?"

"Yeah, let's save those thoughts for later." Casper touched the blade hilts at her boot top, her method of preparation.

"Those drones might be seen by the local authorities."

"True, but believe me when I say that no digital photo will ever make its way into a file. On top of that, Wyatt will wipe any pics from tonight off every phone. I guarantee they'll never be found."

Association with Wyatt and Major Clannahan carried very specific advantages.

The flight of automatic weapons at the fog's edge would cause most sane people to drop their guns. The three Jackyls held tight to their weapons and moved closer to their hostages. A dare of sorts.

Fog had grown thicker between the Jackyls' holding spot and police officials, expanding to prevent their knowledge of events as they unfolded.

Direct sight of both Jackyls and hostages became more obscure, which meant she and Hailey wouldn't be seen approaching. A testament to Cecile's control that the fog's thinner layers in different areas blended to the thicker layers where they needed them most.

"Okay. Ready?" Casper held out her hand and crouched low. No one could identify them if they noted movement. The level of fog had risen to waist-high and the level of horror movie set.

Across the open space and through a few low-lying bushes they ran. Casper's backpack thumped against her spine. Going into battle was nothing new. Going in with a partner not trained with her psychic family raised several alarms in her mind.

As planned, Wyatt herded the three Jackyls together using two military drones.

Approaching the trio unobserved would present the best-case scenario since they had no specific knowledge of how each gang member might react. If they turned their anger and fear in Hailey and Casper's direction, no injuries would occur.

Phasing through the tables eliminated the hassle and noise of trying to leap over them. Casper cleared her throat when touching her knife to the neck of the closest thug. "Drop your guns, assholes. I know you've each got at least one backup weapon too."

Compliance was slow and grudging. Six knives and three pistols topped the three rifles heaped in a pile off to the side.

Charlotte and her entourage still huddled in fear, their heads down and arms wrapped around bent knees. None looked up in light of mumbled commands.

If it stayed that way, Casper's involvement could remain unknown.

"Zip ties, backpack," Casper whispered, keeping an eye on the hostages. "Hands and feet, then hands and feet linked together behind them. Make sure to check their pockets."

She kept herself phased, acknowledging the men's grunts and grumbled threats with a chuckle.

"Nothing of interest." Hailey examined the ID in each wallet and snorted when retrieving a dozen condoms. "Counting on a party?"

"Hope it wasn't planned with hostages in mind." Casper's warning drew the attention of a Jackyl who swiveled his head to glare.

Recognition changed his demeanor to shock tinged with fear. "Oh, shit."

Casper leaned close and whispered near his ear. "Don't worry. I'll know where to find you and what to do with you once I get there." It was one of the idiots confronted in the parking lot at Á La Mode.

"Does this seem a little too easy to you?" Hailey asked, her face in part obscured by fog.

"Yeah. Maybe—"

"That's because you two are idiots." The male voice held the assurance of success. "Put your hands up, or I'll open this bitch's airway."

Casper whirled to see one of the huddled mass surrounding Charlotte stand and haul her to her feet, a knife at her throat.

"What? We missed one? How?" Hailey spun around but kept her hands up.

"Drop your weapons and sit on the ground, bitches." A smirk in the tone declared victory.

"Hey, dude. That took thought. Didn't think you guys had it in you." Casper took one step forward but halted when Charlotte's head yanked back, her neck exposed to show a small trickle of blood.

"Tell your buddy to point the drones away from us. And if you take another step forward, this one dies. After all, I have more."

Casper froze, her mind whirling with possibilities, all ending in at least one death. One Charlotte didn't deserve. She dropped her knife to the ground and kicked it away when ordered.

"Heard about you. You may be untouchable, but this bitch isn't." Short and wiry, he had a flat face and a gaze that flicked between his comrades and the would-be rescuers. A tiger tattoo stitched around his neck disappeared under his t-shirt.

"Looks like you've got us corporeal types. But I think you're forgetting something." Casper dropped her right arm to her side with her elbow bent and fingers extending as if lacking a care in the world. "What d'ya think, Donald, Addy?"

Casper smiled at the concomitant chorus of, "*Yes,*" which followed. Pulling her right arm back before making a sweeping motion forward gave Simon's flight extra momentum. It ended with his feet braced against Charlotte's upper chest and his fingers' sharp claws digging into the Jackyl's tiger tattoo.

Donald's contribution carried a little more substance, his death being more recent. He jumped into the Jackyl's footsteps.

Beside her, Hailey tipped her head back and howled. Long and soulful, her voice carried over the field.

"Um, partner? Whatcha doin'?" Casper asked in confusion.

"Calling a pack meeting, bringing in the *expected* backup. Trenton and Leigh both know I'd call him in an emergency." Hailey winked.

"What's happening to me? Some kind of Vodou curse?" Tattoo's knife hand flung wide while he made swiping motions with his other hand across his face. "I—" His mouth froze, then opened and shut several times without voicing a word. When he spoke again, a guttural rendition of a pirate song emerged on choking gasps.

Charlotte elbowed him in the gut, sending him a step back. She huddled next to a sobbing young woman with her back to the scene unfolding. "Don't watch. You don't need to see this."

Before Tattoo could readjust and take control of the situation, a black ball of fur leaped over the table to land solidly against his shoulder. The wolf dog took his prey to ground with gleaming canines tearing into soft flesh.

"*Aw, this isn't right. I wanted to possess him first,*" Addy complained. "*I need the practice.*"

"You'll get your turn, sis. He's gonna be in jail for a good while." Hailey snagged Gunther's collar to make him disengage.

"I-I..." With arms flung spread eagle, Tattoo spit the words out as best he could with the animal's mouth near his throat. Gurgling sounds and arms flattening against the dirt noted surrender and the ATF agent's possession.

"Damn, girl. Didn't know your dog would do that." Casper guffawed, straightening with the sound of her phone's beep.

One of the hogtied thugs spit on the ground. Filth covered his face, but not the scar under his bulbous nose. "*Putas.* You think you've won? We're just a distraction. Don't think I won't hear about Frederick getting hold of your asses within the next few days. He'll make an example of you both."

"Aw, shit." Casper retrieved her phone, knowing before she called something occurred behind the scenes.

Wyatt answered on the first ring. *"Yeah, I heard everything. I'm tapping into the county feeds now. Give me a sec. Oh, and the SWAT team is there. Time for you to leave."*

In the distance, multiple sets of tires squealed.

"Kiddo, video shows two deputies down outside the cells at the detention center. One down in the office. I'm alerting medical services now."

Bulbous nose hadn't lied.

"Thanks, buddy." Casper disconnected and detailed the situation to her partner.

"I got this. My howl is gonna bring Leigh and Trenton running any minute." Hailey made a shooing motion with her hands. "Go. Quick."

"One second. I need to deliver a warning." Casper knelt beside Tattoo.

The wolf dog sat beside her with one lip curled and a growl in his throat.

"Thanks, Gunther. Appreciate the help." Casper laced her fingers together and cracked her knuckles.

"What? What are you gonna do? I was just following orders."

Casper leaned close to the moron's face while phasing her hand and delving inside his abdomen. "Listen up, asshole," she murmured low. "If I see you again and you're not in jail, I'm gonna walk right through any barrier you place, wood, brick, or concrete. Then I'm gonna rip out your intestines and wrap them around your neck for a noose. Got it? And if you *ever* speak of this night to a soul, whether gang, friend, or cop, well, you can guess what'll happen."

Unphasing her fingers, she listened as a shrill scream tore from his throat.

"Partner, go." Hailey moved to Charlotte, explaining to the hostages without details that Casper's name should not pass their lips during the debriefing to come.

They appeared grateful enough that compliance shouldn't be a problem.

Casper bolted toward the woods as the sound of boots thumped the ground. No way in hell would Wyatt fire at a cop.

"C'mon, girl. They're moving fast." The ATF agent's spirit kept pace beside her, his form floating above the fog, his words not necessary to spur her onward.

A soft chuckle escaped when she heard tables thumping against each other, the noise covering her exit.

Once under the cover of shadows, she paused to make a call.

A minute later, Kiera's portal appeared, her friend stepping through with a sigh. "Where to?"

Having friends with psychic talent had never been so reassuring. Having one that could open a portal to anywhere familiar was even better.

Chapter Nineteen

Hailey

Fog obscured everything from ground level up to Hailey's chest. Thinner layers surrounding the area where Jackyls had held hostages in a tight knot allowed slightly better visibility.

Sudden bright lights from the sports lights brought reality and a tenuous thread of safety after she had given the all-clear signal.

Charlotte was likely the only one to have seen her partner's face and agreed to leave the teen out of her statement.

Tears and adrenaline washout would play havoc with hostage responses, unreliable in the best and clearest of circumstances. There'd be nothing clear to anyone about the night's events.

Trenton, Leigh, and Colson rushed around the small barricade with guns at low rest position after the non-military drones fell to the ground. Frustration would eat the men alive at not being able to account for the others if seen.

Casper was nowhere to be found, another mystery officials wouldn't solve.

Leigh was the first to Hailey's side, wrapping an arm around her shoulders and leading her away from the others. "Where is she?" The low murmur was for Hailey's ears only.

Of course her lifelong friend would know the teen had been there. Intentional misunderstanding seemed the only viable option. "Mom? Oh, God. I left her over—"

"Can it, Sparkles." Trenton had snuck up behind them, quiet in his approach, but now towering over them both. "Your mom said she got lost in this mysterious fog, which seems to be dissipating even as we speak." Trenton swept his hand wide. "Any ideas?"

"Well, it did come in handy, it let me sneak up and get the drop on these idiots. Is she okay? We, um, got separated." Even as she spoke the words, Trenton stepped forward and tapped the ear mic she forgot to remove.

Crap. He's ex-military intelligence.

She pocketed the device and avoided his gaze.

"Fine, then tell me this. Is the mouthy kid safe? I know full well she had a hand in this." Trenton kept a light grip on her upper arm when marching her back to the parking lot then wrapping a blanket around her shoulders.

"Casper's fine, as far as I know."

Her mother had a similar blanket and waited beside a deputy's car, a smirk playing about her lips. Dante, in stark relief, stood beside her, his wary gaze keeping an eye on her and those around them.

"Everything okay, dear?" An arched brow declared her mom's thought, *"Is your partner safe?"*

"Everything's fine, Mom. I just want to go home and sleep for a week."

Hailey watched as deputies led each of the Jackyls past them and toward a cruiser. Hateful glares promised retribution. Knowing their reputation, it would be swift and carry an air of finality if they ever got paroled. Things in her favor included her reputation and their superstitious fear.

"Sleeping is the only way you'll stay out of trouble," Trenton grumbled as he secured part of the blanket slipping from her shoulder. He rested his arm there for a bit longer than necessary, his smirk daring her to retreat. "How about I see you home, just to make sure?"

"I—" Hailey couldn't finish her thought, watching Casper's car pull into a space when a cruiser pulled away.

"Ah." Cecile waved hello. "There she is. I thought she was supposed to meet us earlier."

Dante nodded to Casper and strolled in step with Cecile to gather around Hailey, Trenton, and Leigh.

"Oh, Trent. You were asking about Casper. Here she is." Hailey smiled sweetly into a visage that defied explanation.

Confidence and certainty radiated from the teen exiting her Camaro wearing blue jeans, a long-sleeved tee featuring her favorite band, and sneakers. A look of surprise crossed her features when spotting Hailey.

"Hey, partner. What kind of mess did you find while I was gone? Seems I can't leave you alone for a minute." An exaggerated sigh, open mouth, and palm slapped to cheek mimicked the dramatic display worthy of an Oscar.

"Oh, just the usual. Guns, mystery, mayhem. Did you finish the book you were reading?" Lips nipped between teeth was the only way Hailey could keep from laughing.

"You mean *Federal Standards for Dummies*? Sure. It was slow reading, but I managed." Casper faked a double take then smiled at Trenton. "Oh, hey, dude. How's it going?" Not waiting for an answer, she turned back to Hailey. "What happened here?"

Hailey repeated her talking points and skipped over her partner or mother's involvement. She was careful to vary her sentence structure to make her thoughts appear random and not repeating a memorized script.

"And where have you been?" One of Trenton's intimidation tactics included invasion of his target's private space. He stepped forward, toe to toe with his young quarry. It generally worked on kids and adults alike.

Unfortunately, he hadn't learned it didn't work with this particular one brimming with a combination of defiance and confidence.

Understanding the game, and returning the favor, Casper closed the scant distance until only a thin slice of air moved between them.

Trenton hardened his jaw, glaring.

Cecile chuckled. "Wrong approach, Trent. You should change tactics."

Casper smiled, resting her hand on the agent's chest. "I was home, taking a shower. Care to check that I got all the nooks and crannies dry? I haven't told my dad yet about your penchant for undressing your targets."

Lightning couldn't move faster than Trenton's backstep. Denial sputtered from his lips before taking a deep breath and returning to stand face to face. This time, he left appropriate space between them. Until he learned another method of interaction, he was doomed to failure.

Casper redirected her attention. "Hailey, how about I give you and your mom a ride home? We can come back tomorrow for your car."

"Um, I have to go to the station and give a statement, but I'd appreciate it if you'd give Mom a ride, though. She was stuck in the shed and didn't get to see anything until the lights came on." Both Trenton and Leigh would spot her lie, but neither spoke.

"Why, thank you, Casper. It'll give us a chance to catch up. I'd love to hear about your classes and how you're settling into life here. Hailey said you might have a boyfriend arriving in Texas soon?"

"Great," Trenton murmured. "Now we have to import trouble, because we don't have enough of our own."

"Hopefully in a couple months, yes. He's helping his brother get settled before planning to join me." Casper patted Trenton on the chest in passing. "See ya around, Schmeidel. Take it easy on Hailey, okay? She's had a rough night, and you wouldn't want to send her into a stranger's arms during that, what do they call it? Post life-and-death adrenaline wash."

Trenton remained mute, a slight tinging of his cheeks the only nonverbal response.

Having wrapped her arm around Casper's waist, Cecile fell in step but stopped to look over her shoulder, assessing Dante again. "*Hmm,*" was all she said.

Hailey's eyelids closed the minute her head touched the pillow. Curled up with Gunther on the bed, she knew wild horses wouldn't get her up during the night.

Bright sunshine and Gunther's snuffling at the door woke her. When she stumbled out of her room, she found Trenton sitting at her table drinking coffee.

No wonder Gunther was antsy during the night.

"You've been here all night."

"Which you would know if you actually remembered to turn your security system *on.*"

"I remember... sometimes. The only way I'm forgiving you for invading my space is if you made enough coffee for me."

Gunther had raced to Trenton's side, accepting his due of petting before moving on to her second uninvited guest, Leigh, whom she now noticed standing in her kitchen, attempting to make something edible.

"I'll take him out and spare the officer posted outside the migraine at seeing you in that." Leigh gestured to Hailey's choice of pajamas.

"Sleep well?" Trenton asked, retrieving her the requested morning caffeine infusion after Leigh and Gunther left.

"Like a baby." Her mind had whirled half the night with thoughts of her next step.

Babtiste was safe, as was Charlotte, who had an off-duty officer providing security.

A glance at her phone revealed an early morning text stating Casper would stop by after class. It'd give them a chance to pool information, maybe with a few details of the prior night's backup. She mentally reviewed what she knew.

Wyatt was their computer genius.

Kiera provided mobility.

Though she'd cleaned the small amount of blood from the truck's floor mat after her partner was shot in the foot, she hadn't learned how the skin appeared intact at the police station. She suspected Ouray provided psychic healing. It was one of the growing list of questions tucked in the back of her mind.

"I figure your mother's fog masked you and Casper's movements last night, allowing you to get to Charlotte without being shot." The statement emerged as a Trenton-style fact.

"Are you having a brain fart? You saw Casper drive up minutes after I had those asshats down." She didn't try and deny her mother's help. Trenton surmised Cecile's talent long ago.

If not careful, she'd get backed into a figurative corner. She wasn't as good at covering the truth or her tracks. He'd always been able to tell when she danced around a subject. Tenacious should be the man's middle name.

"I did. What I don't know is *how* the kid managed that particular feat. I'd had an officer check her house during the standoff. Her car was parked out front."

"Which proves my point."

"No, not that I believe she's working against us, I just can't figure out how she's doing it. Does she have a twin?"

"Not that I know about. She doesn't have any blood relatives." At least those statements she could make with complete honesty.

"Well, thank God there's only one of them."

"So, what are you doing today?" Hailey set her stance for Gunther's greeting with his return. Cooler temperatures brought out his boisterous side. He romped around the loft then returned to stand on his hind legs with his front paws braced against her shoulders. "Aw, sweetie. Have a good run?"

The wolf dog licked her face.

"Depends on where you're gonna be." Trenton nodded to three books sitting on the counter beside the microwave. "Who sent you those?"

"How do you know I didn't order them?" Just noticing the stack that wasn't there the day prior, Hailey picked up one book, then another, careful to keep her face a blank mask. She'd never seen the tomes before.

Which meant someone had been in her loft yesterday. The alarm had been set and showed no sign of tampering when she'd arrived last night. The Jackyls wouldn't taunt her this way, even if they could get in and out undetected. Leigh didn't have much interest in cooking. Her friend Laurent would've left a note with it.

That left Dante at the top of her list.

She'd check her security feed later, but had no doubt who'd left her the presents. It didn't answer the *why* of it, however.

Leigh nudged her brother aside to read the spines then snickered. A serious case of side-eye equaled her version of disbelief. "Dijmnal fubslisa clozuaki."

"Oh, no you two don't. No twin speak. I want answers." Trenton's chair tipped over in his haste to stand. With hands fisted on hips, he glared at his sister before settling on Hailey.

Hailey answered Leigh in kind, the short version of "Later." Dante had some 'splaining to do.

But can I consider it stalking after searching his home?

Was it a not-so-subtle gesture that he was a person to take seriously?

"Trent, I'm going to spend the day doing research. I have a client who wants me to find her employee, and I have no leads. So, it's back to square one. Happy?"

"Fine. Leigh and I can check on you later and bring you dinner. I'm sure by now Cecile has a kitchen full of prepared dishes to send."

Her mother used any excuse to bake, which kept an intermittent supply of select dishes and goodies in her fridge.

She sat at her window seat and watched them drive off. Gunther sat beside her and watched the street below. She returned the wave of the new officer posted below.

Needing to do research wasn't a lie, and she'd never told Trent it was internet research. With all that had transpired, she hadn't had time to check out the address Babtiste provided, the intended destination of the guns.

Ditching her assigned security would take thought, but she wanted to check out the house during daylight. She'd had enough nighttime adventure.

Dosing the officer's coffee with something to keep him in the bathroom downstairs long enough for her to slip away was deviant, but him following her wasn't an option. He was young and not familiar with her determination. No doubt, he'd catch hell from both Trenton and Colson, his boss.

It didn't take long for the natural herb to work.

After waiting a few minutes to see the officer didn't return to his post, she hurried out. Her truck purred to life with a low rumble, easing out of the drive and down the street before she gunned it to make the turn. The ride to town included frequent checks in her rearview.

Maybe next time, a little less aloe vera juice.

Her heart thumped hard with the expectation of blaring lights and sirens rushing up behind her. As soon as she was clear, she stopped and removed the tracking puck Trenton had placed in the front wheel well. This was one trip he didn't need to know about.

Gunther rode shotgun as she made her turn down the narrow side street near the edge of town. A few of the homes appeared far from livable but probably sheltered those who didn't have money for lodging.

Pulling up the address on her phone revealed the neighborhood's less-than-stellar ratings. Sagging rooftops, missing shingles and shutters, and peeling paint were all signs of disrepair.

Lots were small; many appeared tiny with knee-high grass and untrimmed living hedges. The first hints of fall color tinged branching maples overshadowing the crushed stone driveway of her target house.

"Gunther, you stay here and guard the truck. I'll leave the windows down just in case. Doesn't look like anyone's here at the moment, and I'll be quick. I just want the nickel tour, and we'll be on our way." A light forehead-to-forehead rub and she exited quietly.

Across the street, no one sat on the only porch in view. No curtains stirred at the windows.

To her left, low shrubs between the two homes wouldn't block a neighbor witnessing her transgression, but no one stood in view on either floor. Material resembling bed sheets covered the lower level windows.

Whoever blackmailed Babtiste into delivering guns to this address had to either be local or have lived in the area at one time. According to his friend Daphne, the Jackyls wanted in on the gun trade and seemed the most likely suspects.

In counterpoint, the local branch of organized crime could've wanted to lure Babtiste into their web in exchange for gang-related information.

Neither scenario justified involving Casper in the mess. Yet their working relationship had snapped into place without a ruffle.

Cecile had voiced doubts initially, but last night seemed to change something in her mother, who also recognized the old soul in a teenager's body.

A rotting privacy fence separated the property from its rear neighbor. Six-foot vertical slats prevented a look at anything lower than the second-story windows.

Sometimes, fate helped the weary.

Hailey made her way along the home's side in the hedge's shadow. The backyard was more of the same—tall grass, an old rose bush struggling to survive the onslaught of advancing morning glory, and a rusted stove with a four-burner cooktop.

Steps leading to the back portico consisted of stacked cement blocks with planks that appeared safe enough, until Hailey took her first step and heard an ominous hiss from the shadows below.

Damn it.

She hated surprising any type of reptile. It rarely ended well.

Avoiding the lower two levels, she moved to the side and gingerly hopped up to the top tier. Nothing hissed, jumped out, or tried to bite her.

Progress.

The doorknob had long since rusted, its angle in the wood planks suggesting its appearance equaled less than a token to security. If this was the rendezvous point for an illegal gun shipment, wouldn't there be more security?

A sixth sense about the ramshackle house raised the hair on her nape and produced a shudder. Leaving Gunther behind might have been a bad idea, but she couldn't call out now without alerting whoever might be on the other side of the solid portal.

If she backtracked, it would allow time for one of the Jackyls to arrange a nasty surprise.

Chapter Twenty

Hailey

Her hand froze inches from the rusted knob. Dots of perspiration dampened her t-shirt. She normally thought of old homes as charming even if needing a bit of TLC.

So far, this one needed a match.

"Stop being a baby and push. There's a surprise inside." If Addy were among the living, her vocal folds would be short and thin to produce the lower-pitched voice.

Her sister's sudden intrusion made Hailey stumble backward, catching herself before she fell off the semi-rotten floorboards. It appeared she'd have to adapt to the arrival of spirits anytime, anywhere, and regardless of the circumstance.

Lacking experience with life outside of the womb might skew Addy's perception of a surprise to hell and back. They were due for some serious conversations about appropriate timing.

Maybe it was because her sister was noncorporeal and couldn't be hurt by knives and bullets, or maybe because Addy was bored and wanted to see inside, but haste was rarely a good option when approaching an unknown situation.

"Ya know, you could spare me the drama and tell me what's in there." If someone were able to watch, they'd think Hailey had lost her mind, turning her head to the side and harshly whispering the chastisement. "And please don't startle me like that again. Okay?"

"Oh, for heaven's sake. How long are you going to procrastinate? Just push. Like this."

Hinges shrieked in protest with the first few inches of the door opening. It morphed into a loud screech worthy of the most high-tech alarm system.

"Oooh, I did it! Eureka!" Addy lowered her tone to a conspiratorial murmur. *"I've been working really hard on that. I can affect little things if I concentrate hard."*

Hailey lowered her head and face-palmed. A gesture usually reserved for Trenton. On the heels of that thought came, *Is that ability because she's my sister and would've had psychic talent or can any spirit learn to do that?*

"Gee thanks for the announcement, Addy." A minute to gather her wits before stepping inside didn't help much.

Interior and exterior were homogenous concerning lack of repair. If the seventies mated with the Addams family, their otherworldly child would love this structure.

Gouges in the yellowed linoleum floor, once-colorful patterned wallpaper that had peeled halfway down the wall, and a laminate countertop missing half its layers deemed the place unfit for anything other than undiscriminating vermin.

Dust covered the kitchen island dotted with intermittent mounds of matted fur where it met a plywood backsplash. *From rats?*

The shiver had nothing to do with the knowledge her sister was trying to urge her farther inside. "Do you mind? I'd like to go at my own pace."

So entranced with studying the kitchen, she hadn't bothered to look in the other direction before entering.

"Don't mind at all, sunshine. And what exactly is your pace?" The tone was smooth, soft, seductive, and decidedly Italian.

Hailey squealed and sidestepped into the countertop. Her hip crashed into a jagged edge and created instant pain. She ignored the question since she had no plausible answer.

Undaunted, her inquisitor asked another question. "Who's Addy? More importantly, *where* is Addy? I didn't see anyone with you."

To her left, Dante leaned against the doorjamb leading into what a small den. A smile tipped up one side of his mouth.

"My imaginary friend," was the only response coming to mind.

"*Hmm*, I wonder about that."

Subtle amusement combined with intense curiosity declared the matter dormant but far from settled.

"I didn't expect a girly scream, but *what* was that?"

"You startled me. What are you doing here?" Hailey snapped out to redirect his attention.

"Thinking about investing. I believe, though, that this is too much of a fixer-upper. How about you?" So calm and serene, not many would mistake him for a cold-blooded mob enforcer, if in fact, that was how he earned his keep.

Initial assessment—the way he dressed, his demeanor, what she'd learned of his lifestyle—all spoke of confidence and experience dealing with problems of various types.

Then, he saved her life in an alley, which didn't fit her tentative typecasting.

Decisive and motivated topped the list of attributes she associated with him. Yet with all her digging, she hadn't learned much of anything useful concerning his employment or background. The sum total left her confused and frustrated.

"Didn't see a For Sale sign out front." Challenging him could be addictive if she had the time.

"*Huh*, must've blown over in the last storm."

His smile generated a host of emotions to contemplate. She didn't know whether to be flattered or scared. "Why were you at the festival last night?"

"Doesn't everybody love a celebration? I was curious, though—how did Casper get to her car, which according to the fed, was parked at her house? He seems like a competent enough chap."

"How would I know? Maybe someone brought it to her."

"Her adopted father isn't in town, and the guardian was accounted for."

"You have someone spying on her?" Another red flag raised. If not careful, she'd give something away. Casper didn't need any more attention.

"I'm curious, is all. In addition, how did she avoid getting shot by a drone? Actually, how did she even *obtain* one of them? No doubt she carries a weapon of some kind, but it was too dark to get an accurate shot, and those things are harder to knock down than you'd think. For that matter, who's backing her?"

"Care to take a breath?"

Dante ignored her. "While we're at it, how did you take down four armed-to-the-teeth gang members without firing a weapon? I'll bet you didn't even pull that Hellcat you usually holster at your back waist."

"Was that supposed to be multiple choice, or do you have a preference? See, I have a bit of a short memory."

Dante stalked forward slowly, giving her time to move.

She couldn't. Her feet stuck to the floor like her tongue did to the spoon used after dipping up her favorite icy snack.

She knew he wouldn't hurt her. There was heat in his gaze, but it wasn't sexual. It was the burning desire to know the truth, and wherever he thought it would lead.

"Maybe I can refresh your memory. Let's start with the last question." His slow approach likened to that of a crouched panther.

She wouldn't give him a chance to ask. He might wield charisma like *Mjölnir*, but she wasn't a blushing schoolgirl. She took a step back. "You seem awfully interested in a young teenager. Should I look into *your* past? Like cross-reference with the national and state registries?"

"I don't mind you looking into me. Probably won't find much as I value my privacy." He held his arms wide to prove a point. "After all, you've been in my house."

"I was just curious, and *ah*, thanks for the books."

"You mean you *both* were just curious. And, you're welcome. I didn't get anything for Casper, because well, she's young and might get the wrong idea. Interesting entrance you made."

"And what ideas do you have about her?" His focus may be directed at her, but Dante's interest centered on Casper.

"Trust me, my curiosity in that kid is professional only. I'm not into sarcastic, undisciplined girls." A sly smile denoted exactly where his interest could lay. "But damned if I don't want to know more about her. Something is very *off* with both of you."

And you intend to discover all the details.

He was intentionally trying to mislead her with his sexy smile and a body no man had a right to have.

Dante didn't move any closer, letting her set the nature of their interaction. She couldn't find the strength to move, only gulp.

A slow glide of his right hand circled her waist until pressing the butt of her gun into her low back. "You should practice more with this if you're going to keep putting yourself in danger."

"Who are you? Really? I can find no trace of you, like, anywhere."

"Just a flesh and blood man. Nothing special."

Hailey shook her head and took a half step outside his bubble of magnetism.

"Why did you save my life? They would have killed me in the alley and tossed my body in the dumpster." Tilting her head back was the only way to meet his gaze, to assess his thought and action.

"Because one such as you likens to a fine wine if allowed to breathe. Discovery is half the journey, but nothing compared to the prize."

His smile detailed knowledge of his effect on her. Her gulp was audible.

"Damn, Hailey. Get right to it, why dontcha?" Addy whistled low in her left ear. Whether meant as a sign of encouragement or a dose of cold water, the result was the same.

Hailey jumped back, her fingers covering her mouth. She wasn't a virgin, but the dating well had been empty for far too long if she reacted like this to a near stranger with such careless behavior.

Knowing she was the only one who could hear Addy's voice didn't calm her racing heart.

"What?" Dante tilted his head to the side then closed his eyes, his right hand brushing his cheek. "That's the second time I've felt this. Each time you were near."

"Felt what?"

"Something… I don't know. Like someone touching my cheek."

"Addy, stop that. Right now."

"You haven't claimed him yet. That means he's fair game."

"No, he's not. You're a ghost, a spirit. Don't confuse him."

"I've investigated your background. Quite colorful. Your mother is reported to be active in the religious sector, if a bit secluded and private about her practices. Quite the humanitarian, though."

"Don't beat around the bush. You've read we're a bunch of Vodou fanatics."

"That's one way to put it. There are other theories, however. Ones I find fascinating. Tell me, are you and the gabby teen related in some way?" Undeterred, he again stepped into her space. He was using sexuality to throw her off balance.

The warm glowing feeling in Hailey's stomach suddenly turned to acid and roiled up into her chest. If he mentioned psychic ability or spirits, she'd hurl her breakfast on the expensive suit costing more than her truck.

"I-I don't know what you're talking about. Casper and I are not related."

"Let's not beat around the bush. You came here looking for the gun shipment."

"Was it yours?"

"No. It belongs to a, shall we say, concerned party. Does Babtiste have it stashed somewhere?"

"No. Someone shot him when he tried to intercept it. He didn't see the shooter."

"And you believe him? Is he safe?"

The fact he didn't ask for Babtiste's location was a definite plus. "He's safe, and I believe him. Someone blackmailed him into getting involved."

Why am I spilling my guts?

"Blackmailed by whom?"

"Doesn't know. All done by phone and email."

"Those can be traced."

"Working on it." If she didn't shore up her mental reserves soon, she'd regret it for all time to come.

"Would that be Casper's aspect of the investigation? After all, she does attend the school for the gifted elite. Not a far reach for a computer genius."

"Casper is staying out of this conversation."

Finally, a voice and a line drawn.

"Because of who's backing her? And, no, I haven't been able to figure out much. Every time I try, it's like I get sucked into a black hole, probably because of her adopted father, Major Clannahan." Dante held one hand up to forestall any argument. "I'm only interested in keeping her and the rest of the GE kids out of harm's way. She just doesn't seem to have an off switch."

"Are you working for the mob?"

"My employer wishes to remain anonymous. I do have an interest in keeping you and your sidekick alive and well. Her, because she's too young to be involved in this crap. And you, well, for other, more personal reasons."

"Again with the diversion? He's good, sis. Real good."

"Babtiste didn't kill Charlotte's assistant." She wanted, no, needed to see his reaction. Sincerity, confusion, a problem solver at work.

"Who did?"

The man appeared honestly baffled at the intricate twist of events.

"Maybe your employer?"

"No. At least not to my knowledge. Please, for your own safety, back out of this."

"I can't. Donald Fitzpatrick died out there in the bayou, his body left to the gators. He deserves justice."

Actual, physical pain crossed Dante's features. "He wasn't a dirty ATF agent. I can tell you that much."

"I know that."

"How? Are you conversant with the recently deceased?"

"Doesn't matter how I found out. I just know. He was working undercover, yes? Did someone make him for an undercover cop?"

"Again, I don't know. Don was a friend. A good one. His wife and daughter are devastated."

That was the first she'd heard of someone speaking about the ATF agent's family. The scenario hit too close to home.

Townsfolk had deemed her father a criminal until recent events brought his innocence to light after years of thinking the worst and enduring pitiful glances and whispered murmurs.

"Will you help them? His family?"

"They will be taken care of, physically and financially. As far as the emotional aspect... time will have to intervene there."

"Yeah, been there, done that." If she didn't leave soon, she'd be caught in his spell again.

"How'd you find me? How'd you know to come here?"

"I've had a small camera watching this place. After last night, I figured you'd come." His tone deepened, his concern heartfelt. "I was worried about you. Is that so hard to believe?"

A shake of her head was the only safe response. He offered limited denials and only in hopes of gaining something in return.

Addy's light slap along her cheek jolted her from her dreamlike state.

"Time to book, Hails. Trouble's coming."

"Shit."

"What?" Dante looked around, his air of casual disregard replaced with wariness. One hand moved to his back waist, under his jacket.

"Trouble. We have to leave, but I need to search this place."

"Don't bother. It's clean. According to surveillance, no one's entered here with anything bigger than a cigar box."

"Damn. Someone's coming. We gotta scoot."

With a hand on her shoulder, he ushered her out the door with murmured words brushing her ear. "One day, I want to know how you anticipate trouble headed your way with such precision."

She couldn't tell if it was a promise or a threat, and right now, didn't care.

When she rounded the corner and headed to her truck, Gunther hopped from one seat to the other. Excited chuffing signaled his anticipation in seeing the Italian.

"Not this time, boy." Hailey slid in and started to close the door, stopped by Dante's hand on the frame.

"Stay safe, Hailey. I look forward to cooking for you." His smile was genuine, showing perfect white teeth with a small gap.

"Thanks again for the books." She couldn't be mad at the thoughtful gift, despite the underhanded delivery.

He slammed the door, and she wasted no time, nor did she spare a thought for gas in jamming her foot on the accelerator.

"*Phew, that was close.*" Addy's voice floated up from the back seat.

"What kind of trouble did you see coming? And how?" Hailey looked in her rearview before making a turn at the end of the street. She didn't see Dante, who'd managed to fade into the shadows.

"Didn't see it, not like I have x-ray vision. I recognized it. I think I have a gift for sounds. As I said, things are different on this side."

Hailey spotted the same vehicle driven by the Jackyl who'd shot at her in an alleyway.

"Thanks, sis."

"*Anytime. Sorry I don't know more. It's so damn hard to navigate your world. I can hear things from a distance, but seeing and moving about—that's a whole different ballgame.*"

"You recognized the sound of the car?"

"Yeah, like I was riding in it."

"I didn't see where Dante—"

"He went out the back."

The morning's excursion raised more questions than it answered. Was Dante's presence a coincidence? Generally speaking, she didn't believe in such things.

By now, both Leigh and Trenton would be searching for her, one madder than hell that she'd removed the tracking device, the other exasperated.

In lieu of returning to the loft, she'd make a stop to check on Charlotte and her associates after last night's ordeal. To her knowledge, no one's statement had brought Casper into the scene.

Trenton would've questioned Charlotte for hours. Maybe that's why he was so surly over coffee this morning. He hated unsolved puzzles.

Chapter Twenty-One

Hailey

Gunther chuffed softly the moment she turned onto the rutted road to Upward Bound.

"Yes, boy. You can play while I talk to Charlotte, but don't get too rambunctious. Okay?"

Her answer came in the form of a sloppy kiss along her cheek.

"Thanks, fella. I love you too."

From what she understood, farm activity would increase during fall break. She still had a few hours before classes ended for the day. Several of the ranch's "new recruits" included two seniors and a junior at Hamchet High.

Charlotte had continued to make inroads and hired a new assistant to help manage the entity that had taken on a life of its own with community support.

How will last night's near tragedy affect them?

All seemed quiet at the moment with Charlotte's golden resting under the outstretched arms of a maple tree. He bounded over when she parked beside the SUV in front of the barn.

The vehicle's rear hatch was open.

Gunther hopped out the moment she slid from the seat. "Alrighty, then. Excited much?" It was good to watch them play. If only people could get along half as well.

"Charlotte?" If the lack of vehicles present stemmed from the threat presented by the Jackyls, life here would change, and not for the better. With Frederick on the loose, maybe Charlotte erred on the side of caution.

On the heels of that, she wondered, *Where's the officer assigned to be here?* Knowing Charlotte, she'd sent him away. The owner's stubborn reputation preceded her.

Gunther hadn't alerted to trouble and the golden retriever didn't appear injured.

The personnel door to the barn stood open, so she went inside where the smell of fresh cut hay reminded her of summers helping Leigh and Trenton stack bales in the Briner's loft. Horses had been Leigh's kryptonite as a teen.

From the office and extending sixty feet were tongue-and-groove stalls with grillwork covering the upper half of each section.

Exit doors locked open to their respective pasture offered each animal shelter or sunshine, whichever it preferred. Light flooded in to emphasize a clean and organized operation.

A door ajar opened to an office, the layout simple. The far side consisted of a brag wall, complete with two large shadow boxes full of ribbons. A freestanding bookcase underneath contained two shelves of trophies, some from the local 4-H chapter and others from nearby community centers. An oversized corkboard with dozens of photos took up most of the second wall.

Scuffing sounds preceded light thumping nearby. Hazy light from behind the desk, similar to landscape up lighting, created a creepy, malformed shadow figure on the wall.

Quiet steps to the wood-slatted chair clarified one question but raised many more. Light did in fact, emanate from below.

She didn't expect to see a hatch door under the knee well of the desk leading to a basement.

Who hides a basement, and does it extend below the entire barn?

At the bottom of the vertical stairs and reaching for a rung with her left hand, Charlotte looked up at the same time Hailey peered over the edge. The bore of the handgun pointing at Hailey's head encouraged her to freeze.

Charlotte let out a weary sigh. "Damn, I should've closed the door. Don't move, hon. I'll explain."

Thoughts whirled through Hailey's mind at lightning speed. The mission statement of Upward Bound openly denounced the use of guns or any kind of weapon, along with drugs.

Through the narrow view, light glinted off the grips of a half dozen handguns on the right-side shelf.

"You can explain a small armory? Great. Looking forward to it." The last thing Hailey should do included aggravating someone holding a gun. "Nice Glock. I have one just like it."

Charlotte emerged from the access and closed the hatch. A large square mat with a smaller extension covered the entry and provided a buffer between chair and floor.

"As you know by last night, tension between the Jackyls and, well, everybody else, has escalated. I have to protect my kids."

"So, your answer is to stock an armory? That goes against everything this place stands for."

Micro air currents against Hailey's right cheek registered Addy's unseen presence with the brush of ethereal fingers. Anything her sister said would remain between family.

"Sis, I've found out something interesting. She's not who you think she is. There's a twenty-by-twenty space down there with a shit load of weapons. All kinds of rifles and weird-looking round balls with pins on the top side."

"So, you've learned a lot about—life—from someone. What the hell is going on?"

"Touch her and find out." Addy's words brushed her ear like the wings of a butterfly.

Charlotte swept her hand back to indicate her sub-level stash. "The space is a panic room if shelter is needed and we can't get to the house, which by the way, also has one."

"You took the shipment and killed the ATF agent?"

Charlotte visibly deflated. "It... wasn't supposed to go like that. Really." She brought the barrel up when Hailey took a step back. "He got the drop on Babtiste, which I didn't expect to happen."

"You blackmailed your own man into doing your bidding? Did he know it was you?"

"No. I used a voice modulator. Survival mode teaches us all kinds of things." A look of desperation crept over the older woman's face. She stared at the corrugated walls as if they held the answers needed then shook her head before retrieving her phone and sending a one-handed text. "Damn. Just damn it."

"Why, Charlotte?"

"It was the only way I could think to get them. Gang life is stealing my kids' lives, both literally and emotionally. You've seen that with the few times you've brushed up against them."

"So you decided to fight fire with fire."

"I can't sit by and watch them kill my kids. When our latest arrivals left the Jackyls with precious information, I had to take the opportunity offered. The gang was planning to ambush the ATF agent farther up the river."

"Donald was relaying the weapons for the local chapter of organized crime?"

"Yes, and the Jackyls wanted a cut of the business. It was a perfect setup. One I couldn't resist. Every year, senseless violence cuts my kids down. You saw that when they locked you in the mausoleum."

"Why'd you shoot the ATF agent?"

"I-I didn't set out to shoot him." Charlotte covered her mouth as if to prevent specific truths from spilling out. "It all went so wrong. I didn't want anyone to get hurt." Anguish and the need for understanding seemed to freeze Charlotte in place.

In part to offer comfort and in part to close the distance between them to wrangle the gun away, Hailey reached out and touched Charlotte's bare forearm. A vision snapped into place, like watching a movie in fast-forward mode.

"The ATF agent was going to arrest Babtiste, and you shot to protect your friend." Hailey made the statement, not expecting a rebuttal.

"I couldn't let Babtiste take the fall." Tears rolled down Charlotte's face. "I'd taken my dad's old rifle. I just meant to scare him off, make him set Babtiste free. I didn't mean to kill him. It was an accident."

"Who shot Babtiste here at the farm?"

Before receiving an answer, another vision assaulted Hailey's mind. This one more vicious. "Why'd you kill your assistant?"

Charlotte flinched but didn't lower the barrel of her gun, a scant inch from Hailey's stomach. "Because she found out I'd gotten the guns."

"So, you collected them and brought them down here. Did Babtiste catch you unloading them?"

"No. I had nothing to do with Babtiste getting shot. Is he okay?"

"He's recovering. He'll be fine."

"I heard a shot that night, but by the time I got outside, I didn't see anyone. I didn't know they'd shot Babtiste."

"You saw blood on the porch, and used bleach to clean it."

"Oh, my god. It's true." Charlotte snatched her arm away as if just realizing what was happening. Her sidestep put distance between them. "You've got some kind of," Charlotte waved her hand in Hailey's general direction, "...thing going on. You're reading me some way." The barrel that had started to sag toward the ground now snapped up waist high.

So intent on solving the puzzle of who did what, Hailey neglected to consider the bigger picture. "No, Charlotte. I'm not."

"How'd you get the drop on them at the festival? That fog. There was nothing natural about that, not the way it appeared, and not the way it vanished after authorities made their arrests."

A new resolve shone from Charlotte's eyes. One boding ill for anyone in her way. No one could doubt the dedication to her mission or the lengths she'd go to protect it.

"I don't create fog, Charlotte. I don't have a magic wand, or whatever." Their tenuous relationship had changed in the space of several heartbeats.

"I won't let you destroy all the work I've done here. This morning, I received a call from Frederick."

Hailey knew what was coming before the next words cleared Charlotte's lips.

"He offered me a truce, a trade, with a bonus. He's willing to forego his vendetta toward me and mine if I deliver you to him. Apparently, he's set his sights on bigger game."

"He's trying to get out of the charges leveled on him from the warehouse fiasco where he shot at me. Plus, there are the items found in his house linking him to multiple murders."

"That all stemmed from you and that girl who hangs around with you... a partner perhaps? Kinda young."

"She's just a kid who misses home and likes attention."

Maybe the first part is true, but sure as hell not the second.

"Shame she couldn't mind her own business. Frederick's gonna get her too."

"If we disappear, so does the case against them," Hailey surmised.

"I'm sorry you got involved in all this. I am. But I'm doing important work that needs to continue. We're saving lives here."

"You'll be setting a killer free."

"The world is full of murderers, and this one has promised to not interfere with me or mine."

"And you're taking the word of a snake like that? How long do you think it will last? A week? A month?"

"It's the best I can do." Her fingers holding the Glock tightened before the barrel wiggled, motioning her to move. "C'mon. Let's get this over with."

"Let me guess. You need to wash your hair?"

Charlotte's mouth flattened into a straight line. "I'm trading one life for those of my kids. The ones who come here seeking asylum."

The soft brush of Addy's fingers along her cheek warned Hailey not to jump. *"Sis, I can nudge the barrel, but you might get shot."*

"Then don't try, Addy. Leigh always says, 'Pick your time.'"

She had minutes to disentangle the mess but was unable to assimilate all she'd taken in. The woman who'd hired her carried so much of the evil she claimed to abhor.

"Charlotte, you're betting the entire enchilada on Frederick not wanting revenge on someone who has humiliated him in front of his following. You've taken those he considers his possessions. The rest would do anything for him, including taking hostages and murder.

"Since he wants to get his hooks into the Gifted Elite school, he's got other things occupying his mind."

Hailey pivoted and walked out at the older woman's urging. Each step drained a little more heat from her face. Her furry companion, so in tune with her emotions and nonverbal body language, stopped romping with his playmate and whined.

"You have a choice. You can leave your dog here where he'll be taken care of, or I can shoot him now."

Gunther stalked forward when Charlotte emerged with a gun, his body tightening, tail out, and white showing around his eyes. Hailey gave him a down command, repeated when the gun jabbed her in the back.

"I don't want to shoot a dog."

"But you don't mind killing me?" Hailey focused and calmed her thoughts. Gunther was perceptive. "Stay there, boy."

"Hails, this bitch is a liter shy of a full tank. I don't know what to do."

"Where are you taking me?"

"For a ride, north to the Big Thicket Preserve. We'll take your truck. Frederick can ditch it somewhere."

Hailey turned her head to the side to give the appearance of speaking to her furry companion. "Go play with Simon, boy." Since Addy could find her from anywhere, she sent her in search of Casper in the hope of getting help.

"My dog's name isn't Simon." Charlotte gestured for Hailey to slide into the driver's seat after opening the door. "If you start the engine before I'm seated behind you, I'll blow your head off."

"Understood." Unfortunately, so did her dog, at least the intent.

Gunther whined but stayed with Hailey's hand signal.

"Don't worry, boy. You're gonna be okay. I'll find a nice home for you. You'll forget your master in no time." Sincere regret didn't alter Charlotte's plan.

The back door opened then a slight dip indicated Charlotte sliding onto the back seat.

"I'm sure you know the way there as much as you tromp around the bayous with your camera."

"That text you sent earlier was to Frederick?"

"Yes. One life versus many. Not a good trade, but the best I can manage."

Hailey had no idea how long it would take Addy to find Casper. If successful, hopefully the teen would call Leigh or Trenton. Hell, even her adoptive father, the one simply called the major. This was a situation even Casper wouldn't walk into blind.

Would she?

An eternity of regrets piled higher with each mile driven. Bayous equaled stereotypical dumping grounds for good reason. Hailey had almost become one of those statistics months ago when she stumbled across a faculty member of the Gifted Elite wanting to expand his distribution ring for counterfeit money.

Now, she had more immediate problems. Would her death be quick and painless?

No, that wasn't Frederick's MO. He was a sadist and reportedly liked his victims to suffer for hours or days so he could enjoy their fear and desperation. She wondered if the officer assigned to watch her loft had called Leigh and Trenton and begun a search.

Even so, they wouldn't know where to start.

"This is murder, Charlotte."

"This is a trade. A noble opportunity to save kids from becoming monsters."

"You're saying it takes a monster to save others?"

"Shut up and drive. This is a necessity. If you'd stayed out of it last night, this wouldn't be happening. It's more your fault than mine."

"If I'd stayed out of it last night, you'd be dead now." Truth held no weight in light of cowardly desperation.

Miles passed in utter silence. What was there to say to a person who'd lost perspective?

Many regrets flitted across Hailey's mind. Trenton and his penchant for overprotection, Leigh and the antics they'd shared growing up, and Casper, a young warrior type who never quit and never backed down.

When she left the world of the living, she hoped to find Casper and guide the young woman away from a lifetime of mistakes.

Though she loved her mother and homespun family with all her heart, she'd never truly loved a man and never known the soft caress of a child's first touch. In her mind, there'd always been time for that in the future, after the next case.

Now, she'd enter her sister's realm.

Prickly pear cactus and yucca passed their blooming stage but dotted the landscape. Rich greens contrasted the bed of pine leaves when scant traffic thinned out to nothing.

Texas consisted of a more diverse topography than most outlanders understood. It was true that parts were a breeding ground for mosquitos, gators, and snakes, yet even that land was magnificent by virtue of unspoiled beauty. Other areas were flat, dry, and desert-like.

Eight unique climate zones spanned the gamut to offer diversity in both topography and the creatures that called it home.

She'd hiked or kayaked through bayous and was vaguely familiar with their destination. It was a relatively high area, especially during a dry spell. Either way, it was obvious they planned to kill her and bury her body where no one would find her.

She'd seen little sign of civilization after their path dwindled to wheel tracks through weedy flatland. Each mile lessened the likelihood of help arriving in time.

Charlotte tapped her on the shoulder with the barrel of her Glock. "Turn left up ahead by that knotty tree and follow the tire tracks."

Heavy stands of Blackjack Oak and loblolly pine took the place of open fields and prairie grass. They entered a section of arid sandy land created when ancient seas and flood events deposited sufficient sand to form dunes and sand hills. Most would see it as a soothing place, a retreat.

Hailey knew it as the last thing she'd see.

The truck dipped on the nonexistent road and slid Hailey into her door, nothing compared to what she'd soon feel at Frederick's behest.

Tire tracks indicated passage over the path to where she suspected they'd leave her body.

Strange that Charlotte remained mute. Maybe she thought her trade justified, more likely, she just wanted to save her own skin.

There was little time to contemplate what lay ahead, torture or a bullet to the back of her head. Two vehicles sat parked beside a grouping of tall pines ahead. A small berm with a variety of beer cans and plastic cans filled with sand formed a gang-style pistol range.

"For what it's worth, Hailey. I *am* sorry."

"Sure you are." *How is it she can excuse murder with an apology.*

Her truck rolled to a stop in front of her executioners. She took a deep breath and left the keys in the ignition. She wouldn't need them unless a miracle unfolded.

Four Jackyl members leaned against their hoods, smiles stretched over each face. One was toothless with a nose that had probably been broken more times than he could count.

Bird tattoos covered the bald head of the wiry man beside him.

One was young with eyes continuously flicking between his comrades and Hailey. Fear and uncertainty characterized his nervous twitching and repeated motion of stuffing his hands in his pockets and then crossing his arms over his chest.

The last man stood out.

Frederick.

He pushed off the hood and ambled forward with his thumbs hooked in the front of his jeans.

In stepping out, she noted the bayou perfume that permeated miles of deserted land. It'd always smelled like home. Now, it would be.

Charlotte exited the truck behind her and kept her gun pressed tight to her prisoner's back. "Frederick, here she is. All yours. This makes us square, yes?"

The gang leader offered a noncommittal shrug. "Looks like you delivered her after all. I was wonderin' if I'd have to send my crew to pick her up again. That was real thoughtful." Frederick's wary gaze assessed Hailey as he might a snake.

"You have no idea what trouble's heading your way, asshole." Dissing the killer who held her life in his hands wasn't smart. It was, however, unavoidable.

Hailey wanted him to know, if he did succeed in his initial plan, eventually he'd fail, and suffer. If not by her own hand, then by Addy's.

The leader's sneer faltered for a second before he regained his composure. He made no move to come closer. "Bet you're not bulletproof now, without your little friend. Can't wait to get a hold of that one. Maybe you'll get lucky, and I'll bury you side by side. You two can keep each other company for eternity."

"You have no idea what happens after death, about the spirit world or their vengeful natures." Hailey offered a malicious smile and took a small pleasure in seeing Frederick and his men blanch.

A faint brushing along her cheek advised she was no longer alone.

"Addy? You getting a good look at all these faces?" Speaking out loud and seeing their reaction gave her small pleasure.

"Yeah, sis. I'm here."

"Why don't you let every person here feel your presence?" Each gang member stood up straight, tense.

"My pleasure, sis."

One by one, the men shuddered and moved in a disjointed manner.

"Hailey, I don't know what Casper's got up her sleeve, but she said to stall them as long as you can. Help is coming."

"Enough of this," Frederick commanded at the same time slapping the back of his neck. "When the puta is dead, the problem is over.

Hailey's question remained. Would help come in time?

Chapter Twenty-Two

Hailey

Sunlit swaths lanced through gaps in the canopy above to create a dappled effect on the carpet of pine leaves underfoot. It was a world unto itself if left unsullied by human contact. Not many appreciated the beauty or serenity.

Hailey stumbled forward when Charlotte shoved using the barrel of her gun. Windmilling her arms didn't prevent her graceless landing on all fours.

She stood immediately.

Toothless chuckled and offered lewd comments.

"Ouch." Charlotte rubbed the back of her head. "Damn mosquitos are bigger than starlings and just as irritating."

"Bitch. Hurt my sister and I'll make it my afterlife's mission to haunt your ass. Every. Waking. Moment," Addy hissed behind Hailey. She was able to affect small things, but nothing on the scale that would facilitate an escape.

Three of the Jackyls remained aloof, off to the side, with Frederick standing and taking point.

Redness and swelling around the tattoos on Frederick's knuckles indicated a recent fight, probably during his escape from the detention center. The left side of his mouth sported signs of a split lip.

"She's all yours now," Charlotte murmured in turning to go. "I trust we'll have no further involvement."

"Just one thing," Frederick said with a slight hand gesture to his crew.

Charlotte hadn't gone three steps when a single gunshot rang out, fired from Toothless, the oldest of the three leaning against his car. After spitting in the dirt, he smiled.

Charlotte's body swiveled in slow motion as the gun she'd held dropped to the ground. Blood spread in a widening circle on her shirt. A mask of utter disbelief slid from her face, her gaze accusing Hailey of betrayal. Sputtering gasps emitted crimson spittle from the corner of her mouth as she face-planted in the soft pine bedding.

Her body twitched several times in an attempt to move, denied with the release of her last breath. No dignity, no compassion, not a care for what they treated as the lowest form of animal.

It was no way to die.

Frederick spat on the body. "Stupid bitch. You were never gonna walk away after stealing what I intended to take. I'll tear your place apart board by board and kill every animal there until I find that shipment."

He shuffled to stand face to face with Hailey, having gained a measure of confidence after ordering Charlotte's death. "Not so tough or proud now, *perra.* I own your ass. Soon, I'll have the little black-haired she-devil too."

Foul breath washed down her face, smelling worse than the bodies in the mausoleum where they'd left her for dead days prior.

In a preemptive attempt to direct the conversation away from Casper, Hailey snorted. "It's only a matter of time before the cops hunt you down. They'll find another way to link you to those murders."

"Cops won't be a problem for me or mine." Frederick shrugged as if he had no pressing cares. "Their case will crumble without any witnesses. 'Cuz you see, they no longer have any evidence."

The gang leader leaned down to study her face. His eyes narrowed with closer scrutiny. "You're not wearing contacts... so the rumors are true?"

"Frankly, there are so many rumors, you'll have to be more specific."

"They claim you're a Vodou priestess."

"Why? You want a sample of my work?"

"Addy, I could sure use your help about now."

"I don't have any chickens for you to slaughter, *puta.*" Frederick made a point of leaning around Hailey to stare at Charlotte's body. "I think it's all smoke and mirrors. Party tricks."

"I don't kill. Period."

"Then what good are you? What other talents do you have?"

The word talent hit too close to the mark. "How'd you like to feel ants crawling across your scalp and skin for the rest of your life?"

Whether by suggestion or Addy's influence, Frederick scratched the back of his head and scrubbed a hand down his face.

"Oooh, Hails. I could do this forever. Watch this."

Frederick's eyes widened, his jaw dropped. Both hands flew to his crotch, rubbed while squirming. "What are you doing?" With obvious Herculean effort, he dropped his hands to his sides and stood tall. His men couldn't see the way he scrunched his eyes tight.

The knife he whipped out from his back pocket extended with a flick of his wrist. "Stop it or I'll start cutting."

"*Addy, want to try a little possession?*"

"*I've been trying but haven't gotten the hang of it yet.*"

"*It's all right. There's four of them here anyway, and they all look damned determined to see me dead.*"

Again, Addys' voice rung strong in Hailey's ear. "*I'm sorry. I'm trying, but it's not working.*"

"Stupid *puta*." Frederick sneered. "I don't have many enemies yet, but I'm gearing up for war. I'm afraid your little stunt has no value."

In a lightning-fast move belying her fear, Hailey latched onto Frederick's hand. It might be the last useful thing she did, and she might take the knowledge to her grave, but she'd get the information out there through Casper.

A flood of visions assaulted her mind.

"You stole your first car in Amaranth when still a kid, got sent to juvie. As soon as you ran away, you were a lookout while your buddies robbed a guy in the laundry mat."

Frederick's eyes widened and he tried to yank his hand away. "I never got caught for that. Who you been talking to?"

Hailey held tight and ignored him, continuing, "You raped an elderly lady in her home outside of Grandbury. Didn't get caught for that either. You stole her ring, which you gave to a girl to lure her into your lifestyle. Didn't work, though. She saw the real you."

Frederick's hand whipped back and slapped her hard, knocking her backward. If they were one on one, she could handle herself.

Unfortunate for her, Frederick had backup, and she wasn't bulletproof.

"You're gonna take those secrets to your grave."

"Kill me and you'll never know a minute's peace. In fact, not only will I haunt you into eternity, I'll call all the other local spirits to join me. You'll go mad within months, but I think we can manage to draw it out longer."

"Liar. The minute you die, so does your influence over the spirit world, if you can control them at all." Glancing over his shoulder, he nodded to the one still holding his gun. "Stick her in the box. She'll have a day to contemplate her mistakes in life."

She had no choice other than to move when Toothless waved his gun. Short and wiry with a grin no one should see, he pointed to a trampled footpath leading deeper into the shadowy interior. "Your spot is all ready."

His two companions picked up Charlotte's lifeless body by the shoulders and dragged her along behind them.

Hailey barely heard Addy's words over the thundering of her heart. Acid churned in her belly. Her breaths became shorter.

"They're gonna put you in a box, sis. Alive."

Panic set in. She wasn't claustrophobic, but she had a very strict aversion to death.

They didn't walk far, thirty yards at best, before trees thinned to reveal a small clearing with two piles of dirt next to grave-size holes. A shovel protruded from each dirt pile.

"Don't worry, *puta*. We have a special surprise for you." Toothless grinned. "Because you are special, you get your very own box. Charlotte here gets nothing."

To prove his point, he jutted his chin toward the first shallow grave. Two feet deep, it wouldn't prevent animals from investigating and digging up the remains in the coming weeks.

They dumped Charlotte's body unceremoniously, as if her worth equaled no more than a dead rat.

Toothless grabbed Hailey by the back of the neck and leaned in close. "While you're still alive, think about all the things you could've done with your life instead of meddling in our business. It didn't have to be this way."

She barely heard the words. What drew her attention was the vision inspired by his touch.

"It was you. You shot Babtiste when he returned to Upward Bound." The accusation or response meant little.

Toothless smiled. "Yeah. Thought he was so clever, a regular James Bond. Always did hate that wimp. Serves him right to die like a dirty pig."

With that revelation, he turned her head to face her fate.

The second grave contained a wooden box, a crude homemade coffin. When she turned to voice her refusal, all she saw was the butt end of a gun flying toward her head.

Pain spread from impact with a narrowing of her visual field. A lifetime of regrets passed in a heartbeat. All the things she hadn't done and things she hadn't said.

She felt weightless, her body crumbling as she fell forward.

She never felt the landing.

* * * *

Casper hated the very thought of asking Trenton for help. It went against her nature. He wasn't part of her makeshift family. He had no talent and might be a giant pain in the ass when it came to battle. Not that he was worthless. He was just... normal. Well, maybe above normal, but still nosy as hell.

An anonymous tip wouldn't cut it, nor would it direct him to the right location in time. *She* wouldn't even find it in time without Addy's help. The spirit's only exchange with the living included Casper and Hailey.

To his credit, Trenton answered her call on the first ring with a, *"Where is she?"* Without receiving explanations other than, *"In deep shit,"* he'd arrived at her designation in a screech of wheels.

He now drove like a madman, taking curves on less than four wheels while talking on his Bluetooth, forming and coordinating his plan on the fly.

She respected that. For a non-psychic, he was turning out to be handy. Maybe there was hope for him after all.

It sounded like Leigh on the other end of the conversation fared about the same. *"How is it you're heading toward the preserve and not know exactly where to go? I'm heading in that direction. Send me your coordinates as you can."*

Trenton disconnected the call using the steering wheel control and growled. "Where is she, Casper?"

"I think it's a place near Surly Knots?"

"You don't know? You're the one leading this posse."

"I know the name of the park, but I haven't hiked every inch of the area. So... no. But, there's an old shack out there in need of razing. She heard that name, and from there will guide us."

"She? Who is she?" Trenton glared at her in the passenger seat.

"What? Nothing. Just drive. We have bigger problems."

"Really?"

"The shack used to be a bar that trafficked drugs on the side. Hence its position in the middle of nowhere. They catered to those exiting the national park."

"For not knowing where we're going, you're spewing a lot of history. I barely remember that and I used to live in the area." Trenton swerved to miss a possum scurrying across the dirt road.

"Well, obviously I'm too young to drink and don't frequent bars." Casper smirked. "And I don't do drugs. I hear they're bad for your health."

"Right. Tell me again how you know all this?"

"I heard one of the Jackyls bragging to his buddies he was gonna be out here taking care of a problem. When I couldn't get hold of Hailey, I knew it was her. Especially after last night."

"How many am I facing?"

Casper closed her eyes and held tight to the amulet. A minute later, she nodded. "Four, one of which is Frederick. See? I can be of use. You'll save the girl and catch the fugitive, all in one swipe."

Again, she received a glare. "You have no business being involved in this."

"Hey, these assholes are trying to gain a foothold at the school. Do you have any idea what they succeeded in influencing even a few of those kids?"

"Yet you're not really one of them, and don't belong there. Care to elaborate?"

Casper crossed her arms over her chest and shoved back into the passenger seat. "Jeez. Try and do a good deed and all you get is a bunch of shit. I should've handled this myself. My way."

"And what exactly is your way, Miss Decuir?"

"Not involving federal assholes who constantly poke me with questions, that's for sure."

"Look. I know you're more like Hailey than the other kids at that school. Even if we all come out of this relatively unscathed, *I* know it's not the last time you and Hails will find trouble. I swear I won't divulge your secrets. After all, I keep the ones Hailey holds tight. You've got to trust someone sometime."

"I have an entire family back home I trust."

"Yeah, in Pennsylvania. They're not close enough to help. I am. Think about it."

"You'd be surprised," she snapped while finishing with the thought, *At what my family can do.* But the truth was, Casper did think about it. Having a fed in her corner could be a big help. At one time, her family had questioned whether or not to let Major Clannahan in on their secrets, and that turned out fine.

If he used her cover name to drive home a point, Casper missed it entirely. "You should save your energy, you know, since you're at least five minutes ahead of your backup."

"You said Hailey might not have the time."

"She does now." Casper knew she'd made a mistake with the last words uttered. She currently dealt with a man who bore no psychic talent, just an in-depth perception and determination to save a friend. They had that in common.

"Uh-huh. Care to elaborate?"

"No." Nervous tension wasn't relieved when Simon patted her head. The capuchin monkey wrapped his tail around her neck and laid his cheek against her own.

"Surly teen."

"Uptight fed. Ya know, if you'd remove the stick from your ass, you'd have a much better chance with Hailey."

Trenton's hands tightened on the steering wheel. "Hailey and I are friends. That is all we'll ever be."

It was Casper's turn with, "*Uh-huh.*"

"We're just a couple minutes out. How about I drop you behind—"

"No."

"You didn't hear me out. This is for your own safety."

"Still no. You won't find her without my help. I'm more qualified than you realize."

"Yeah, I've been picking up that vibe. Would love an explanation."

Heavily forested land protected by the state and federal governments offered miles of hiding places and possible burial sites. When all was said and done, Casper would have to come back for a long hike. The dead deserved justice too.

"Trent," she tried out his shortened name used by his sister and friends. "The more time you waste with useless probing, the less time you have to figure out what to do when we get there."

"Well, it's not like I can assess the situation before I arrive." One brow arched and his lips twisted with his next side-glance. "Care to help with that?"

"How?"

"It could save her life."

"I don't think it'll change anything at this point, but there are four Jackyls you'll need to fend off while I help Hailey." Her friend lay unconscious in a coffin, buried under several feet of loamy dirt. What she couldn't discern was the amount of blood seeping from the head wound or the stability of her vital signs.

Trenton started to slam on the brakes then apparently thought better of it. "When we get there, you follow orders. Got it?"

"I hear you." *But I don't take orders.*

She should've called Kiera. Maybe. Using a portal, they could've gotten Hailey out safe and healed. While the fed already knew too much, chipping away at Casper's secrets, nothing compared to saving her partner.

In counterpoint, the current operation also offered the ability to collect evidence that would be viable in court. Working semi-within the law was a new thing she was trying out.

What if Hailey ends up with permanent brain damage?

By the time she'd tapped Trenton, she figured Frederick intended Hailey to survive and suffer, at least until suffocating in the coffin.

Grabbing hold of her amulet, Casper projected an image of Addy, willing her to come forward so she could ask, "How's she doing?"

"Who are you talking to?" Trenton stared, his jaw slack, then refocused on the road and jerked the wheel to avoid a turkey vulture.

"Not now, Trenton. I'm busy."

Subtle throat clearing from the back seat, unheard by Trenton, drew her attention. Addy's translucent form appeared, flickering in and out of focus. *"She's alive. Frederick's thug knocked her unconscious and she's still bleeding. I did what I could to stop it. I tried, but I couldn't possess any of them."*

The spirit's words radiated a mix of sorrow, worry, and low self-esteem.

"Don't worry. We'll work on it." Again, she'd spoken aloud, realized when witnessing Trenton's expression.

"What exactly are *we* going to work on?" he asked.

"Not now, dude."

Addy pointed to a giant oak with three large burls, developed as a protective response to disease. *"There. Tell him to turn left there."*

"Hey, turn left by that deformed tree sticking out over the road."

"How'd you know that?"

"Because it's under the cloud shaped like an elephant. That's where we turn."

"Could you be a little more specific?"

"Shaped like Dumbo. Now. Do you want to save your *friend* or talk shit?" *There, fed. Set your priorities.*

Trenton grumbled something too low to discern, but turned onto the rutted path. Rounding the last of a snaking S-turn, a bone-chilling view opened up.

"Over there. That's Hailey's truck."

"Damn. And another car."

"Yeah, I told you there are four of them. You should give me a gun."

Trenton made an irritated noise in the back of his throat, ignoring her suggestion.

"Sorry, fed. I didn't think they'd all still be here. We got this, just the same."

"And how can you be sure how many Jackyls are present?"

"Talk, Trenton. I heard them talking."

"Do you even know how to shoot?" The words slipped out as if he considered giving her his backup weapon.

"Well, I have favorites, to be sure. I prefer a Sig Sauer Cross PRS rifle for long-range. Its steel structure, even weight distribution, and folding stock make for easy movement. For close range, I prefer a Glock, though. But I've been eyeing Hailey's Hellcat Pro. I like that grip better."

Trenton stared in disbelief before jerking the wheel to correct his course after veering off the path. "Dear God. What is happening? I cannot in good conscience consider giving a gun to a kid."

"And yet you bring one to an active crime scene. We are all more than the sum of our parts, fed man. You'll figure that out soon enough."

"They must be in the woods." Trenton scanned the area, letting his foot lighten on the gas pedal.

Grabbing the amulet that facilitated her connection with the spirit realm, Casper asked, "Where are these yahoos, Addy?"

"Who's Addy?"

Casper merely shook her head. Damn it, she'd lost focus and spoken out loud instead of inside her head.

The spirit again appeared in the back seat, playing with Trenton's hair. "*They're partying over the graves.*"

"Who are you talking to?" Trenton asked.

"The great cosmos. Now, quiet while I figure this out. Is your distraction ready?" At this point, it didn't matter what Trenton heard.

"What distraction?" Trenton's expression darkened.

Addy's voice came lower, more urgent. "*Yes, Simon's gonna help me keep Frederick busy until Colson arrives.*"

Casper ignored the fed's question in favor of, "Okay, Trenton. Looks like these guys are in the woods."

"Yeah, but not for long. They'll hear our approach." Obviously preferring a fast entrance over a quiet one, Trenton gunned the engine.

Deep potholes sent Casper against the roof, causing her to grab the door handle with one hand and the center console with the other. "Jeez, you drive like Dacien."

"Who's Dacien?"

"A friend who drives worse than a blind man." No doubt, he's quiz her without end about Dacien too.

Trenton skidded to a halt behind Hailey's truck, just as a hole appeared in his windshield with a loud popping noise.

Concordial fractures radiated from the central breach like misshapen spokes of a bike's wheel. The coordinating exit in the passenger window determined the angle and position of the shooter.

Casper grabbed Trenton's forearm, refocusing his attention. "I'm gonna hold onto you, for just a minute."

"What, like you're scared? Duck! And keep your head down." Trenton drew his service weapon and opened his door.

Three more shots hit the SUV. The second would've killed the agent before he'd had a chance to return fire if not for Casper keeping her grip on his arm.

"It's coming more from my side." If she let him get hurt, Hailey would never forgive her.

Three of the four gang members took cover behind trees. Only two appeared to be popping out to shoot. They'd lack Trenton's training, but a stray bullet could catch him just the same.

Frederick was nowhere in sight.

Trenton slid out and used his door for cover. Taking aim, he fired two rounds in quick succession, nailing the tree where a Jackyl hid.

Casper opened her door and slid out despite Trenton's shouted warning. By phasing her body, she could make it to cover and slip through to where they'd buried her partner.

If the shooters followed her, so much the better for protecting the fed. No doubt, Frederick's entire gang hunted her with equal fervor. She was a more open target than the federal officer.

The roar of another engine changed her direction before she'd taken her second step. Casper rushed to the back of the SUV and waited for Leigh to emerge.

In the driver's seat, Leigh's eyes rounded with shock. The local detective was out of the vehicle with her gun drawn when a shot pierced her vehicle's grill.

She met Casper and urged her to crouch. "Is he crazy? What are you doing here?"

"Hey, I'm here to help. There's three at the wood line, at least two with guns. Frederick is hanging back. He's being, uh, held by others."

"Others? Others who? Colson's ETA is seven minutes. He'll be coming from over there." The sheriff's deputy pointed toward the woods.

"Yeah, help Trenton. I can bolt around the edge of that small berm and find Hailey." Casper tried to give Leigh a light shove in the direction that offered more cover.

"No." She was having none of it. "Get in my truck and get the hell out of here. Keys are inside."

"No... I'm more like Hailey than you realize. I'm going to get her." Casper pointed toward Trenton. "You help him."

Casper bolted toward the small berm that would shield her from the fed's view. If one of the gang members moved and happened to get a lucky shot, the bullet would pass through her phased body. Something she didn't care to explain.

Twice, she heard the whiz of a leaded projectile passing nearby. Apparently, the thugs hadn't learned their lesson. They could see her in living color, but targeting her was a different matter. Chipped bark from trees flew in various directions, some through her torso.

"*Straight this way, Casper. Follow me.*"

"*Is Simon with Frederick?*"

"*Actually, he's on Frederick. He's really getting the hang of moving physical objects. He picked up a small rock!*"

"Good. Maybe he can teach you how it's done when this is over."

Casper flailed her phased arms, reaching out but not connecting with viny briars in passing. A little distraction for the criminal element could help the badges. If the asshats engaged in a firefight with both local and federal authorities then saw and decided on what they'd suspect a softer target, she'd educate them into an early grave.

Psychic style.

She didn't flinch when stepping on a riled copperhead. It couldn't bite through the bottom of her boot.

"*Addy, show me where exactly Hailey's buried.*"

With the next footfalls, she broke into a small meadow and saw the noncorporeal help floating next to her.

"*This way. She just woke up and is starting to panic.*"

Casper corrected her course and ran toward the freshly turned dirt.

"She's buried in a coffin here." Addy's translucent arm pointed to one of two mounds, between which lay two shovels.

"What's Frederick doing now?" she asked.

"Being entertained by the ATF agent." Addy giggled. *"Fitzpatrick is using a small stick to whip the bastard."*

Termination of loud pops signaled Trenton's firefight over. That left her little time to extract her friend and concoct a sufficient story to explain current events.

She dropped to hands and knees and phased her right arm into the earth as deep as she could go. It wasn't far enough to reach the coffin.

"Damn. I'm gonna have to dig a bit first." She could hear the echo of Hailey's enraged screams.

Hold on. Hold on. I'm coming.

"Addy, go assess her. Tell her I'm digging her out now."

One shovelful of dirt after another slung over her shoulder. Her muscles ached within minutes. Judging by the muffled sounds heard, she guessed Hailey's position, her head on the right side of the grave.

She needed to get her out before Trenton and Leigh found them. Otherwise, she'd have to devise a suitable explanation of how she found the graves to begin with, not to mention all the other details they'd demand.

Once she'd cleared enough dirt to reach into the crude box, she lay on the ground and stretched. She'd just reached the other side of the wooden barrier when hearing Trenton and Leigh calling from a distance.

Damn.

Hailey grasped her hand after a touch on her head.

Casper tugged her up and out. Dirt smudged both their faces, but each breathed a sigh of relief.

"Thanks, partner." Hailey wrapped Casper in a tight hug. "I knew Addy could find you."

"No problem, but we need to open this up more because, well, I can't explain how you escaped a half-covered grave and a closed coffin. So, grab a shovel. Let's get our stories straight before company arrives."

"Casper?" Trenton called from a distance with as much aggravation as trepidation.

Both women huffed with each shovelful of dirt flung over their shoulders.

"Is Addy still here?" Hailey asked. Touching her cheek a second later, she said, "Thanks, sis. I owe you again."

"I don't know where Frederick and the others are." Hailey bent at the waist to rest her hands on her knees when Casper reached down to open the crude box. "But I owe those assholes a solid kick in the groin."

"Hailey?" From deeper in the shadows, Colson and one of his deputies stepped forward holding a wild-eyed Frederick between them. "You okay?"

Frederick dug in, his legs stiffening along with his body at the sight of Hailey. "Keep me away from that bitch. She's possessed."

"Aw, now, Freddy. Is that any way to speak to a lady?" Casper ambled forward, slowed when Hailey slung an arm around her shoulders.

"Easy, partner. We've got eyes watching and enough questions to answer. Let's not create more."

Frederick twisted in Colson's grasp. "No, man. I'm serious. She's, like, really possessed. Don't let her touch you. She can hex you. Hell, she can do it from a distance."

As if to prove his point, Frederick suddenly screamed and tried to grab his head. On the heels of that, he rubbed his hands over his arms and chest as much as his constraints allowed. "Get her off me. Get her off!"

Hailey, still ten yards away, merely rolled both shoulders. "I think he's been doing too many of his own drugs."

"Where're Leigh and Trenton?" Colson asked, struggling to contain his prisoner.

"They've got the other three jackasses secured," Casper advised, then added with the back of her hand on her forehead, an imitation of a drama queen. "And thank heavens for that. I was so scared."

Behind them, a low snort heralded Trenton's arrival. "Try again, kiddo. This time with more feeling." The fed ignored Casper's mock outrage and stalked toward Hailey, grabbing her upper arms and pulling her in tight for a hug. "Good to have you back. Are you done investigating this now?" He kissed the top of her head and closed his eyes. "Please don't do this again. Okay?"

"I'm fine. And I'd like a large coffee with beignets." The feel of his arms around her was so right, so welcome. She felt the steady beat of his heart against her cheek and knew she was where she belonged. An involuntary shudder coursed through her body when he toyed with her long hair.

"How 'bout a shower first." Trenton sniffed conspicuously then chuckled but didn't let go.

Hailey filled in the details on the trek back to their vehicles. If gaps existed in their accounting of events while they gave statements, Addy would act the go between to iron them out. Funny that no one thought to separate Hailey and Casper, a normal procedure with such events.

EMS arrived along with the coroner's van. The designated snoops were wrapped in blankets and vital signs checked.

Frederick required multiple restraints to keep him in place. He had no visible injuries. His babbling about ghosts holding him to the ground and doing unspeakable things before Lt. Colson's arrival earned serious side-eye from the medics. As he spoke, his body contorted, his gasping pleas contributed to drugs he must have taken.

Hailey watched the spectacle sitting on the ambulance's bumper and listening to Casper's rude comments while Trenton watched, rubbing the back of his neck.

Leigh sidled up to where Casper stood and stared directly at the teen. "Friends of yours or hers?"

"I've no idea what you're talking about." Casper couldn't contain her smirk. "I'd like to think we could all be friends."

"Lookin' forward to that," Trenton replied with a shit-eating grin. "Come to think of it—when they started shooting at us, I happened to look *through* a hole in the windshield. From where I was standing, I should have an extra hole in my head, yet I don't." Running his fingers over his face and head, he feigned confusion, then met Casper's gaze directly. "Any ideas?"

"None that you'd like, fed. None you'd like."

"You might be surprised, kid." Trenton nodded in concession, but he'd not forget, and he wouldn't give up. He'd bide his time.

The gang leader's contortions stretched the straps covering his thighs and chest. Blood-curdling screams continued until he was hoarse.

"Enough, guys. I'm fine." Hailey brushed away the EMT's hand when he tried to wipe crusted blood from her face.

"Head wounds bleed a lot," the medic advised but capitulated, putting away his gauze.

One of the gang members suffered a fatal wound. The other two stabilized before transport.

"Hey, Trenton." Hailey looked up when Colson added another set of cuffs between Frederick and the gurney.

"Yeah, Sparkles?"

"The one without teeth, he shot Babtiste. Check his gun." She had a lot of questions to answer, but at least they'd see justice done.

Explanations coming from her would earn less hours of interrogation since Trenton understood she'd gathered information through skin-to-skin contact.

Major Clannahan would probably make an appearance at the station.

Chapter Twenty-Three

Casper

Not the tiniest dust mote or stray dog hair called Cecile's kitchen home. The well-used space bore evidence of love with the scent of fresh-baked cookies wafting from the countertop.

Casper had learned the value of family from the men and women in Pennsylvania who'd adopted her. It wasn't until meeting Hailey and her mom she realized there existed room for expansion. And like any family, this one had its black sheep and those deemed a pain in the ass. Across from her sat the latter.

Dinner had been great. Hailey and her mom were good people. Even Leigh was starting to grow on her. She'd made polite conversation without specific nosy questions.

Sitting cattycorner and at the head of the table, Trenton smiled before taking a sip of his wine. "How are your classes coming, Casper?"

The fact he relented in not calling her Olivia equaled a step in the right direction. She ignored the question in favor of one of her own. "Do cops take courses on how to ask the same question in twenty different ways?" A smile she considered sweet induced a cringe in Trenton before he covered it with a blank mask.

"The only academy I've been through is Quantico. Tell me, have you had any special training? You seem to navigate trouble with specific grace and an eye for detail."

"I'm in high school, fed," she huffed out. "It's dangerous enough."

Despite the exhaustive questions about her non-involvement with Frederick, he hadn't given up. Instinct dictated he wouldn't.

"Casper, dear. Have you been to the Alamo or the Space Center in Houston? They can be quite interesting." Cecile arched a brow in Trenton's direction, the admonishment clear.

"No, but I—"

The doorbell chimed throughout the open space, prompting Hailey to stand. On her way past Trenton, she patted him on the shoulder. "Ease up, cowboy."

Trenton's faux relaxed posture didn't fool anyone, but it was a start.

Gunther bounded to the door by Hailey's side and waited for it to open. He greeted the newcomer with a raised paw.

From her seat, Casper recognized the newest arrival and groaned. "Really? Like life isn't complicated enough?"

"Hi, I'm Tom Clannahan. I was hoping to have a minute with my, uh, ward. Is Olivia here?"

Hailey paused with her hand resting on the door's edge, her head tilted in question. "Olivia?" A second later, she smiled. "Oh, Casper? Yes. Come in. We're just finishing dinner."

Her adoptive father, according to legal documents, held out a bottle of wine to Cecile when she approached. Major Thomas Clannahan knew how to charm ladies and was the best friendly interrogator she knew. Keeping him away from Trenton Briner became paramount.

"Come in and have a seat. Would you like a bite to eat? There's plenty here." Cecile pointed to an empty chair beside Leigh.

"Ah, thanks, I'm not hungry, but I wouldn't mind sitting a spell. I just got off the plane and heard my girl found a spot of trouble. Wanted to check on her."

"Hi, Major. What's up?" If the man came to stick his nose where it didn't belong, Casper would find a way to retaliate.

"You call your adopted father by his title?" Trenton also stood to greet the newest arrival.

"Well," Casper thought about it, "...if you were in a room with a bunch of kids and their parents, then yelled, Dad, that *could* be awkward, if you know what I mean."

Cecile ushered Clannahan to sit before grabbing the plate of cookies from the counter and placing it on the table. "Dig in, everyone."

The major proved as adept at avoiding questions as he was at asking them. Casper smirked at Trenton when his best attempts failed specific information.

"So, I hear there's been quite the stir down here. Gun shipments, an ATF agent's murder, and a hostage situation? Your small town doesn't lack for significant events. That's for sure." Clannahan directed his sideways question at Trenton.

Over the next half-hour, details came to light and fleshed out particulars along with their consequences, ending with Charlotte's death.

Clannahan summarized. "So, let me get this straight. The ATF agent worked undercover. He was killed while trying to make an arrest. Shot by the woman who'd blackmailed her employee/ex-gang member to intercept the shipment of guns."

"Yes," Trenton confirmed. "Then Babtiste, the ex-gang member, gets shot by a Jackyl who wanted to steal the shipment. Damn. Convoluted mess."

"And Charlotte killed her assistant because she discovered the gun shipment."

"Yep." Casper took up the story. "Local gang members who intended to intercept the guns figured Babtiste was involved. They tried to kill him, but failed."

Clannahan stared at Hailey. "And the local thugs set their sights on you?"

Hailey nodded. "Seems I ticked them off at the festival."

"Then I say, good work." Clannahan pushed his chair back and crossed one ankle over the other knee. It was a stalling tactic when he wanted to say something but wasn't sure how to proceed.

Casper had seen the scenario play out before and wondered what was on the major's mind, so she asked. "You didn't come down here to check on me, at least not only for that, did you?"

"Of course, I did. I just haven't figured out how to be in two places at once." Drumming his fingers on his knee, he proceeded, "I'm sure Agent Briner and his sister appreciate your help in all this, but I worry you'll get in over your head without the rest of your *family* here."

By now, her guardian had vetted each member present up one side and down the other. *Cagey bugger.*

"Uh-huh." Casper couldn't commit to anything else, feeling the other shoe about to drop.

Clannahan continued with, "I think Agent Briner has a good head on his shoulders, as does his sister Leigh." Clannahan nodded to Hailey. "Not to put you down, young lady. I just don't know you well. Though, I hear good things about your work."

"Kiera and the others are only a phone call away," Casper hedged, waiting, sucking her bottom lip between her teeth.

"True, but you don't always have a phone handy," Clannahan countered.

"Hailey and I make a good team." Casper heard the defiance in her voice spilling out before Clannahan clamped down in whatever devious way he'd planned.

"Yes. I believe you do. It's great to find *like-minded* people."

The way he emphasized keywords sent a sliver of uncertainty up her spine. He knew well her adopted family in Pennsylvania and their psychic talents. But there was no way in hell she'd spill Hailey's secrets without consent.

"And sometimes, opposites attract. Take us, for example." Casper pasted a sweet if insincere smile on her face.

A soft guffaw muffled by Clannahan's hand rubbing his chin. "Yep. I suppose so. Here's the thing. Helping others is fine and great. Endangering your life isn't. Your Uncle Nicholai will have my scalp if anything happens to you down here."

"Maybe we should invite him for dinner, let him get to know us," Hailey suggested, perking up.

"I was thinking about that, but they're pretty busy 'bout now."

"He's one whose orders you follow without question, yes?" Clannahan smiled.

He was baiting her, Casper just couldn't figure out with what. "Of course. But other than from him, I don't take orders well." She stood and took her plate to the sink.

"I have information about your parents. We can talk later." Clannahan crossed his arms over his chest, the challenge issued.

Casper spun around, realizing too late the trap he'd sprung. Searching for information concerning her parents and possible remaining family had instigated her move to Texas.

"I guess orders aren't *always* a bad thing," Casper relented. "They help maintain status quo and keep everyone on the same page, as long as they make sense."

Clannahan smiled and canted his head toward Trenton. "I think when an FBI agent tells you something, you should listen. Of course, do your own evaluation, but there is something to be said for life experience."

Casper groaned. "Fine. I'll listen to him. Happy now?" Without waiting, she turned to the back door. "I'm taking Gunther for a walk."

Before the back door closed, she heard the smirk in Clannahan's words, "And that, folks, is how it's done."

Outside, the evening had cooled, but nothing like she'd expect to feel in Pennsylvania. Despite the familiar surroundings beginning to feel like home, there were times she missed her friends, her extended family.

Always in tune with what she felt, Simon brushed his tiny fingers along her cheek.

"Yeah, buddy. I love you too. I just never expected to feel so comfortable other than in PA, never thought I'd be accepted for who I am." Hailey, Cecile, and even Leigh and Trenton had grown on her during her short time in southeast Texas.

As if internalizing her feelings, Simon cooed softly against her hair.

The night was quiet, except for intermittent hoots of an owl and a whip-poor-will chanting its name. She was starting to understand why her parents came here.

Deep notes of her favorite horror movie erupting from her phone alerted her to an expected call. She swiped the screen and thought of her boyfriend, awaiting the results of his decision.

If he stayed in Pennsylvania to be closer to his brother, she'd understand. After all, the search for relatives is what brought her to Texas.

"Colin, how goes it?" Leaning against an old oak in the backyard, she smiled and leaned her head back to close her eyes.

"Good. Still trying to get things settled here. I was planning on visiting next week, but it doesn't look like that's going to happen. My brother's having a hard go of it."

Delays weren't optimal, but there wasn't much she could do about it. "Okay, so when will I see you?"

"Open your eyes."

"What?"

Simon tapped her temple at the same time she opened her eyes.

He stood five feet away, backlit by Cecile's porch lighting.

"Really?" Dropping her phone, she rushed forward and into his open arms.

"Miss me?"

"Yes. All the time." Warm breath brushed her forehead before she buried it against his chest. Soft flannel reminded her of the mountains from where he'd come.

Stepping away, he adopted a serious expression. "We need to talk."

The bottom dropped out of her stomach. No good conversation ever began with those words.

"Why'd you come by astral projection?" Leaving his body in Pennsylvania wasn't an issue with Kiera and the others watching over his inert form. Although she preferred him present in totality, she'd take what she could get.

"Kiera offered to bring me, but I didn't want an audience."

Soft-spoken with brown hair and hazel eyes, he took a step back. After a glance over his shoulder, he nodded to himself.

"You've decided to stay in Pennsylvania with the others?"

"I know it's not what you want to hear, but you deserved to hear it in person."

"Oh." It's all the energy she could muster to say.

"Casper, I also came because trouble's headed your way. Actually, it might already be here."

"What do you mean?"

"Nicholai had a vision. Things are about to change."

Epilogue

Pain and hard work.

That's what it took to reinvent a life. That and a few hundred grand, which he'd tucked away.

Nothing died harder than old, well-established habits. Some people were slaves to them.

The meddlesome shop owner would die a horrid death. He'd go out screaming at the top of his lungs. Each note screamed would blend with the sounds of the bayou.

In truth, the task would be finished all too soon, but the time would be well-spent and allow for contemplation on what to do with the woman left behind.

Killing her would make the daughter motherless, but leave him free to raise her in a style befitting a proper assassin.

Decisions. Decisions.

The End

Thank you for reading *Deceptive Silence.*

Hailey and Casper's adventures continue in southeast Texas as the past comes back to haunt the newly formed team.

Read farther for an excerpt from *Unlikely Justice.*

If you'd like to know when my next book is ready, take a second and sign up for my NEW RELEASE email alerts at reilygarrett (dot) com. My original release dates always have time padded in for, you know, life events and such. They usually move up by several months. Plus, I don't spend a lot of time on social media. You can find a complete list of all my books on my website.

Unlikely Justice
Clarence

The soft ditty Clarence Burke hummed while heading to his car halted the chittering of two nearby squirrels that stopped to stare. The night had been full of wonder, his excitement magnified when his girlfriend said yes to the ultimate question. Due to her prior husband's abandonment, there'd be legal hurdles to navigate, but what was life's journey without a few bumps in the road?

They hadn't discussed specifics of where they'd live; though, it didn't matter as they both had nice homes. He liked her location, remote enough to enjoy privacy but within reasonable distance to town and the hardware store co-owned with his brother.

His sedan purred to life in the cool morning air, reflecting his contentment despite the grim feeling suddenly inducing goose bumps on his forearms. The sensation didn't liken to that produced earlier when photographing white-winged crossbills deep in the bayou.

He'd captured the penultimate photo before discovering a stranger, an unidentified phenomenon flitting through the trees.

This carried a direct, personal vibe to it.

He squashed the ill-timed feelings with the knowledge he'd soon become a husband and father, well, stepfather, each a first for him. It'd be good for Eleanor to have a man around the house again, one who'd take an interest in raising her vivacious toddler.

A three-point turn headed him down the dirt driveway lined by vibrant Shumard Oaks on the right and brown flatlands on the left. A vast unspoiled beauty.

At the tip of the winding entrance, he stopped to observe the passage of three deer darting from the woods. He hadn't thought to ask Eleanor if poaching was an issue during the hunting season, a plight to consider when outdoors with small children.

Still, his future had never looked so bright.

So, why did the muscles around his right eye twitch? And why was his heart beating to the rhythm of heavy metal drum rolls?

Turning toward town, he accelerated and pushed the button on the wheel's digital media. Classical country music soothed the perception of a thousand eyes watching him. Paranoia had never been a quirk in his personality, despite living alone all his adult life.

Ahead, he saw a large sandy-colored lump in the middle of the road. It didn't move.

Someone had hit a deer and left it where it'd fallen. Few people lived farther along the road. Small-town living dictated he knew of them, if not by sight.

Braking to a stop, he got out to first make sure it wasn't suffering, and then move it to the shoulder to prevent an accident.

Lack of carrion creatures decreed it hadn't been present long, and yet, he saw no skid marks indicating a motorist hit their brakes or swerved to miss the animal.

A quick nudge of its hindquarters produced no response, but the slow and even rise and fall of the animal's chest confirmed it alive. There existed no blood or obvious deformity.

He'd never hit an animal but reckoned vehicular collision would produce some overt sign.

Poachers were known to bring bucks down and take their antlers for trophies. This was a doe. That left the possibility of drugging, which made no sense. What was the motive?

Beads of sweat rolled down his spine despite the slight chill in the air. His first impulse dictated he get in his car and peel out, but he couldn't run over the helpless creature. It wasn't in his nature.

Hind legs twitched in his grasp when dragging it to the side, indicating life. Once he got to his store, he'd notify Parks and Wildlife of its status.

Eleanor wasn't scheduled to go anywhere and didn't need to be burdened with the animal's plight.

He estimated the deer's weight to be a few pounds shy of a hundred, its grating slide over dirt and small rocks producing a sound that turned his stomach.

"Poor thing. I hope you get back to your family safe and sound."

Why would anyone do such a thing?

He took a moment to examine the creature's legs for signs of injury or swelling and confirmed them intact.

It reminded him of a classic movie plot, except he wasn't a high-value target. The store he co-owned made just enough to keep him and his brother well-fed, and their employees content.

He wasn't a hunter, nor did he embrace the killer instinct. But in the blink of an eye, he knew trouble barreled his way at high velocity.

Reacting as a basic survival mechanism, the primitive part of his brain, the amygdala, activated the part of the nervous system that released hormones. His breathing quickened, muscles tensed, and awareness heightened with a change in the atmosphere. If fear had a scent, he'd reek of it.

Having finished his task, he peered through the wooded shadows across the road. Nothing moved other than viny growth with the caress of a light breeze. No beady red eyes shone to contrast the blackness.

A small voice felt rather than heard declared the warning as clear as mud. He understood the physical responses but couldn't define the instigating reason. It didn't matter. Survival of early ancestors had proven the necessity of reacting to perceived danger. It wasn't a question of intelligence, simply a survival instinct. Even a humble shop owner should heed natural responses.

He stood and rushed toward his car, having left the door open. As he bent to slide onto the seat, a sharp pain stabbed his right shoulder. Stinging, burning sensations sizzled down his arm and into his hand like he'd hit his funny bone on a corner shelf.

He wasn't laughing.

A dart protruded three inches from his bicep. It felt like the other half was buried in his bone. He pulled it out and tossed it over his shoulder.

The likely scenario registered in the next heartbeat. Unlike in the movies, tranquilizers injected into muscle didn't take effect as quickly as when inserted into the veinous system. A matter of simple anatomy and physiology.

A suggestive throat clearing snapped his attention toward the tree line.

"Hello, Clarence. Let's go for a ride. Shall we?" Amusement laced the deep voice.

He didn't recognize the voice, but the mannerism, the way the stranger twisted his lips to the side and tilted his head seemed familiar. Neither matched his memory of someone he feared.

Thank God.

He felt lucky to not be facing the most dangerous and quite likely the most deranged man known for his sociopathic streak. Too late he'd learned of the deranged mind underneath the pleasant façade of one he'd called friend. The memory created a shudder.

It was then he noticed the first hazing of his vision, a numbness of his thoughts. Most likely, the deviant had modified the drug to his own parameters.

One thing became abundantly clear as Clarence stared at the face of his unknown enemy. He'd not live long enough to slip a wedding ring on Eleanor's finger or adopt the beautiful toddler, so full of life and joy.

Disjointed thoughts and hazed vision accompanied rough hands guiding him to, and shoving him into, his own trunk.

His car wasn't so old to lack an interior trunk release. If he wasn't so tired, he'd be able to pull it.

Utter and complete despair matched the total blackness enfolding him when the lid slammed shut. The last thing he saw was a smile.

He knew that smile.

REILY GARRETT

Romantic Thrillers
McAllister Justice Series
Tender Echoes
Digital Velocity
Bound By Shadows
Inconclusive Evidence
Carbon Replacements
Shattered Reflections
Remnants of Evil
Moonlight and Murder Series
Shifting Targets
A Critical Tangent
Pivotal Decisions
Seeds of Murder
An Unlikely Grave
Deadly Interception
Love You To Death
Psychic Thrillers
Mind Stalkers Series
Bending Fate
Silent Depths
Shadow Guard
Whispers After Death
Mind Hunters
Guardian Series
Shadowed Horizons
Shadowed Origins
Shadowed Passages
Shadowed Spirits
Shadowed Intent
Shadowed Visions
Shadowed Deliverance

DECEPTIVE SILENCE

Hailey Arquette Murder Files
Perfect In Death
Deceptive Silence
Unlikely Justice
Phantom Reunion
North Side OF The Grass
Paranormal Romance
Immortal Lovers Series
Unholy Alliance
Blood Union
Standalone paranormal romance
Tiago

About Reily

Reily Garrett is a writer, mother, and companion to three long coat German shepherds. When not working with her dogs, she's sitting at her desk with her fur kids by her side.

Author of chilling suspense and snarky romance, her stories span the distance of romantic thrillers, paranormal romance, and erotic romance. Regardless of genre, each book delves into a dark and twisted imagination yet is tempered with romance and a touch of humor.

Reviews by Kirkus Reviews, San Francisco Bay Review, and BestThrillers.com best describe her work:

"This could be James Patterson, Lee Child, and Tess Gerritsen rolled into one, but the dark, twisted methods used by the serial killer could surprise even those readers..." - San Francisco Bay Review

"...steamy, seductive police procedural..." - BestThrillers.com

"...well-researched thriller that remains romantically genuine throughout." - Kirkus Review

Prior experience in the Military Police, private investigations, and as an ICU nurse gives her fiction a real-world flavor.